one of SF's brightest talents takes you on thirteen amazing leaps from the mind of man to the final, starstudded frontier

"Twice the winner of the Hugo, once of the Nebula, Joe Haldeman is possibly the best young science fiction writer to emerge in the past few years. This, his first book of short fiction, amply demonstrates his mastery of the form. . . . Especially fine are the subtly moving 'Counterpoint' and 'A Mind of His Own' and the dazzlingly inventive 'Armaja Das' and 'Jury Rigged'. . . . The reader will find here some of the purest and most classically constructed SF since the Golden Age of *Astounding*."

Publishers Weekly

"He breezes through the narrative with an effortlessly appropriate pacing which convinces you that you are confronting an idea rather than a gimmick. . . . Fluent craftsmanship, with tantalizing hints of something more."

Kirkus Reviews

SELECTED BY THE
SCIENCE FICTION BOOK CLUB

INFINITE DREAMS
JOE HALDEMAN

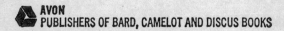
AVON
PUBLISHERS OF BARD, CAMELOT AND DISCUS BOOKS

AVON BOOKS
A division of
The Hearst Corporation
959 Eighth Avenue
New York, New York 10019

First Avon Printing, October, 1979

FOR THE GUILFORD GAFIA:

And the three men I admire the most
The father, son, and the holy ghost
They caught the last train for the coast
The day the music died.

Contents

COUNTERPOINT 9

ANNIVERSARY PROJECT 21

THE MAZEL TOV REVOLUTION 34

TO HOWARD HUGHES: A MODEST
  PROPOSAL 54

A MIND OF HIS OWN 74

ALL THE UNIVERSE IN A MASON JAR 94

THE PRIVATE WAR OF PRIVATE JACOB 108

A TIME TO LIVE 115

JURYRIGGED 125

SUMMER'S LEASE 141
  (called TRUTH TO TELL in *Analog*)

26 DAYS, ON EARTH 157

ARMAJA DAS 177

TRICENTENNIAL 198

AFTERWORD 220

Counterpoint

The good people who agreed to publish this book asked me to say a few words about each story: where it came from, how it was written. In the trade, we call this the "Where do you get your crazy ideas?" syndrome.

I always liked Roger Zelazny's answer. He says that every night he leaves a bowl of milk and some crackers on the back stoop; in the morning, the milk and crackers are gone, but there's a stack of crazy ideas by the empty bowl.

An apology may be in order for the significant number of readers who think a story ought to speak for itself, and everything else is irrelevant blather. I like the blather myself, though, and I think most readers do. The rest can skip it easily enough: it's in a different type face.

The story that follows is important to me because it's the first one I wrote after learning that I might some day be a writer. I'd sold a few stories before, but always figured that it would be a sideline, a hobby that managed to pay for itself with a little beer money left over. I learned that it might be more in June of 1970.

For twenty years science fiction has had an annual rite of spring called the Milford Conference. For some, it's a rite of passage as well. Milford used to be held in Milford, Pennsylvania, at the home of its founder, Damon Knight (its geography changes as Damon moves around, but it's still called "the Milford"). Damon invites a mixture of established writers and newcomers for a week of intensive roundtable criticism: manuscripts are passed around and sometimes praised, sometimes literally torn to bits.

It was a real feeling of privilege to be allowed to sit with people like Bova, Dickson, Ellison, Knight, Laumer, Wilhelm; but I was a nervous wreck by the time my story came up for appraisal. One fellow neophyte had been re-

duced to tears by having his manuscript referred to as "this piece of shit" and flung to the floor. By the time my turn came around I knew *my* story was cretinous, subliterate, an insult to everyone's intelligence, and poorly Xeroxed besides.

But most of the people liked it, and some people whose opinions were important to me liked it very much.* I was able to relax after that, and talk with the established pros about practical things like agents and editors, and important things like how to fill an empty page, how to restart a dead story. I found out that they weren't all that different from me, and that if I really wanted to, I could make my living as a writer, eventually (it took about six years, much less time than I'd expected).

I went home from the conference and wrote this story, and started my first novel, and eventually sold both. In the "crazy ideas" department, all I want to say, to avoid muting the story's suspense, is that it's loosely patterned after a Greek myth. Followers of Dr. Jung will be glad to know that I'd never heard of the myth when I wrote the story.

---

* My memory is as selective and self-reinforcing as anybody's; what I remember is that *everybody* thought the story was the best thing since sliced yoghurt. But according to my notes, several people didn't like it, and one positively (or negatively) frothed at the mouth in his dislike. He went on to his just reward, though: now he's a critic.

Michael Tobias Kidd was born in New Rochelle, N.Y., at exactly 8:03:47 on 12 April 1943. His birth was made as easy as the birth of a millionaire's son can be.

Roger William Wellings was born in New Orleans, La., at exactly 8:03:47 on 12 April 1943. His prostitute mother died in giving birth, and his father could have been any one of an indeterminate number of businessmen she had serviced seven months before at a war matériel planning convention.

Michael's mother considered herself progressive. She alternated breast-feeding with a sterilized bottle of scientifically prepared formula. An army of servants cared for the mansion while she lavished time and affection on her only son.

Roger's wet nurse, a black woman hired by the orphanage, despised the spindly pink premature baby and hoped he would die. Somehow, he lived.

Both babies were weaned on the same day. Michael had steak and fresh vegetables laboriously minced and mortared and pestled by a skilled dietician on the kitchen staff. Roger had wartime Gerber's, purchased by the orphanage in gallon jars that were left open far too long.

In a sunny nursery on that glorious morning of 16 March 1944, Michael said "Mama," his first word. It was raining in New Orleans, and unseasonably cold, and that word was one that Roger wouldn't learn for some time. But at the same instant, he opened his mouth and said "No" to a spoonful of mashed carrots. The attendant didn't know it was Roger's first word, but was not disposed to coax, and Roger went hungry for the rest of the morning.

And the war ground on. Poor Michael had to be without his father for weeks at a time, when he journeyed to

Washington or San Francisco or even New Orleans to confer with other powerful men. In these times, Mrs. Kidd redoubled her affection and tried to perk up the little tyke with gifts of toys and candy. He loved his father and missed him, but shrewdly learned to take advantage of his absences.

The orphanage in New Orleans lost men to the armed forces and the stronger women went out to rivet and weld and slap grey paint for the war. Roger's family winnowed down to a handful of old ladies and bitter 4-F's. Children would die every month from carelessness or simple lack of attention. They would soil their diapers and lie in the mess for most of the day. They would taste turpentine or rat poison and try to cope with the situation without benefit of adult supervision. Roger lived, though he didn't thrive.

The boys were two years old when Japan capitulated. Michael sat at a garden party in New Rochelle and watched his parents and their friends drink champagne and kiss and laugh and wipe each other's tears away. Roger was kept awake all night by the drunken brawl in the next room, and twice watched with childish curiosity as white-clad couples lurched into the ward and screwed clumsily beside his crib.

September after Michael's fourth birthday, his mother tearfully left him in the company of ten other children and a professionally kind lady, to spend half of each day coping with the intricacies of graham crackers and milk, crayons and fingerpaints. His father had a cork board installed in his den, where he thumbtacked Michael's latest creations. Mr. Kidd's friends often commented on how advanced the youngster was.

The orphanage celebrated Roger's fourth birthday the way they celebrated everybody's. They put him to work. Every morning after breakfast he went to the kitchen, where the cook would give him a paper bag full of potatoes and a potato peeler. He would take the potatoes out of the bag and peel them one by one, very carefully making the peelings drop into the bag. Then he would take the bag of peelings down to the incinerator, where the colored janitor would thank him for it very gravely. Then he would return to wash the potatoes after he had scrubbed his own hands.

This would take most of the morning—he soon learned that haste led only to cut fingers, and if there was the slightest spot on one potato, the cook would make him go over all of them once again.

Nursery school prepared Michael quite well for grade school, and he excelled in every subject except arithmetic. Mr. Kidd hired a succession of tutors who managed through wheedling and cajoling and sheer repetition to teach Michael first addition, then subtraction, then multiplication, and finally long division and fractions. When he entered junior high school, Michael was actually better prepared in mathematics than most of his classmates. But he didn't understand it, really—the tutors had given him a superficial facility with numbers that, it was hoped, might carry him through.

Roger attended the orphanage grade school, where he did poorly in almost every subject. Except mathematics. The one teacher who knew the term thought that perhaps Roger was an *idiot savant* (but he was wrong). In the second grade, he could add up a column of figures in seconds, without using a pencil. In the third grade, he could multiply large numbers by looking at them. In the fourth grade, he discovered prime numbers independently and could crank out long division orally, without seeing the numbers. In the fifth grade someone told him what square roots were, and he extended the concept to cube roots, and could calculate either without recourse to pencil and paper. By the time he got to junior high school, he had mastered high school algebra and geometry. And he was hungry for more.

Now this was 1955, and the boys were starting to take on the appearances that they would carry through adult life. Michael was the image of his father; tall, slim, with a slightly arrogant, imperial cast to his features. Roger looked like one of nature's lesser efforts. He was short and swarthy, favoring his mother, with a potbelly from living on starch all his life, a permanently broken nose, and one ear larger than the other. He didn't resemble his father at all.

Michael's first experience with a girl came when he was twelve. His riding teacher, a lovely wench of eighteen, supplied Michael with a condom and instructed him in its use, in a pile of hay behind the stables, on a lovely May afternoon.

On that same afternoon, Roger was dispassionately fellating a mathematics teacher only slightly uglier than he was, this being the unspoken price for tutelage into the mysteries of integral calculus. The experience didn't particularly upset Roger. Growing up in an orphanage, he had already experienced a greater variety of sexual adventure than Michael would in his entire life.

In high school, Michael was elected president of his class for two years running. A plain girl did his algebra homework for him and patiently explained the subject well enough for him to pass the tests. In spite of his mediocre performance in that subject, Michael graduated with honors and was accepted by Harvard.

Roger spent high school indulging his love for mathematics, just doing enough work in the other subjects to avoid the boredom of repeating them. He applied to several colleges, just to get the counselor off his back, but in spite of his perfect score on the College Boards (Mathematics), none of the schools had an opening. He apprenticed himself to an accountant and was quite happy to spend his days manipulating figures with half his mind, while the other half worked on a theory of Abelian groups that he was sure would one day blow modern algebra wide open.

Michael found Harvard challenging at first, but soon was anxious to get out into the "real world"—helping Mr. Kidd manage the family's widespread, subtle investments. He graduated *cum laude,* but declined graduate work in favor of becoming a junior financial adviser to his father.

Roger worked away at his books and at his theory, which he eventually had published in the SIAM *Journal* by the simple expedient of adding a Ph.D. to his name. He was found out, but he didn't care.

At Harvard, Michael had taken ROTC and graduated with a Reserve commission in the infantry, at his father's behest. There was a war going on now, in Vietnam, and his father, perhaps suffering a little from guilt at being too young for the first World War and too old for the second, urged his son to help out with the third.

Roger had applied for OCS at the age of twenty, and

had been turned down (he never learned it was for "extreme ugliness of face"). At twenty-two, he was drafted; and the Army, showing rare insight, took notice of his phenomenal ability with numbers and sent him to artillery school. There he learned to translate cryptic commands like "Drop 50" and "Add 50" into exercises in analytic geometry that eventually led to a shell being dropped exactly where the forward observer wanted it. He loved to juggle the numbers and shout orders to the gun crew, who were in turn appreciative of his ability, as it lessened the amount of work for them—Roger never had a near miss that had to be repeated. Who cares if he looks like the devil's brother-in-law? He's a good man to have on the horn.

Michael became a company commander, leader of seventy infantrymen who patrolled the verdant hills and valleys of the Central Highlands, each one cursing and killing and sweating out his individual year. He hated it at first; it scared him and put a great weight on his heart when he ordered men out with the certain knowledge that some of them would come back dead and already rotting, and some screaming or whimpering with limbs or organs shattered, and some just grey with horror, open-mouthed, crying . . . but he got hardened to it and the men came to respect him and by 9 June 1966 he had to admit that he had come to enjoy it, just a little.

Roger wasn't disappointed when he got orders for Vietnam and was relieved to find that, once there, they let him do what he enjoyed most: taking those radioed commands and translating them into vernier readings for his gun crew, a group of men manning a 155-millimeter howitzer. In the Central Highlands.

Michael's company had settled into a comfortable routine the past few weeks. They would walk for a day and dig in, and he'd let them rest for a day, setting out desultory ambushes that never trapped any enemy. The consensus was that Charlie had moved out of this area, and they were getting a long-deserved rest. Michael even found time to play some poker with his men (being careful to keep the stakes down), even though it was strictly against regulations. It increased his popularity tremendously, as he was also careful to lose consistently. It was 9 June 1966 and he had been in Vietnam for five months.

It was 9 June 1966 and Roger had been with his gun crew for six months. They liked him at first, because he was so good. But they were getting distant now—he spent all of his free time writing strange symbols in a fat notebook, he never took leave to go into Pleiku and fuck the slope whores, and the few times they had invited him to play poker or craps he had gotten that funny look on his face and taken all their money, slowly and without seeming to enjoy it. Most of the guys thought he was a faggot, and though he said he'd never been to college, everybody knew that was a lie.

It was 9 June 1966 and Michael was dealing five-card stud when he heard the rattle of machine-gun fire on his southern perimeter. His educated ear separated the noises and, before he dropped the cards, he knew it was one M-16 against two Chinese AK-47's. He scrambled out of the bunker that had provided shade for card playing and ran in the direction of the firing. He was halfway there when fire broke out on the western and northern quadrants. He checked his stride and returned to the command bunker.

Roger was amusing himself with an application of point-set topology to stress analysis of concrete structures when the radio began to squawk: "One-one, this is Tiger-two. We're under pretty heavy contact and need a coupla dozen rounds. Over." Roger dumped his notebook and carried the radio to his gun crew. He had to smile—Tiger-two, that was Cap'n Kidd, of all the unlikely names. He hollered into the radio as he ran. "Tiger-two, this is One-one. We got your morning coordinates on file and we'll drop a smoke round by you. You correct. Okay? Over."

Michael rogered Roger's suggestion; he would look and listen for the harmless smoke round and tell him how much to drop or add.

The fire to the south had stepped up quite a bit now, and Michael was pretty sure that was where the enemy would make his play. The smoke round came whining in and popped about a hundred meters from the perimeter. "Drop seventy-five, one HE," Michael yelled into the radio.

Roger had worked with this Captain Kidd before and found him to be notoriously conservative. Which wasted shells, as he walked the artillery in little by little toward the action. So Roger yelled out the string of figures for one hundred meters' drop instead of seventy-five. His crew set the verniers and the charge and pulled the lanyard that sent the high explosive, "one HE," round singing toward Michael's position.

It landed smack on the perimeter, in a stand of bamboo right next to a hardworking machine-gun bunker. The two men inside the bunker died instantly, and the two men in a bunker on the other side were knocked out by the concussion. The bamboo exploded in a flurry of woden shrapnel.

Before Michael could react, a six-inch sliver of bamboo traveling with the speed of a bullet hit him one inch above the left eyebrow and buried itself in his cerebral cortex. He dropped the binoculars he had been holding, put a hand to his head, and fell over in a state of acute tetanic shock; muscles bunched spastically, legs working in a slow run, mouth open wide saying nothing.

A medic rushed to the captain and was puzzled to find no apparent wound save a scratch on the forehead. Then he took Michael's helmet off and saw a half inch of bamboo protruding from the back of his head. He told a private to tell the lieutenant he was commander now.

The lieutenant got on the horn and asked who the fuck fired that round, we have at least two killed, landed right on the perimeter, give us some more but for Chrissake add fifty.

The gun crew overheard and Roger told them not to worry, he'd cover for them. Then he gave them the appropriate figures and they sent a volley of six HE rounds that providentially landed right in the middle of the enemy force grouping for the attack. Then he put volleys to the west and north, knocking out the diversionary squads. By the time air support arrived, there were no live enemy targets left. Roger got a commendation.

Michael was evacuated by helicopter to Banmethuot, where they couldn't do anything for him. They flew him to Bienhoa, where a neurosurgeon attempted to extract the bamboo splinter but gave up after an hour's careful exploration. They sent him to Japan, where a better, or at least more confident, surgeon removed the missile.

There was a board of inquiry where Roger testified that

his men could not possibly have made such an elementary error and, after demonstrating his own remarkable talent, suggested that it had been either a faulty round or an improper correction by the captain. The board was impressed and the captain couldn't testify, so the matter was dropped.

After a few months Michael could say a few words and his body seemed to have adjusted to being fed and emptied through various tubes. So they flew him from Japan to Walter Reed, where a number of men experienced in such things would try to make some sort of rational creature out of him again.

Roger's esteem was now very high with the rest of the artillery battery, and especially with his own crew. He could have dumped the whole mess into their laps, but instead had taken on the board of inquiry by himself.

Michael was blind in his right eye, but with his left he could distinguish complementary colors and tell a circle from a square. The psychiatrists could tell because his pupil would dilate slightly at the change, even though the light intensity was kept constant.

A company of NVA regulars took Roger's fire base by surprise and, in the middle of the furious hand-to-hand battle, Roger saw two enemy sappers slip into the bunker that was used to store ammunition for the big guns. The bunker also contained Roger's notebook, and the prospect of losing eight months' worth of closely reasoned mathematical theorizing drove Roger to take his bayonet, run across a field of blistering fire, dive in the bunker and kill the two sappers before they could set off their charge. In the process, he absorbed a rifle bullet in the calf and a pistol wound in his left tricep. A visiting major who was cowering in a nearby bunker saw the whole thing, and Roger got a medical discharge, the Congressional Medal of Honor, and a fifty percent disability pension. The wounds were reasonably healed in six months, but the pension didn't stop.

Michael had learned to say "mama" again, but his mother wasn't sure he could recognize her during her visits, which became less and less frequent as cancer spread through her body. On 9 June 1967, she died of the cervical cancer that had been discovered exactly one year before. Nobody told Michael.

On 9 June 1967, Roger had finished his first semester at

the University of Chicago and was sitting in the parlor of the head of the mathematics department, drinking tea and discussing the paper that Roger had prepared, extending his new system of algebraic morphology. The department head had made Roger his protégé, and they spent many afternoons like this, the youth's fresh insight cross-pollinating the professor's great experience.

By May of 1970, Michael had learned to respond to his name by lifting his left forefinger.

Roger graduated *summa cum laude* on 30 May 1970 and, out of dozens of offers, took an assistantship at the California Institute of Technology.

Against his physician's instructions, Mr. Kidd went on a skiing expedition to the Swiss Alps. On an easy slope his ski hit an exposed root and, rolling comfortably with the fall, Michael's father struck a half-concealed rock which fractured his spine. It was June of 1973 and he would never ski again, would never walk again.

At that same instant on the other side of the world, Roger sat down after a brilliant defense of his doctoral thesis, a startling redefinition of Peano's Axiom. The thesis was approved unanimously.

On Michael's birthday, 12 April 1975, his father, acting through a bank of telephones beside his motorized bed, liquidated ninety percent of the family's assets and set up a tax-sheltered trust to care for his only child. Then he took ten potent pain-killers with his breakfast orange juice and another twenty with sips of water and he found out that dying that way wasn't as pleasant as he thought it would be.

It was also Roger's thirty-second birthday, and he celebrated it quietly at home in the company of his new wife, a former student of his, twelve years his junior, who was dazzled by his genius. She could switch effortlessly from doting *Hausfrau* to randy mistress to conscientious secretary and Roger knew love for the first time in his life. He was also the youngest assistant professor on the mathematics faculty of CalTech.

On 4 January 1980, Michael stopped responding to his name. The inflation safeguards on his trust fund were eroding with time and he was moved out of the exclusive private clinic to a small room in San Francisco General.

The same day, due to his phenomenal record of publica-

19

tions and the personal charisma that fascinated students and faculty alike, Roger was promoted to be the youngest full professor in the history of the mathematics department. His unfashionably long hair and full beard covered his ludicrous ears and "extreme ugliness of face," and people who knew the history of science were affectionately comparing him to Steinmetz.

There was nobody to give the tests, but if somebody had they would have found that on 12 April 1983, Michael's iris would no longer respond to the difference between a circle and a square.

On his fortieth birthday, Roger had the satisfaction of hearing that his book, *Modern Algebra Redefined,* was sold out in its fifth printing and was considered required reading for almost every mathematics graduate student in the country.

Seventeen June 1985 and Michael stopped breathing; a red light blinked on the attendant's board and he administered mouth-to-mouth resuscitation until they rolled in an electronic respirator and installed him. Since he wasn't on the floor reserved for respiratory disease, the respirator was plugged into a regular socket instead of the special fail-safe line.

Roger was on top of the world. He had been offered the chairmanship of the mathematics department of Penn State, and said he would accept as soon as he finished teaching his summer post-doctoral seminar on algebraic morphology.

The hottest day of the year was 19 August 1985. At 2:45:20 p.m. the air conditioners were just drawing too much power and somewhere in Central Valley a bank of bus bars glowed cherry red and exploded in a shower of molten copper.

All the lights on the floor and on the attendant's board went out, the electronic respirator stopped, and while the attendant was frantically buzzing for assistance, 2:45:25 to be exact, Michael Tobias Kidd passed away.

The lights in the seminar room dimmed and blinked out. Roger got up to open the Venetian blinds, whipped off his glasses in a characteristic gesture and was framing an acerbic comment when, at 2:45:25, he felt a slight tingling in his head as a blood vessel ruptured and quite painlessly he went to join his brother.

Anniversary Project

~~~~~~

This story was a real problem child. Harry Harrison asked me to do a story for an anthology of science fiction set one million years in the future. I ran home and wrote the first three pages of "Anniversary Project," and then stopped dead. Started again, stopped again.

After a half-dozen tries I was all the way up to four pages, and I really liked those four pages, but I had to stop wasting time on it. I wrote Harry and told him to go on without me.

Several years later I came across the fragment and it was immediately obvious what was wrong with it. Painfully obvious, and so was the solution.

I had taken as a basic premise that "people" a million years in the future would have evolved into something totally alien, and I'd done too good a job; they were the most convincing aliens I'd ever invented. But they did lack certain interesting attributes: love, hate, fear, birth, death, sex, appetites, politics. About all they had was slight differences of opinion regarding ontology. Pretty dry stuff.

Yet I thought I was onto something. Most aliens in science fiction aren't truly alien, and that's not because science fiction writers lack imagination, but because the purpose of an alien in a story is usually to provide a meaningful distortion of human nature. My purpose was not nearly so elevated; my aliens were there as unwitting vehicles for absurdist humor. All the story needed was a couple of bewildered humans, to serve as foils for alien nature. Once I saw that, the story practically wrote itself.

In the process of writing itself, the story generated two dreadful puns. I'm not responsible.

His name is Three-phasing and he is bald and wrinkled, slightly over one meter tall, large-eyed, toothless and all bones and skin, sagging pale skin shot through with traceries of delicate blue and red. He is considered very beautiful but most of his beauty is in his hands and is due to his extreme youth. He is over two hundred years old and is learning how to talk. He has become reasonably fluent in sixty-three languages, all dead ones, and has only ten to go.

The book he is reading is a facsimile of an early edition of Goethe's *Faust*. The nervous angular Fraktur letters goose-step across pages of paper-thin platinum.

The *Faust* had been printed electrolytically and, with several thousand similarly worthwhile books, sealed in an argon-filled chamber and carefully lost, in 2012 A.D.; a very wealthy man's legacy to the distant future.

In 2012 A.D., Polaris had been the pole star. Men eventually got to Polaris and built a small city on a frosty planet there. By that time, they weren't dating by prophets' births any more, but it would have been around 4900 A.D. The pole star by then, because of precession of the equinoxes, was a dim thing once called Gamma Cephei. The celestial pole kept reeling around, past Deneb and Vega and through barren patches of sky around Hercules and Draco; a patient clock but not the slowest one of use, and when it came back to the region of Polaris, then 26,000 years had passed and men had come back from the stars, to stay, and the book-filled chamber had shifted 130 meters on the floor of the Pacific, had rolled into a shallow trench, and eventually was buried in an underwater landslide.

The thirty-seventh time this slow clock ticked, men had moved the Pacific, not because they had to, and had found the chamber, opened it up, identified the books and carefully sealed them up again. Some things by then were more important to men than the accumulation of knowledge: in half of one more circle of the poles would come the millionth anniversary of the written word. They could wait a few millennia.

As the anniversary, as nearly as they could reckon it, approached, they caused to be born two individuals: Ninehover (nominally female) and Three-phasing (nominally male). Three-phasing was born to learn how to read and speak. He was the first human being to study these skills in more than a quarter of a million years.

Three-phasing has read the first half of *Faust* forwards and, for amusement and exercise, is reading the second half backwards. He is singing as he reads, lisping.

"Fain' Looee w'mun . . . wif all'r die-mun ringf . . ." He has not put in his teeth because they make his gums hurt.

Because he is a child of two hundred, he is polite when his father interrupts his reading and singing. His father's "voice" is an arrangement of logic and aesthetic that appears in Three-phasing's mind. The flavor is lost by translating into words:

"Three-phasing my son-ly atavism of tooth and vocal cord," sarcastically in the reverent mode, "couldst tear thyself from objects of manifest symbol, and visit to share/ help/learn, me?"

"?" he responds, meaning "with/with/of what?"

Withholding mode: "Concerning thee: past, future."

He shuts the book without marking his place. It would never occur to him to mark his place, since he remembers perfectly the page he stops on, as well as every word preceding, as well as every event, no matter how trivial, that he has observed from the precise age of one year. In this respect, at least, he is normal.

He thinks the proper coordinates as he steps over the mover-transom, through a microsecond of black, and onto his father's mover-transom, about four thousand kilometers away on a straight line through the crust and mantle of the earth.

Ritual mode: "As ever, father." The symbol he uses for "father" is purposefully wrong, chiding. Crude biological connotation.

23

His father looks cadaverous and has in fact been dead twice. In the infant's small-talk mode he asks, "From crude babblings of what sort have I torn your interest?"

"The tale called *Faust,* of a man so named, never satisfied with { symbol for slow but continuous accretion } of his knowledge and power; written in the language of Prussia."

"Also depended-ing on this strange word of immediacy, your Prussian language?"

"As most, yes. The word of 'to be': *sein.* Very important illusion in this and related languages/cultures; that events happen at the 'time' of perception, infinitesimal midpoint between past and future."

"Convenient illusion but retarding."

"As we discussed 129 years ago, yes." Three-phasing is impatient to get back to his reading, but adds:

"Obvious that to-be-ness $\left\{ \begin{array}{l} \text{same order of illusion as} \\ \text{three-dimensionality of external world.} \\ \\ \text{thrust upon observer by geometric limitation of synaptic degrees of freedom.} \end{array} \right\}$ "

"You always stick up for them."

"I have great regard for what they accomplished with limited faculties and so short lives." Stop beatin' around the bush, Dad. *Tempus fugit,* eight to the bar. Did Mr. Handy Moves-dat-man-around-by-her-apron-strings, 20th-century American poet, intend cultural translation of *Lysistrata*? If so, inept. African were-beast legendry, yes.

Withholding mode (coy): "Your father stood with Nine-hover all morning."

"," broadcasts Three-phasing: well?

"The machine functions, perhaps inadequately."

The young polyglot tries to radiate calm patience.

"Details I perceive you want; the idea yet excites you. You can never have satisfaction with your knowledge, either. What happened-s to the man in your Prussian book?"

"He lived-s one hundred years and died-s knowing that

a man can never achieve true happiness, despite the appearance of success."

"For an infant, a reasonable perception."

Respectful chiding mode: "One hundred years makes-ed Faust a very old man, for a Dawn man."

"As I stand," same mode, less respect, "yet an infant." They trade silent symbols of laughter.

After a polite tenth-second interval, Three-phasing uses the light interrogation mode: "The machine of Nine-hover. . . ?"

"It begins to work but so far not perfectly." This is not news.

Mild impatience: "As before, then, it brings back only rocks and earth and water and plants?"

"Negative, beloved atavism." Offhand: "This morning she caught two animals that look as man may once have looked."

"!" Strong impatience, "I go?"

"." His father ends the conversation just two seconds after it began.

Three-phasing stops off to pick up his teeth, then goes directly to Nine-hover.

A quick exchange of greeting-symbols and Nine-hover presents her prizes. "Thinking I have two different species," she stands: uncertainty, query.

Three-phasing is amused. "Negative, time-caster. The male and female took very dissimilar forms in the Dawn times." He touches one of them. "The round organs, here, served-ing to feed infants, in the female."

The female screams.

"She manipulates spoken symbols now," observes Nine-hover.

Before the woman has finished her startled yelp, Three-phasing explains: "Not manipulating concrete symbols; rather, she communicates in a way called 'non-verbal,' the use of such communication predating even speech." Slipping into the pedantic mode: "My reading indicates that such a loud noise occurs either { following a stimulus that produces pain { under conditions of extreme agitation { since she seems not in pain, then she must fear me or you or both of us.

"Or the machine," Nine-hover adds.

Symbol for continuing. "We have no symbol for it but in Dawn days most humans observed 'xenophobia,' reacting to the strange with fear instead of delight. We stand as strange to them as they do to us, thus they register fear. In their era this attitude encouraged-s survival.

"Our silence must seem strange to them, as well as our appearance and the speed with which we move. I will attempt to speak to them, so they will know they need not fear us."

Bob and Sarah Graham were having a desperately good time. It was September of 1951 and the papers were full of news about the brilliant landing of U.S. Marines at Inchon. Bob was a Marine private with two days left of the thirty days' leave they had given him, between boot camp and disembarkation for Korea. Sarah had been Mrs. Graham for three weeks.

Sarah poured some more bourbon into her Coke. She wiped the sand off her thumb and stoppered the Coke bottle, then shook it gently. "What if you just don't show up?" she said softly.

Bob was staring out over the ocean and part of what Sarah said was lost in the crash of breakers rolling in. "What if I what?"

"Don't show up." She took a swig and offered the bottle. "Just stay here with me. With us." Sarah was sure she was pregnant. It was too early to tell, of course; her calendar was off but there could be other reasons.

He gave the Coke back to her and sipped directly from the bourbon bottle. "I suppose they'd go on without me. And I'd still be in jail when they came back."

"Not if—"

"Honey, don't even talk like that. It's a just cause."

She picked up a small shell and threw it toward the water.

"Besides, you read the *Examiner* yesterday."

"I'm cold. Let's go up." She stood and stretched and delicately brushed sand away. Bob admired her long naked dancer's body. He shook out the blanket and draped it over her shoulders.

"It'll all be over by the time I get there. We'll push those bastards—"

"Let's not talk about Korea. Let's not talk."

He put his arm around her and they started walking back toward the cabin. Halfway there, she stopped and enfolded the blanket around both of them, drawing him toward her. He always closed his eyes when they kissed, but she always kept hers open. She saw it: the air turning luminous, the seascape fading to be replaced by bare metal walls. The sand turns hard under her feet.

At her sharp intake of breath, Bob opens his eyes. He sees a grotesque dwarf, eyes and skull too large, body small and wrinkled. They stare at one another for a fraction of a second. Then the dwarf spins around and speeds across the room to what looks like a black square painted on the floor. When he gets there, he disappears.

"What the hell?" Bob says in a hoarse whisper.

Sarah turns around just a bit too late to catch a glimpse of Three-phasing's father. She does see Nine-hover before Bob does. The nominally female time-caster is a flurry of movement, sitting at the console of her time net, clicking switches and adjusting various dials. All of the motions are unnecessary, as is the console. It was built at Three-phasing's suggestion, since humans from the era into which they could cast would feel more comfortable in the presence of a machine that looked like a machine. The actual time net was roughly the size and shape of an asparagus stalk, was controlled completely by thought, and had no moving parts. It does not exist any more, but can still be used, once understood. Nine-hover has been trained from birth for this special understanding.

Sarah nudges Bob and points to Nine-hover. She can't find her voice. Bob stares open-mouthed.

In a few seconds, Three-phasing appears. He looks at Nine-hover for a moment, then scurries over to the Dawn couple and reaches up to touch Sarah on the left nipple. His body temperature is considerably higher than hers, and the unexpected warm moistness, as much as the suddenness of the motion, makes her jump back and squeal.

Three-phasing correctly classified both Dawn people as Caucasian, and so assumes that they speak some Indo-European language.

"GutenTagsprechensieDeutsch?" he says in a rapid soprano.

"Huh?" Bob says.

"Guten-Tag-sprechen-sie-Deutsch?" Three-phasing clears his throat and drops his voice down to the alto he uses to sing about the St. Louis woman. *"Guten Tag,"* he says, counting to a hundred between each word. *"Sprechen sie Deutsch?"*

"That's Kraut," says Bob, having grown up on jingoistic comic books. "Don't tell me you're a—"

Three-phasing analyzes the first five words and knows that Bob is an American from the period 1935-1955. "Yes, yes—and no, no—to wit, how very very clever of you to have identified this phrase as having come from the language of Prussia, Germany as you say; but I am, no, not a German person; at least, I no more belong to the German nationality than I do to any other, but I suppose that is not too clear and perhaps I should fully elucidate the particulars of your own situation at this, as you say, 'time' and 'place.' "

The last English-language author Three-phasing studied was Henry James.

"Huh?" Bob says again.

"Ah. I should simplify." He thinks for a half-second and drops his voice down another third. "Yeah, simple. Listen. Mac. First thing I gotta know's whatcher name. Whatcher broad's name."

"Well . . . I'm Bob Graham. This is my wife, Sarah Graham."

"Pleasta meetcha, Bob. Likewise, Sarah. Call me, uh . . ." The only twentieth-century language in which Three-phasing's name makes sense is propositional calculus. "George. George Boole.

"I 'poligize for bumpin' into ya, Sarah. That broad in the corner, she don't know what a tit is, so I was just usin' one of yours. Uh, lack of immediate culchural perspective, I shoulda knowed better."

Sarah feels a little dizzy, shakes her head slowly. "That's all right. I know you didn't mean anything by it."

"I'm dreaming," Bob says. "Shouldn't have—"

"No you aren't," says Three-phasing, adjusting his diction again. "You're in the future. Almost a million years. Pardon me." He scurries to the mover-transom, is gone for a second, reappears with a bedsheet, which he hands to Bob. "I'm sorry, we don't wear clothing. This is the best I can do, for now." The bedsheet is too small for Bob to wear the way Sarah is using the blanket. He folds it over and tucks it around his waist, in a kilt. "Why us?" he asks.

"You were taken at random. We've been time-casting" —he checks with Nine-hover—"for twenty-two years, and have never before caught a human being. Let alone two. You must have been in close contact with one another when you intersected the time-caster beam. I assume you were copulating."

"What-ing?" Bob says.

"No we weren't!" Sarah says indignantly.

"Ah, quite so." Three-phasing doesn't pursue the topic. He knows that humans of this culture were reticent about their sexual activity. But from their literature he knows they spent most of their "time" thinking about, arranging for, enjoying, and recovering from a variety of sexual contacts.

"Then that must be a time machine over there," Bob says, indicating the fake console.

"In a sense, yes." Three-phasing decides to be partly honest. "But the actual machine no longer exists. People did a lot of time-travelling about a quarter of a million years ago. Shuffled history around. Changed it back. The fact that the machine once existed, well, that enables us to use it, if you see what I mean."

"Uh, no. I don't." Not with synapses limited to three degrees of freedom.

"Well, never mind. It's not really important." He senses the next question. "You will be going back . . . I don't know exactly when. It depends on a lot of things. You see, time is like a rubber band." No, it isn't. "Or a spring." No, it isn't. "At any rate, within a few days, weeks at most, you will leave this present and return to the moment you were experiencing when the time-caster beam picked you up."

"I've read stories like that," Sarah says. "Will we remember the future, after we go back?"

"Probably not," he says charitably. Not until your brains evolve. "But you can do us a great service."

Bob shrugs. "Sure, long as we're here. Anyhow, you did us a favor." He puts his arm around Sarah. "I've gotta leave Sarah in a couple of days; don't know for how long. So you're giving us more time together."

"Whether we remember it or not," Sarah says.

"Good, fine. Come with me." They follow Three-phasing to the mover-transom, where he takes their hands and transports them to his home. It is as unadorned as the time-caster room, except for bookshelves along one wall, and a low podium upon which the volume of *Faust* rests. All of the books are bound identically, in shiny metal with flat black letters along the spines.

Bob looks around. "Don't you people ever sit down?"

"Oh," Three-phasing says. "Thoughtless of me." With his mind he shifts the room from utility mood to comfort mood. Intricate tapestries now hang on the walls; soft cushions that look like silk are strewn around in pleasant disorder. Chiming music, not quite discordant, hovers at the edge of audibility, and there is a faint odor of something like jasmine. The metal floor has become a kind of soft leather, and the room has somehow lost its corners.

"How did that happen?" Sarah asks.

"I don't know." Three-phasing tries to copy Bob's shrug, but only manages a spasmodic jerk. "Can't remember not being able to do it."

Bob drops into a cushion and experimentally pushes at the floor with a finger. "What is it you want us to do?"

Trying to move slowly, Three-phasing lowers himself into a cushion and gestures at a nearby one, for Sarah. "It's very simple, really. Your being here is most of it.

"We're celebrating the millionth anniversary of the written word." How to phrase it? "Everyone is interested in this anniversary, but . . . nobody reads any more."

Bob nods sympathetically. "Never have time for it myself."

"Yes, uh . . . you *do* know how to read, though?"

"He knows," Sarah says. "He's just lazy."

"Well, yeah." Bob shifts uncomfortably in the cushion.

"Sarah's the one you want. I kind of, uh, prefer to listen to the radio."

"I read all the time," Sarah says with a little pride. "Mostly mysteries. But sometimes I read good books, too."

"Good, good." It was indeed fortunate to have found this pair, Three-phasing realizes. They had used the metal of the ancient books to "tune" the time-caster, so potential subjects were limited to those living some eighty years before and after 2021 A.D. Internal evidence in the books indicated that most of the Earth's population was illiterate during this period.

"Allow me to explain. Any one of us can learn how to read. But to us it is like a code; an unnatural way of communicating. Because we are all natural telepaths. We can read each other's minds from the age of one year."

"Golly!" Sarah says. "Read minds?" And Three-phasing sees in her mind a fuzzy kind of longing, much of which is love for Bob and frustration that she knows him only imperfectly. He dips into Bob's mind and finds things she is better off not knowing.

"That's right. So what we want is for you to read some of these books, and allow us to go into your minds while you're doing it. This way we will be able to recapture an experience that has been lost to the race for over a half-million years."

"I don't know," Bob says slowly. "Will we have time for anything else? I mean, the world must be pretty strange. Like to see some of it."

"Of course; sure. But the rest of the world is pretty much like my place here. Nobody goes outside any more. There isn't any air." He doesn't want to tell them how the air was lost, which might disturb them, but they seem to accept that as part of the distant future.

"Uh, George." Sarah is blushing. "We'd also like, uh, some time to ourselves. Without anybody . . . inside our minds."

"Yes, I understand perfectly. You will have your own room, and plenty of time to yourselves." Three-phasing neglects to say that there is no such thing as privacy in a telepathic society.

But sex is another thing they don't have any more.

They're almost as curious about that as they are about books.

So the kindly men of the future gave Bob and Sarah Graham plenty of time to themselves: Bob and Sarah reciprocated. Through the Dawn couple's eyes and brains, humanity shared again the visions of Fielding and Melville and Dickens and Shakespeare and almost a dozen others. And as for the 98% more, that they didn't have time to read or that were in foreign languages—Three-phasing got the hang of it and would spend several millennia entertaining those who were amused by this central illusion of literature: that there could be order, that there could be beginnings and endings and logical workings-out in between; that you could count on the third act or the last chapter to tie things up. They knew how profound an illusion this was because each of them knew every other living human with an intimacy and accuracy far superior to that which even Shakespeare could bring to the study of even himself. And as far Sarah and as for Bob:

Anxiety can throw a person's ovaries 'way off schedule. On that beach in California, Sarah was no more pregnant than Bob was. But up there in the future, some somatic tension finally built up to the breaking point, and an egg went sliding down the left Fallopian tube, to be met by a wiggling intruder approximately halfway; together they were the first manifestation of the organism that nine months later, or a million years earlier, would be christened Douglas MacArthur Graham.

This made a problem for time, or Time, which is neither like a rubber band nor like a spring; nor even like a river nor a carrier wave—but which, like all of these things, can be deformed by certain stresses. For instance, two people going into the future and three coming back, on the same time-casting beam.

In an earlier age, when time travel was more common, time-casters would have made sure that the baby, or at least its aborted embryo, would stay in the future when the mother returned to her present. Or they could arrange for the mother to stay in the future. But these subtleties had long been forgotten when Nine-hover relearned the dead art. So Sarah went back to her present with a hitch-hiker, an interloper, firmly imbedded in the lining of her womb. And its dim sense of life set up a kind of eddy in the flow of time, that Sarah had to share.

The mathematical explanation is subtle, and can't be comprehended by those of us who synapse with fewer than four degrees of freedom. But the end effect is clear: Sarah had to experience all of her own life backwards, all the way back to that embrace on the beach. Some highlights were:

In 1992, slowly dying of cancer, in a mental hospital.

In 1979, seeing Bob finally succeed at suicide on the American Plan, not quite finishing his 9,527th bottle of liquor.

In 1970, having her only son returned in a sealed casket from a country she'd never heard of.

In the 1960's, helplessly watching her son become more and more neurotic because of something that no one could name.

In 1953, Bob coming home with one foot, the other having been lost to frostbite; never having fired a shot in anger.

In 1952, the agonizing breech presentation.

Like her son, Sarah would remember no details of the backward voyage through her life. But the scars of it would haunt her forever.

They were kissing on the beach.

Sarah dropped the blanket and made a little noise. She started crying and slapped Bob as hard as she could, then run on alone, up to the cabin.

Bob watched her progress up the hill with mixed feelings. He took a healthy slug from the bourbon bottle, to give him an excuse to wipe his own eyes.

He could go sit on the beach and finish the bottle; let her get over it by herself. Or he could go comfort her.

He tossed the bottle away, the gesture immediately making him feel stupid, and followed her. Later that night she apologized, saying she didn't know what had gotten into her.

The Mazel Tov Revolution

~~~~~~~~~~~~~~~~~~~~~~~~~~~~~~~~~~~~~~~

I know exactly where this story comes from. One evening I was sitting with good friend Jack Dann, discussing anthologies. He wanted to edit a "theme" anthology—these are Great Science Fiction About Root Vegetables–type books—and we were bouncing around various topics that hadn't been done yet, or at least not recently, and might be saleable. I suggested he do an anthology of Jewish science fiction, as he is quite Jewish (try to imagine a creature that's a cross between Isaac Bashevis Singer and Henny Youngman) and does write science fiction. We even made up a list of various stories he might be able to use.

Lo and gevalt, he sold it. He wrote asking me for a Jewish science fiction story—but for three cents a word. I wrote back saying, Jack, my friendship knows no bounds, but there is a lower bound on my word rate for original stories. Five cents a word, boychik. He didn't write back.

A year or so later, he sold another anthology, this time needing stories about faster-than-light travel. Again, three cal power. Word rate, three cents. Again, he would not beg.

And then yet another: science fiction stories about political power. Word rate, three cents. Again he would not beg.

Finally, he writes saying he's putting together another anthology of Jewish science fiction. I begin to feel like Dr. Frankenstein. Three cents, take it or leave it. So I sit down and write "The Mazel Tov Revolution": a Jewish story about the effect of faster-than-light travel on political power. Sell it to Analog for a nickel a word.

Moral: I may prostitute my art, but at least I'm not a cheap whore.

This is the story of the □venerated/ □despised Chaim Itzkhok (check one). And me. And how we □made 238 worlds safe for democracy/ □really screwed everything up (check another). With twenty reams of paper and an old rock. I know you probably think you've heard the story before. But you haven't heard it all, not by a long way—things like blackmail and attempted murder, however polite, have a way of not getting in the history books. So read on, OK?

It all started out, for me at least, when I was stranded on Faraway a quarter of a century ago. You're probably thinking *you* wouldn't mind getting stranded on Faraway, right? Garden spot of the Confederation? Second capital of humanity? Monument to human engineering and all that, terraformed down to the last molecule. I tell kids what it was like back in '09 and they just shake their heads.

Back then, Faraway was one of those places where you might see an occasional tourist, only because it was one of the places that tourists just didn't go. It was one of the last outposts of George's abortive Second Empire, and had barely supported itself by exporting things like lead and cadmium. Nice poisonous heavy metals whose oxides covered the planet instead of grass. You had to run around in an asbestos suit with an air conditioner on your back, it was so damned close to Rigel.

Still is too damned close, but the way they opaqued the upper atmosphere, they tell me that Rigel is just a baby-blue ball that makes spectacular sunrises and sunsets. I've never been too tempted to go see it, having worked under its blue glare in the old days; wondering how long it'd be before you went sterile, lead underwear notwithstanding, feeling skin cancers sprouting in the shortwave radiation.

I met old Chaim there at the University Club, a run-down bar left over from the Empire days. How I got to that godforsaken place is a story in itself—one I can't tell because the husband is still alive—but I was down and out with no ticket back, dead-ended at thirty.

I was sitting alone in the University Club, ignoring the bartender, nursing my morning beer and feeling desperate when old Chaim came in. He was around seventy but looked older, all grizzled and seamed, and I started getting ready an excuse in case he was armed with a hard-luck story.

But he ordered a cup of real coffee and when he paid, I sneaked a look at his credit flash. The number was three digits longer than mine. Not prejudiced against million-aires, I struck up a conversation with him.

There was only one opening gambit for conversation on Faraway, since the weather never changed and there were no politics to speak of: What the hell are you doing here?

"It's the closest place to where I want to go," he said, which was ridiculous. Then he asked me the same, and I told him, and we commiserated for a few minutes on the unpredictability of the other sex. I finally got around to asking him exactly where it was he wanted to go.

"It's interesting enough," he said. Two other people had come into the bar. He looked at them blandly. "Why don't we move to a table?"

He got the bartender's attention and ordered another cup of coffee, and must have seen my expression—the tariff on two cups of coffee would keep me drunk for a week—and ordered me up a large jar of beer. We carried them to a table and he switched on the sound damper, which was the kind that works both ways.

"Can I trust you to keep a secret?" He took a cautious sip of his coffee.

"Sure. One more won't hurt."

He looked at me for a long time. "How would you like to get a share of a couple of million CU's?"

A ticket back cost about a hundred thousand. "That depends on what I'd have to do." I wouldn't have, for instance, jumped off a high building into a vat of boiling lead. Boiling water, yes.

"I can't say, exactly, because I really don't know. There may be an element of danger, there may not be. Certainly a few weeks of discomfort."

"I've had several of those, here."

He nodded at the insignia on my fading fatigue jacket. "You're still licensed to pilot?"

"Technically."

"Bonded?"

"No, like I told you, I had to skip out. My bond's on Perrin's World. I don't dare—"

"No problem, really. This is a system job." You need to be bonded for interstellar flight, but planet-to-planet, within a stellar system, there's not that much money involved.

"System job? Here? I didn't know Rigel had any other—"

"Rigel has one other planet, catalogued as Biarritz. It never got chartered or officially named because there's nothing there."

"Except something you want."

"Maybe something a lot of people want."

But he wouldn't tell me any more. We talked on until noon, Chaim feeling me out, seeing whether he could trust me, whether he wanted me as a partner. There were plenty of pilots stranded on Faraway; I later found out that he'd talked to a half-dozen or so before me.

We were talking about children or some damn thing when he suddenly sat up straight and said, "All right. I think you'll be my pilot."

"Good . . . now, just what—"

"Not yet, you don't need to know yet. What's your credit number?"

I gave it to him and he punched out a sequence on his credit flash. "This is your advance," he said; I checked my flash and, glory, I was fifty thousand CU's richer. "You get the same amount later, if Biarritz doesn't pan out. If it works, you'll also get a percentage. We'll talk about that later."

The other fifty thousand was all I wanted—get back to

civilization and I could hire a proxy to go to Perrin and rescue my bond. Then I'd be in business again.

"Now. The first thing you have to do is get us a ship. I'll arrange the financing." We left the bar and went to Faraway's only public (or private) stenographer, and he made out a letter of credit for me.

"Any kind of a ship will do," he said as I walked him back to his hotel. "Anything from a yacht to a battlewagon. We just have to get there. And back."

On any civilized world, I could have stepped into a booth and called Hartford; then strolled down to the nearest port and picked up a vessel: local, interplanetary or, if I was bonded and could wait a day or two, interstellar. But Faraway was Faraway, so it was a little more complicated.

Let me digress, in case you were born less than twenty years ago and fell asleep in history class.

Back then, we had two governments: the Confederation we all know and love, and New Hartford Transportation Rentals, Ltd. There was nothing on paper that connected the Confederation with Hartford, but in reality they were as intertwined as the skeins of a braid.

New Hartford Transportation Rentals, Ltd., owned virtually all of the basic patents necessary for interstellar travel as well as every starship, including the four clunkers left over from George VIII's disastrous imperialistic experiment.

Tired of your planet? Seek religious freedom, adventure, fresh air? Want to run from creditors? Get enough people together and Hartford would lease you a ship—for an astronomical sum, but at very generous rates. In fact, the first couple of generations hardly paid anything at all (while the interest built up), but then—

Talk about the sins of the fathers coming home to roost! Once a colony began to be a going concern, Hartford was empowered to levy a tax of up to fifty percent on every commercial transaction. And Hartford would carefully keep the tax down to a level where only the interest on the loan was being paid—the principal resting untouched, to provide Hartford an income in perpetuity. It was a rigged game (enforced by the Confederation), and everybody knew it. But it was the only game in town.

Hartford had a representative on every planet, and they kept him fueled with enough money so that he was always the richest, and usually the most influential, citizen of the planet. If a planetary government tried to evolve away from the rapacious capitalism that guaranteed Hartford a good return on its investment, their representative usually had enough leverage to put it back on the right road.

There were loopholes and technicalities. Most planets didn't pass the Hartford tax on directly, but used a sliding income tax, so the rich would get poorer and the poor, God bless them, would go home and make more taxpayers rather than riot in the streets.

If you ever patronized the kind of disreputable tavern that caters to pilots and other low types, you may have heard them singing that ancient ballad, "My Heart Belongs to Mother, But Hartford Owns My Ass."

Hartford owned that fundamental part of everybody on Faraway, too. But that didn't mean they'd supplied Faraway with a nice modern spaceport, bristling with ships of all sizes and ranges. No, just the bi-weekly vessel from Steiner that dropped off supplies and picked up some cadmium.

I had to admit there wasn't much reason for Faraway to have a short-run, plain old interplanetary ship—what good would it be? All you could do with it would be to orbit Faraway—and it looked bad enough from the *ground* —or take a joyride out to Biarritz. And there were more entertaining ways to throw away your money, even on Faraway.

It turned out that there actually was one interplanetary ship on Faraway, but it was a museum piece. It had been sitting for two hundred years, the *Bonne Chance,* the ship Biarritz herself had used to survey the clinker that retained her name by default. It was being held for back taxes, and we picked it up for six figures.

Then the headaches began. Everything was in French— dial markings, instruction manual, log. I got a dictionary and walked around with an indelible pencil, relabeling; and Chaim and I spent a week of afternoons and evenings translating the manual.

The fusion engine was in good shape—no moving parts bigger than a molecule—but the rest of the ship was pretty ragged. Faraway didn't have much of an atmosphere, but it was practically pure oxygen, and *hot*. The hull was all pitted and had to be reground. The electronic components of the ship had been exposed to two hundred years of enough ionizing radiation to mutate a couple of fruit flies into a herd of purple cattle. Most of the guidance and communications gimcrackery had to be repaired or replaced.

We kept half the drifter population of Faraway—some pretty highly trained drifters, of course—employed for over a week, hammering that antique wreck into some kind of shape. I took it up alone for a couple of orbits and decided I could get it twenty AU's and back without any major disaster.

Chaim was still being the mystery man. He gave me a list of supplies, but it didn't hold any clue as to what we were going to do once we were on Biarritz: just air, water, food, coffee and booze enough for two men to live on for a few months. Plus a prefab geodesic hut for them to live in.

Finally, Chaim said he was ready to go and I set up the automatic sequencing, about two hours of systems checks that were supposed to assure me that the machine wouldn't vaporize on the pad when I pushed the *Commence* button. I said a pagan prayer to Norbert Weiner and went down to the University Club for one last round or six. I could afford better bars, with fifty thousand CU's on my flash, but didn't feel like mingling with the upper classes.

I came back to the ship a half-hour before the sequencing was due to end, and Chaim was there, watching the slavies load a big crate aboard the *Bonne Chance*. "What the hell is that?" I asked him.

"The Mazel Tov papers," he said, not taking his eyes off the slavies.

"Mazel Tov?"

"It means good luck, maybe good-bye. Doesn't translate all that well. If you say it like this"—and he pronounced the words with a sarcastic inflection—"it can mean 'good riddance' or 'much good shall it do you.' Clear?"

"No."

"Good." They finished loading the crate and sealed the

hold door. "Give me a hand with this." It was a gray metal box that Chaim said contained a brand-new phased-tachyon transceiver.

If you're young enough to take the phased-tachyon process for granted, just step in a booth and call Sirius, I should point out that when Chaim and I met, they'd only had the machines for a little over a year. Before that, if you wanted to communicate with someone light-years away, you had to write out your message and put it on a Hartford vessel, then wait around weeks, sometimes months, while it got shuffled from planet to planet (at Hartford's convenience) until it finally wound up in the right person's hands.

Inside, I secured the box and called the pad authorities, asking them for our final mass. They read it off and I punched the information into the flight computer. Then we both strapped in.

Finally the green light flashed. I pushed the *Commence* button down to the locked position, and in a few seconds the engine rumbled into life. The ship shook like the palsied old veteran that it was, and climbed skyward trailing a cloud of what must have been the most polluting exhaust in the history of transportation: hot ionized lead, slightly radioactive. Old Biarritz had known how to economize on reaction mass.

I'd programmed a quick-and-dirty route, one and a half G's all the way, flip in the middle. Still it was going to take us two weeks. Chaim could have passed the time by telling me what it was all about, but instead he just sat around reading—*War and Peace* and a tape of Medieval Russian folk tales—every now and then staring at the wall and cackling.

Afterwards, I could appreciate his fetish for secrecy (though God knows enough people were in on part of the secret already). Not to say I might have been tempted to double-cross him. But his saying a couple of million were involved was like inviting someone to the Boston Tea Party by asking him if he'd like to put on a loincloth and help you play a practical joke.

So I settled down for two weeks with my own reading, earning my pay by pushing a button every couple of hours to keep a continuous systems check going. I could have programmed the button to push itself, but hell . . .

At the end of two weeks, I did have to earn my keep. I watched the "velocity relative to destination" readout crawl down to zero and looked out the viewport. Nothing.

Radar found the little planet handily enough. We'd only missed it by nine thousand and some kilometers; you could see its blue-gray disc if you knew where to look.

There's no trick to landing a ship like the *Bonne Chance* if you have a nice heavy planet. It's all automated except for selecting the exact patch of earth you want to scorch (port authorities go hard on you if you miss the pad). But a feather-light ball of dirt like Biarritz is a different proposition—there just isn't enough gravity, and the servomechanisms don't respond fast enough. They'll try to land you at the rock's center of mass, which in this case was underneath forty-nine kilometers of solid basalt. So you have to do it yourself, a combination of radar and dead reckoning—more a docking maneuver than a landing.

So I crashed. It could happen to anybody.

I was real proud of that landing at first. Even old Chaim congratulated me. We backed into the surface at less than one centimeter per second, all three shoes touching down simultaneously. We didn't even bounce.

Chaim and I were already suited up, and all the air had been evacuated from the ship; standard operating procedure to minimize damage in case something did go wrong. But the landing had looked perfect, so we went on down to start unloading.

What passes for gravity on Biarritz comes to barely one-eightieth of a G. Drop a shoe and it takes it five seconds to find the floor. So we half-climbed, half-floated down to the hold, clumsy after two weeks of living in a logy G-and-a-half.

While I was getting the hold door open, we both heard a faint bass moan, conducted up from the ground through the landing shoes. Chaim asked whether it was the ground settling; I'd never heard it happen before, but said that was probably it. We were right.

I got the door open and looked out. Biarritz looked just like I'd expected it to: a rock, a pockmarked chunk of useless rock. The only relief from the grinding monotony of the landscape was the silver splash of congealed lead directly below us.

We seemed to be at a funny angle. I thought it was an optical illusion—if the ship hadn't been upright on landing, it would have registered on the attitude readout. Then the bright lead splash started moving, crawling away under the ship. It took me a second to react.

I shouted something unoriginal and scrambled for the ladder to the control room. One short blip from the main engine and we'd be safely away. Didn't make it.

The situation was easy enough to reconstruct, afterwards. We'd landed on a shelf of rock that couldn't support the weight of the *Bonne Chance*. The sound we had heard was the shelf breaking off, settling down a few meters, canting the ship at about a ten-degree angle. The force of friction between our landing pads and the basalt underfoot was almost negligible, in so little gravity, and we slid downhill until we reached bottom, and then gracefully tipped over. When I got to the control room, after quite a bit of bouncing around in slow-motion, everything was sideways and the controls were dead, dead, dead.

Chaim was lively enough, shouting and sputtering. Back in the hold, he was buried under a pile of crates, having had just enough time to unstrap them before the ship went over. I explained the situation to him while helping him out.

"We're stuck here, eh?"

"I don't know yet. Have to fiddle around some."

"No matter. Inconvenient, but no matter. We're going to be so rich we could have a fleet of rescuers here tomorrow morning."

"Maybe," I said, knowing it wasn't so—even if there were a ship at Faraway, it couldn't possibly make the trip in less than ten days. "First thing we have to do, though, is put up that dome." Our suits weren't the recycling kind; we had about ten hours before we had to start learning how to breathe carbon dioxide.

We sorted through the jumble and found the various components of the pop-up geodesic. I laid it out on a piece of reasonably level ground and pulled the lanyard. It assembled itself very nicely. Chaim started unloading the ship while I hooked up the life-support system.

He was having a fine time, kicking crates out the door and watching them float to the ground a couple of meters below. The only one that broke was a case of whiskey—every single bottle exploded, damn it, making a cloud of brownish crystals that slowly dissipated. So Biarritz was the only planet in the universe with a bonded-bourbon atmosphere.

When Chaim got to *his* booze, a case of gin, he carried it down by hand.

We set up housekeeping while the dome was warming. I was still opening boxes when the bell went off, meaning there was enough oxygen and heat for life. Chaim must have had more trust in automatic devices than I had; he popped off his helmet immediately and scrambled out of his suit. I took off my helmet to be sociable, but kept on working at the last crate, the one Chaim had said contained "the Mazel Tov papers."

I got the top peeled away and looked inside. Sure enough, it was full of paper, in loose stacks.

I picked up a handful and looked at them. "Immigration forms?"

Chaim was sitting on a stack of food cartons, peeling off his suit liner. "That's right. Our fortune."

" 'Mazel Tov Immigration Bureau,' " I read off one of the sheets. "Who—"

"You're half of it. I'm half of it. Mazel Tov is the planet under your feet." He slipped off the box. "Where'd you put our clothes?"

"What?"

"This floor's cold."

"Uh, over by the kitchen." I followed his naked wrinkled back as he climbed across the dome. "Look, you can't just . . . *name* a planet . . ."

"I can't, eh?" He rummaged through the footlocker and found some red tights, struggled into them. "Who says I can't?"

"The Confederation! Hartford! You've got to get a charter."

He found an orange tunic that clashed pretty well and slipped it over his head. Muffled: "So I'm going to get a charter."

"Just like that."

He started strapping on his boots and looked at me with amusement. "No, not 'just like that.' Let's make some coffee." He filled two cups with water and put them in the heater.

"You can't just charter a rock with two people on it."

"You're right. You're absolutely right." The timer went off. "Cream and sugar?"

"Look—no, black—you mean to say you printed up some fake—"

"Hot." He handed me the cup. "Sit down. Relax. I'll explain."

I was still in my suit, minus the helmet, so sitting was no more comfortable than standing. But I sat.

He looked at me over the edge of his cup, through a veil of steam rising unnaturally fast. "I made my first million when I was your age."

"You've got to start somewhere."

"Right. I made a million and paid eighty-five percent of it to the government of Nueva Argentina, who skimmed a little off the top and passed it on to New Hartford Transportation Rentals, Ltd."

"Must have hurt."

"It made me angry. It make me think. And I did get the germ of an idea." He sipped.

"Go on."

"I don't suppose you've ever heard of the Itzkhok Shipping Agency."

"No . . . it probably would have stuck in my mind."

"Very few people have. On the surface, it's a very small operation. Four interplanetary ships, every one of them smaller than the *Bonne Chance*. But they're engaged in interstellar commerce."

"Stars must be pretty close together."

"No . . . they started about twenty years ago. The shortest voyage is about half over. One has over a century to go."

"Doesn't make any sense."

"But it does. It makes sense on two levels." He set down the cup and laced his fingers together.

"There are certain objects whose value almost has to go up with the passage of time. Jewelry, antiques, works of art. These are the only cargo I deal with. Officially."

"I see. I think."

"You see half of it. I buy these objects on relatively poor

planets and ship them to relatively affluent ones. I didn't have any trouble getting stockholders. Hartford wasn't too happy about it, of course."

"What did they do?"

He shrugged. "Took me to court. I'd studied the law, though, before I started Itzkhok. They didn't press too hard—my company didn't make one ten-thousandth of Hartford's annual profit—and I won."

"And made a credit or two."

"Some three billion, legitimate profit. But the important thing is that I established a concrete legal precedent where none had existed before."

"You're losing me again. Does this have anything to do with . . ."

"Everything, patience. With this money, and money from other sources, I started building up a fleet. Through a number of dummy corporations . . . buying old ships, building new ones. I own or am leasing some two thousand ships. Most of them are loaded and on the pad right now."

"Wait, now." Economics was never my strong suit, but this was obvious. "You're going to drive your own prices down. There can't be that big a market for old paintings and—"

"Right, precisely. But most of these ships aren't carrying such specialized cargo. The closest one, for instance, is on Tangiers, aimed for Faraway. It holds nearly a hundred thousand cubic meters of water."

"Water . . ."

"Old passenger liner, flooded the damn thing. Just left a little room for ice expansion, in case the heating—"

"Because on Faraway—"

"—on Faraway there isn't one molecule of water that men didn't carry there. They recycle every drop but have to lose one percent or so annually."

"Tonight or tomorrow I'm going to call up Faraway and offer to sell them 897,000 kilograms of water. At cost. Delivery in six years. It's a long time to wait, but they'll be getting it for a hundredth of the usual cost, what Hartford charges."

"And you'll lose a bundle."

"Depends on how you look at it. Most of my capital is tied up in small, slow spaceships; I own some interest in three-quarters of the interplanetary vessels that exist. If my scheme works, all of them will double in value overnight.

"Hartford, though, is going to lose more than a bundle. There are 237 other planets, out of 298, in a position similar to Faraway's. They depend on Hartford for water, or seed, or medical supplies, or something else necessary for life."

"And you have deals set up—"

"For all of them, right. Underbidding Hartford by at least a factor of ten." He drank off the rest of his coffee in a gulp.

"What's to stop Hartford from underbidding *you?*"

"Absolutely nothing." He got up and started preparing another cup. "They'll probably try to, here and there. I don't think many governments will take them up on it.

"Take Faraway as an example. They're in a better position than most planets, as far as their debt to Hartford, because the Second Empire financed the start of their colonization. Still, they owe Hartford better than ten billion CU's—their annual interest payment comes to several hundred million.

"They keep paying it, not because of some abstract obligation to Hartford. Governments don't have consciences. If they stopped paying, of course, they'd dry up and die in a generation. Until today, they didn't have any choice in the matter."

"So what you're doing is giving all of those planets a chance to welsh on their debts."

"That bothers you?" He sat back down, balanced the cup on his knee.

"A little. I don't love Hartford any more than—"

"Look at it this way. My way. Consider Hartford as an arm of the government, the Confederation."

"I've always thought it was the other way around."

"In a practical sense, yes. But either way. A government sends its people out to colonize virgin lands. It subsidizes them at first; once the ball is rolling, it collects allegiance and taxes.

"The 'debt' to Hartford is just a convenient fiction to justify taking these taxes."

"There are services rendered, though. Necessary to life."

"Rendered and paid for, separately. I'm going to prove

47

to the 'colonies' that they can provide these services to each other. It will be even easier once Hartford goes bankrupt. There'll be no monopoly on starships. No Confederation to protect patents."

"Anarchy, then."

"Interesting word. I prefer to call it revolution . . . but yes, things will be pretty hectic for a while."

"All right. But if you wanted to choreograph a revolution, why didn't you pick a more comfortable planet to do it from? Are you just hiding?"

"Partly that. Mostly, though, I wanted to do everything legally. For that, I needed a very small planet without a charter."

"I'm lost again." I made myself another cup of coffee and grieved for the lack of bourbon. Maybe if I went outside and took a deep breath . . .

"You know what it takes to charter a planet?" Chaim asked me.

"Don't know the numbers. Certain population density and high enough gross planetary product."

"The figures aren't important. They look modest enough on paper. The way it works out, though, is that by the time a planet is populated enough and prosperous enough to get its independence, it's almost guaranteed to be irretrievably in debt to Hartford.

"That's what all those immigration forms are for. Half of those stacks are immigration forms and the other half, limited powers of attorney. I'm going to claim this planet, name it Mazel Tov, and accept my own petition for citizenship on behalf of 4,783 immigrants. Then I make one call, to my lawyer." He named an Earth-based interplanetary law firm so well-known that even I had heard of it.

"They will call about a hundred of these immigrants, each of whom will call ten more, then ten more, and so on. All prearranged. Each of them then pays me his immigration fee."

"How much is that?"

"Minimum, ten million CU's."

"God!"

"It's a bargain. A new citizen gets one share in the Mazel Tov Corporation for each million he puts in. In thirty minutes MTC should have almost as much capital behind it as Hartford has."

"Where could you find four thousand—"

"Twenty years of persuasion. Of coordination. I've tried to approach every living man of wealth whose fortune is not tied up with Hartford or the Confederation. I've showed them my plan—especially the safeguards on it that make it a low-risk, high-return investment—and every single one of them has signed up."

"Not one betrayal?"

"No—what could the Confederation or Hartford offer in return? Wealth? Power? These men already have that in abundance.

"On the other hand, I offer them a gift beyond price: independence. And incidentally, no taxes, ever. That's the first article of the charter."

He let me absorb that for a minute. "It's too facile," I said. "If your plan works, everything will fall apart for the Confederation and Hartford—but look what we get instead. Four thousand-some independent robber barons, running the whole show. That's an improvement?"

"Who can say? But that's revolution: throw the old set of bastards out and install your own set. At least it'll be different. Time for a change."

I got up. "Look, this is too much, too fast. I've got to think about it. Digest it. Got to check out the ship, too."

Chaim went along with me halfway to the air lock. "Good, good. I'll start making calls." He patted the transceiver with real affection. "Good thing this baby came along when it did. It would have been difficult coordinating this thing, passing notes around. Maybe impossible."

It didn't seem that bloody easy, even with all those speedy little tachyons helping us. I didn't say anything.

It was a relief to get back into my own element, out of the dizzying fumes of high finance and revolution. But it was short-lived.

Things started out just dandy. The reason the control board was dead was that its cable to the fuel cells had jarred loose. I plugged it back in and set up a systems check. The systems check ran for two seconds and quit. What was wrong with the ship was number IV-A-1-a. It took me a half-hour to find the manual, which had slid into the head and nestled up behind the commode.

"IV" was fusion power source. "IV-A" was generation of magnetic field for containment thereof. "IV-A-1" was disabilities of magnetic field generator. And "IV-A-1-a," of course, was permanent disability. It had a list of recommended types of replacement generators.

Well, I couldn't run down to the store and pick up a generator. And you can't produce an umpty-million-gauss fusion mirror by rubbing two sticks together. So I kicked Mlle. Biarritz's book across the room and went back to the dome.

Chaim was hunched over the transceiver, talking to somebody while he studied his own scribblings in a notebook.

"We're stuck here," I said.

He nodded at me and kept up the conversation. "—that's right. Forty thousand bushels, irradiated, for five hundred thousand CU's . . . so *what?* So it's a gift. It's guaranteed. Delivery in about seven years, you'll get details . . . all right, fine. A pleasure to do business. Thank *you,* sir."

He switched off and leaned back and laughed. "They all think I'm crazy!"

"We're stuck here," I said again.

"Don't worry about it, don't *worry,*" he said, pointing to an oversized credit flash attached to the transceiver. It had a big number on it that was constantly changing, going up. "That is the total assets of Mazel Tov Corporation." He started laughing again.

"Minims?"

"No, round credits."

I counted places. "A hundred and twenty-eight billion . . . credits?"

"That's right, right. You want to go to Faraway? We'll have it *towed* here."

"A hundred and twenty-nine billion?" It was really kind of hard to grasp.

"Have a drink—celebrate!" There was a bowl of ice and a bottle of gin on the floor beside him. God, I hate gin.

"Think I'll fix a cup of tea." By the time I'd had my cup, cleaned up and changed out of my suit, Chaim was through with his calls. The number on the credit flash was up to 239,605,967,000 and going up slowly.

He took his bottle, glass and ice to his bunk and asked me to start setting up the rescue mission.

I called Hartford headquarters on Earth. Six people referred me to their superiors and I wound up talking to the Coordinator of Interstellar Transit himself. I found out that bad news travels fast.

"Mazel Tov?" his tinny voice said. "I've heard of you, new planet out by Rigel? Next to Faraway?"

"That's right. We need a pickup and we can pay."

"Oh, that's not the problem. Right now there just aren't any ships available. Won't be for several months. Maybe a year."

"What? We only have three months' worth of air!" By this time Chaim was standing right behind me, breathing gin into my ear.

"I'm really very sorry. But I thought that by the time a planet gets its charter, it should be reasonably self-sufficient."

"That's murder!" Chaim shouted.

"No, sir," the voice said. "Just unfortunate planning on your part. You shouldn't have filed for—" Chaim reached over my shoulder and slapped the switch off, hard. He stomped back to his bunk—difficult to do with next to no gravity—sat down and shook some gin into his glass. He looked at it and set it on the floor.

"Who can we bribe?" I asked.

He kept staring at the glass. "No one. We can try, but I doubt that it's worth the effort. Not with Hartford fighting for its life. Its corporate life."

"I know lots of pilots we could get, cheap."

"Pilots," Chaim said without too much respect.

I ignored the slur. "Yeah. Hartford programs the main jump. Nobody'd get a jump to Rigel."

We sat in silence for a while, the too-sober pilot and the Martian-Russian Jew who was the richest person in the history of mankind. Less than too sober.

"Sure there's no other ship on Faraway?"

"I'm sure," I said. "Took me half a day to find someone who remembered about the *Bonne Chance*."

He considered that for a minute. "What does it take to build an interplanetary ship? Besides money."

"What, you mean could they build one on Faraway?"

"Right."

"Let me see." Maybe. "You need an engine. A cabin and life-support stuff. Steering jets or gyros. Guidance and commo equipment."

"Well?"

"I don't know. The engine would be the hard part. They don't have all that much heavy industry on Faraway."

"No harm in finding out."

I called Faraway. Talked to the mayor. He was an old pilot (having been elected by popular vote) and I finally reached him at the University Club, where he was surrounded by other old pilots. I talked to him about engineering. Chaim talked to him about money. Chaim shouted and wept at him about money. We made a deal.

Faraway having such an abundance of heavy metals, the main power generator for the town, the only settlement on the planet, was an old-fashioned fission generator. We figured out a way they could use it.

After a good deal of haggling and swearing, the citizens of Faraway agreed to cobble together a rescue vehicle. In return, they would get control of forty-nine percent of the stock of Mazel Tov Corporation.

Chaim was mad for a while, but eventually got his sense of humor back. We had to kill two months with six already-read books and a fifty-bottle case of gin. I read *War and Peace* twice. The second time I made a list of the characters. I made crossword puzzles out of the characters' names. I learned how to drink gin, if not how to like it. I felt like I was going slowly crazy—and when the good ship *Hello There* hove into view, I knew I'd gone 'round the bend.

The *Hello There* was a string of fourteen buildings strung along a lattice of salvaged beams; a huge atomic reactor pushing it from the rear. The buildings had been uprooted whole, life-support equipment and all, from the spaceport area of Faraway. The first building, the control room, was the transplanted University Club, Olde English decorations still intact. There were thirty pairs of wheels along one side of the "vessel," the perambulating shanty-town.

We found out later that they had brought along a third of the planet's population, since most of the buildings on Faraway were without power and therefore uninhabitable. The thing (I still can't call it a ship) had to be put on wheels because they had no way to crank it upright for launching. They drove it off the edge of a cliff and pulled for altitude with the pitch jets. The pilot said it had been pretty harrowing, and after barely surviving the landing I could marvel at his power of understatement.

The ship hovered over Mazel Tov with its yaw jets and they lowered a ladder for us. Quite a feat of navigation. I've often wondered whether the pilot could have done it sober.

The rest, they say, is history. And current events. As Chaim had predicted Hartford went into receivership, MTC being the receiver. We did throw out all of the old random bastards and install our own hand-picked ones.

I shouldn't bitch. I'm still doing the only thing I ever wanted to do. Pilot a starship; go places, do things. And I'm moderately wealthy, with a tenth-share of MTC stock.

It'd just be a lot easier to take, if every ex-bum on Faraway didn't have a hundred times as much. I haven't gone back there since they bronzed the University Club and put it on a pedestal.

To Howard Hughes: A Modest Proposal

≈≈≈≈≈≈≈≈≈≈≈≈≈≈≈≈≈≈≈≈≈≈≈≈≈

One good reason for a novelist to write short stories is that they serve as a proving ground for new techniques. If a structure or texture doesn't work in a short story, you've only lost a few days, and learned something. If a novel goes sour, and I do speak from experience, you lose a thick stack of paper and more. And you might not learn as well, because of your deeper involvement, as a parent might see his child go wrong and never see how he'd caused it.

I admire the work of John Dos Passos, especially the USA trilogy, and wanted to borrow his intricate technique for a science fiction novel.* I wanted to boil it down, make it even more rapid and nervous. This story was the test case, and I liked it, so I used the technique for Mindbridge (St. Martin's Press, 1976), which I think is my best novel, so far.

When I wrote this I was in the process of putting together an anthology of science fiction alternatives to war, which languished for some years before St. Martin's Press published it as Study War No More (1977). The story was written for the anthology, and was meant to be sarcastic. But at that time its basic premise seemed rather absurd.

Some few predictive elements of some of my stories have come true. I'm afraid this one will add to the list.

---

* In the real world it's against the law to take something that somebody else is trying to sell. But since John Brunner already adapted Dos Passos's technique in his powerful novels *Stand on Zanzibar* (Doubleday, 1968) and *The Sheep Look Up* (Harper & Row, 1972), I guess my crime is the receiving of stolen goods rather than kleptomania.

1.   13 October 1975

Shark Key is a few hundred feet of sand and scrub between two slightly larger islands in the Florida Keys: population, one.

Not even one person actually lives there—perhaps the
name has not been attractive to real estate developers—but
there is a locked garage, a dock and a mailbox fronting on
US 1. The man who owns this bit of sand—dock, box, and
carport—lives about a mile out in the Gulf of Mexico and
has an assistant who picks up the mail every morning, and
gets groceries and other things.

Howard Knopf Ramo is the sole "resident" of Shark
Key, and he has many assistants besides the delivery boy.
Two of them have doctorates in an interesting specialty, of
which more later. One is a helicopter pilot, one ran a lathe
under odd conditions, one is a youngish ex-Colonel (West
Point, 1960), one was a contract killer for the Mafia, five
are doing legitimate research into the nature of gravity,
several dozen are dullish clerks and technicians, and one,
not living with the rest off Shark Key, is a U.S. Senator
who does not represent Florida but nevertheless does look
out for the interests of Howard Knopf Ramo. The research-
ers and the delivery boy are the only ones in Ramo's em-
ploy whose income he reports to the IRS, and he only
reports one-tenth at that. All the other gentlemen and ladies
also receive ten-times-generous salaries, but they are all
legally dead, so the IRS has no right to their money, and it
goes straight to anonymously numbered Swiss accounts
without attrition by governmental gabelle.

Ramo paid out little more than one million dollars in

salaries and bribes last year; he considered it a sound investment of less than one-fourth of one per cent of his total worth.

2.   7 May 1955

Our story began, well, many places with many people. But one pivotal person and place was 17-year-old Ronald Day, then going to high school in sleepy Winter Park, Florida.

Ronald wanted to join the Army, but he didn't want to just *join* the Army. He had to be an officer, and he wanted to be an Academy man.

His father had served gallantly in WWII and in Korea until an AP mine in Ch'unch'on (Operation "Ripper") forced him to retire. At that time he had had for two days a battlefield commission, and he was to find that the difference between NCO's retirement and officer's retirement would be the difference between a marginal life and a comfortable one, subsequent to the shattering of his leg. Neither father nor son blamed the Army for having sent the senior Day marching through a muddy mine field, 1955 being what it was, and neither thought the military life was anything but the berries. More berries for the officers, of course, and the most for West Pointers.

The only problem was that Ronald was, in the jargon of another trade, a "chronic underachiever." He had many fascinating hobbies and skills and an IQ of 180, but he was barely passing in high school, and so had little hope for an appointment. Until Howard Knopf Ramo came into his life.

That spring afternoon, Ramo demonstrated to father and son that he had the best interests of the United States at heart, and that he had a great deal of money (nearly a hundred million dollars even then), and that he knew something rather embarrassing about senior Day, and that in exchange for certain reasonable considerations he would get Ronald a place in West Point, class of 1960.

Not too unpredictably, Ronald's intelligence blossomed in the straitjacket discipline at the Point. He majored in physics, that having been part of the deal, and took his commission and degree—with high honors—in 1960. His commission was in the Engineers and he was assigned to the Atomic Power Plant School at Fort Belvoir, Virginia. He took courses at the School and at Georgetown University nearby.

He was Captain Ronald Day and bucking for major, one step from being in charge of Personnel & Recruitment, when he returned to his billet one evening and found Ramo waiting for him in a stiff-backed chair. Ramo was wearing the uniform of a brigadier general and he asked a few favors. Captain Day agreed gladly to cooperate, not really believing the stars on Ramo's shoulders; partly because the favors seemed harmless if rather odd, but reasonable in view of past favors; mainly because Ramo told him something about what he planned to do over the next decade. It was not exactly patriotic but involved a great deal of money. And Captain Day, O times and mores, had come to think more highly of money than of patriotism.

Ramo's representatives met with Day several times in the following years, but the two men themselves did not meet again until early 1972. Day eventually volunteered for Vietnam, commanding a battalion of combat engineers. His helicopter went down behind enemy lines, such lines as there were in that war, in January, 1972, and for one year he was listed as MIA. The North Vietnamese eventually released their list and he became KIA, body never recovered.

By that time his body, quite alive and comfortable, was resting a mile off Shark Key.

3.   5 December 1969

Andre Charvat met Ronald Day only once, at Fort Belvoir, five years before they would live together under Ramo's roof. Andre had dropped out of Iowa State as a sophomore, was drafted, was sent to the Atomic Power Plant School, learned the special skills necessary to turn radioactive metals into pleasing or practical shapes, left the Army and got a job running a small lathe by remote control, from behind several inches of lead, working with plutonium at an atomic power applications research laboratory in Los Alamos—being very careful not to waste any plutonium, always ending up with the weight of the finished piece and the shavings exactly equal to the weight of the rough piece he had started with.

But a few milligrams at a time, he was substituting simple uranium for the precious plutonium shavings.

He worked at Los Alamos for nearly four years, and brought 14.836 grams of plutonium with him when he arrived via midnight barge off Shark Key, 12 November 1974.

Many other people in similar situations had brought their grams of plutonium to Shark Key. Many more would, before the New Year.

4.   1 January 1975

"Ladies. Gentlemen." Howard Knopf Ramo brushes long white hair back in a familiar, delicate gesture and with the other hand raises a tumbler to eye level. It bubbles with good domestic champagne. "Would anyone care to propose a toast?"

An awkward silence, over fifty people crowded into the television room. On the screen, muted cheering as the Allied Chemical ball begins to move. "The honor should be yours, Ramo," says Colonel Day.

Ramo nods, gazing at the television. "Thirty years," he whispers and says aloud: "To *our* year. To our world."

Drink, silence, sudden chatter.

5.   2 January 1975

Curriculum Vitae

My name is Philip Vale and I have been working with Howard Knopf Ramo for nearly five years. In 1967 I earned a doctorate in nuclear engineering at the University of New Mexico and worked for two years on nuclear propulsion systems for spacecraft. When my project was shelved for lack of funding in 1969, it was nearly impossible for a nuclear engineer to get a job; literally impossible in my specialty.

We lived off savings for a while. Eventually I had to take a job teaching high school physics and felt lucky to have any kind of a job, even at $7000 per year.

But in 1970 my wife suffered an attack of acute glomerulonephritis and lost both kidneys. The artificial dialysis therapy was not covered by our health insurance, and to keep her alive would have cost some $25,000 yearly. Ramo materialized and made me a generous offer.

Three weeks later, Dorothy and I were whisked incognito to Shark Key, our disappearance covered by a disastrous automobile accident. His artificial island was mostly unoccupied in 1970, but half of one floor was given over to medical facilities. There was a dialysis machine and two of the personnel were trained in its use. Ramo called it "benevolent blackmail" and outlined my duties for the next several years.

6.   4 April 1970

When Philip Vale came to Ramo's island, all that showed above water was a golden geodesic dome supported by massive concrete pillars and armthick steel cables that sang basso in the wind. Inside the dome were living quarters for six people and a more-or-less legitimate research establishment called Gravitics, Inc. Ramo lived there with two technicians, a delivery boy and two specialists in gravity research. The establishment was very expensive but Ramo claimed to love pure science, hoped for eventual profit, and admitted that it made his tax situation easier. It also gave him the isolation that semi-billionaires traditionally prefer; because of the delicacy of the measurements necessary to his research, no airplanes were allowed to buzz overhead and the Coast Guard kept unauthorized ships from coming within a one-mile radius. All five employees did do research work in gravity; they published with expected frequency, took out occasional patents, and knew they were only a cover for the actual work about to begin downstairs.

There were seven underwater floors beneath the golden dome, and Dr. Philip Vale's assignment was to turn those seven floors into a factory for the construction of small atom bombs. 29 Nagasaki-sized fission bombs.

7.   August 1945

Howard Knopf Ramo worked as a dollar-a-year man for several years, the government consulting him on organizational matters for various projects. The details of many of these projects were quite secret, but he gave as good advice as he could, without being told classified details.

In August 1945 Ramo learned what that Manhattan Project had been all about.

8.   5 April 1970—3 February 1972

Dr. Philip Vale was absorbed for several weeks in initial planning: flow charts, lists of necessary equipment and personnel, timetables, floor plans. The hardest part of his job was figuring out a way to steal a lot of plutonium without being too obvious about it. Ramo had some ideas, on this and other things, that Vale expanded.

By the middle of 1971 there were thirty people living under Gravitics, Inc., and plutonium had begun to trickle in, a few grams at a time, to be shielded with lead and cadmium and concrete and dropped into the Gulf of Mexico at carefully recorded spots within the one-mile limit. In July they quietly celebrated Ramo's 75th birthday.

On 3 February 1972, Colonel Ronald Day joined Vale and the rest. The two shared the directorship amicably, Day suggesting that they go ahead and make several mock-up bombs, both for time-and-motion studies within the plant and in order to check the efficiency of their basic delivery system: an Econoline-type van, specially modified.

9.   Technological Aside

One need not gather a "critical mass" of plutonium in order to make an atom bomb of it. It is sufficient to take a considerably smaller piece and subject it to a neutron density equivalent to that which prevails at standard temperature and pressure inside plutonium at critical mass. This can be done with judiciously shaped charges of high explosive.

The whole apparatus can fit comfortably inside a Ford Econoline van.

10.   9 September 1974

Progress Report

Delivery Implementation Section

TO: Ramo, Vale, Day, Sections 2, 5, 8.

As of this date we can safely terminate R & D on the following vehicles: Ford, Fiat, Austin, VW. Each has performed flawlessly on trial runs to Atlanta.

On-the-spot vehicle checks assure us that we can use Econolines for Ghana, Bombay, Montevideo, and Madrid, without attracting undue attention.

The Renault and Soyuz vans have not been road-tested because they are not distributed in the United States. One mockup Renault is being smuggled to Mexico, where they are fairly common, to be tested. We may be able to modify the Ford setup to fit inside a Soyuz shell. However, we have only two of the Russian vans to work with, and will proceed with caution.

The Toyota's suspension gave out in one out of three Atlanta runs; it was simply not designed for so heavy a load. We may substitute Econolines or VW's for Tokyo and Kyoto.

90% of the vehicles were barged to New Orleans before the Atlanta run, to avoid suspicion at the Key Largo weigh station.

We are sure all systems will be in shape well before the target date.

(signed) Supervisor Maxwell Bergman

11.   14 October 1974

Today they solved the China Problem: automobiles and trucks are still fairly rare in China, and its border is probably the most difficult to breach. Ramo wants a minimum of three targets in China, but the odds against being able to smuggle out three vans, load them with bombs, smuggle them back in again and drive them to the target areas without being stopped—the odds are formidable.

Section 2 (Weapons Research & Development) managed to compress a good-sized bomb into a package the size of a large suitcase, weighing about 800 pounds. It is less powerful than the others, and not as subtly safeguarded— read "boobytrapped"—but should be adequate to the task. It will go in through Hong Kong in a consignment of Swiss heavy machinery, bound for Peking; duplicates will go to Kunming and Shanghai, integrated with farm machinery and boat hulls, respectively, from Japan. Section 1 (Recruiting) has found delivery agents for Peking and Shanghai, is looking for a native speaker of the dialect spoken around Kunming.

12. Naming

Ramo doesn't like people to call it "Project Blackmail," so they just call it "the project" when he's around.

13. 1 July 1975

Everything is in order: delivery began one week ago. Today is Ramo's 79th birthday.

His horoscope for today says "born today, you are a natural humanitarian. You aid those in difficulty and would make a fine attorney. You are attracted to the arts, including writing. You are due for domestic adjustment, with September indicated as a key month."

None of the above is true. It will be in October.

14. 13 October 1975

7:45 on a grey Monday morning in Washington, D.C., a three-year-old Econoline van rolls up to a Park-yourself lot on 14th Street. About a quarter-mile from the White House.

The attendant gives the driver his ticket. "How long ya gonna be?"

"Don't know," he says. "All day, probably."

"Put it back there then, by the Camaro."

The driver parks the van and turns on a switch under

the dash. With a tiny voltmeter he checks the dead-man switch on his arm: a constant-readout sphygmomanometer wired to a simple signal generator. If his blood pressure drops too low too quickly, downtown Washington will be a radioactive hole.

Everything in order, he gets out and locks the van. This activates the safeguards. A minor collision won't set off the bomb, and neither would a Richter-6 earthquake. It will go off if anyone tries to X-ray the van or enter it.

He walks two blocks to his hotel. He is very careful crossing streets.

He has breakfast sent up and turns on the *Today* show. There is no news of special interest. At 9:07 he calls a number in Miami. Ramo's fortune is down to fifty million, but he can still afford a suite at the Beachcomber.

At 9:32, all American targets having reported, Ramo calls Reykjavik.

"Let me speak to Colonel Day. This is Ramo."

"Just a moment, sir." One moment. "Day here."

"Things are all in order over here, Colonel. Have your salesmen reported yet?"

"All save two, as expected," he says: everyone but Peking and Kunming.

"Good. Everything is pretty much in your hands, then. I'm going to go down and do that commercial."

"Good luck, sir."

"We're past the need for luck. Be careful, Colonel." He rings off.

Ramo shaves and dresses, white Palm Beach suit. The reflection in the mirror looks like somebody's grandfather; not long for this world, kindly but a little crotchety, a little senile. Perhaps a little senile. That's why Colonel Day is coordinating things in Iceland, rather than Ramo. If Ramo dies, Day can decide what to do. If Day dies, the bombs all go off automatically.

"Let's go," he shouts into the adjoining room. His voice is still clear and strong.

Two men go down the elevator with him. One is the ex-hit man, with a laundered identity (complete to plastic surgery) and two hidden pistols. The other is Philip Vale, who carries with him all of the details of Project Blackmail and, at Ramo's suggestion, a .44 Magnum single-shot derringer. He watches the hit man, and the hit man watches everybody else.

The Cadillac that waits for them outside the Beachcomber is discreetly bulletproof and has under the front and rear seats, respectively, a Thompson submachine gun and a truncated 12-gauge shotgun. The ex-hit man insisted on the additional armament, and Ramo provided them for the poor man's peace of mind. For his own peace of mind Ramo, having no taste for violence on so small a scale, had the firing pins removed last night.

They drive to a network-affiliated television station, having spent a good deal of money for ten minutes of network time. For a paid political announcement.

It only cost a trifle more to substitute their own men for Union employees behind the camera and in the control room.

15. Transcript

FADE IN LONG SHOT: RAMO, PODIUM, GLOBE

RAMO

My name is Howard Knopf Ramo.

SLOW DOLLY TO MCU RAMO

RAMO

Please don't leave your set; what I have to say is extremely important to you and your loved ones. And I won't take too much of your time.

You've probably never heard of me, though some years ago my accountants told me I was the richest man in the world. I spent a good deal of those riches staying out of the public eye. The rest of my fortune I spent on a project that has taken me thirty years to complete.

I was born just twenty-one years after the Civil War. In my lifetime, my country has been in five major wars and dozens of small confrontations. I didn't consider the reasons for most of them worthwhile. I didn't think that any of them were worth the price we paid.

And at that, we fared well compared to many other countries, whether they won their wars or lost them. Still, we continue to have wars. Rather . . .

TIGHT ON RAMO

. . . our *leaders* continue to declare wars, advancing their own political aims by sending sons and brothers and fathers out to bleed and die.

CUT TO:

MEDIUM SHOT, RAMO SLOWLY TURNING GLOBE

RAMO

We have tolerated this situation through all of recorded history. No longer. China, the Soviet Union, and the United States have stockpiled nuclear weapons sufficient to destroy all human life, twice over. It has gone beyond politics and become a matter of racial survival.

I propose a plan to take these weapons away from them —every one, simultaneously. To this end I have spent my fortune constructing 29 atomic bombs. 28 of them are hidden in various cities around the world. One of them is in an airplane high over Florida. It is the smallest one; a demonstration model, so to speak.

CUT TO:

REMOTE UNIT; PAN SHORELINE

RAMO

VOICE OVER SURF SOUND

This is the Atlantic Ocean, off one of Florida's Keys. The bomb will explode seven miles out, at exactly 10:30. All shipping has been cleared from the area and prevailing winds will disperse the small amount of fallout harmlessly.

Florida residents within fifty miles of Shark Key are warned not to look directly at the blast.

FILTER DOWN ON REMOTE UNIT

Watch. There!

AFTER BLAST COMES AND FADES

CUT TO:

TIGHT ON RAMO

RAMO

Whether or not you agree with me, that all nations must give up their arms, is immaterial. Whether I am a saint or a power-drunk madman is immaterial. I give the governments of the world three days' notice—not just the atomic powers, but their allies as well. Perhaps less than three days, if they do not follow my instructions to the letter.

Atomic bombs at least equivalent to the ones that devastated Hiroshima and Nagasaki have been placed in the following cities:

MCU RAMO AND GLOBE

RAMO

TOUCHES GLOBE AS HE NAMES EACH CITY

Accra, Cairo, Khartoum, Johannesburg, London, Dublin, Madrid, Paris, Berlin, Rome, Warsaw, Budapest, Moscow, Leningrad, Novosibirsk, Ankara, Bombay, Sydney, Peking, Shanghai, Kunming, Tokyo, Kyoto, Honolulu, Akron, San Francisco, New York, Washington.

The smaller towns of Novosibirsk, Kunming and Akron —one for each major atomic power—are set to go off eight hours before the others, as a final warning.

These bombs will also go off if tampered with, or if my representatives are harmed in any way. The way this will be done, and the manner in which atomic weapons will be collected, is explained in a letter now being sent through diplomatic channels to the leader of each threatened country. Copies will also be released to the world press.

A colleague of mine has dubbed this effort "Project Blackmail." Unflattering, but perhaps accurate.

CUT TO:

LONG SHOT RAMO, PODIUM, GLOBE

RAMO

Three days. Goodbye.

FADE TO BLACK

16. Briefing

"They didn't *catch* him?" The President was livid.

"No, sir. They had to find out what studio the broadcast originated from and then get—"

"Never mind. Do they know where the bomb is?"

"Yes, sir, it's on page six." The aide tentatively offered the letter, which a courier from the Polish embassy had brought a few minutes after the broadcast.

"Where? Has anything been done?"

"It's in a public parking lot on 14th Street. The police—"

"Northwest?"

"Yes, sir."

"Good God. That's only a few blocks from here."

"Yes, sir."

"No respect for . . . nobody's fiddled with it, have they?"

"No, sir. It's boobytrapped six ways from Sunday. We have a bomb squad coming out from Belvoir, but it looks pretty foolproof."

"What about the 'representative' he talked about? Let me see that thing." The aide handed him the report.

"Actually, he's the closest thing we've got to a negotiator. But he's also part of the boobytrap. If he's hurt in any way . . ."

"What if the son of a bitch has a heart attack?" The President sat back in his chair and lowered his voice for the first time. "The end of the world."

17. Statistical Interlude

One bomb will go off if any of 28 people dies in the next three days. They will all go off if Ronald Day dies.

All of these men and women are fairly young and in good physical condition. But they are under considerable strain and also perhaps unusually susceptible to "accidental" death. Say each of them has one chance in a thousand of dying within the next three days. Then the probability of accidental catastrophe is one minus .999 to the 29th power.

This is .024 or about one chance out of 42.

A number of cautionary cables were exchanged in the first few hours, related to this computation.

18. Evening

The Secretary of Defense grips the edge of his chair and growls: "That old fool could've started World War III. Atom . . . bombing . . . Florida."

"He gave us ample warning," the Chairman of the AEC reminds him.

"Principle of the goddam thing."

The President isn't really listening; what's past is over and there is plenty to worry about for the next few days. He is chainsmoking, something he never does in public and rarely in conference. Camels in a long filtered holder.

"How can we keep from handing over all of our atomics?" The President stubs out his cigarette, blows through the holder, lights another.

"All right," the Chairman says. "He has a list of our holdings, which he admits is incomplete." Ticks off on his fingers. "He will get a similar list from China: locations, method of delivery, yield. Chinese espionage has been pretty efficient. Another list from Russia. Between the three, that is among the three I guess—" Secretary of Defense make a noise. "—he will probably be able to disarm us completely."

He makes a tent of his fingers. "You've thought of making a deal, I suppose. Partial lists from—"

"Yes. China's willing, Russia isn't. And Ramo is also

getting lists from England, France and Germany. Fairly complete, if I know our allies."

"Wait," says the Secretary, "France has bombs too—"

"Halfway to Reykjavik already."

"What the hell are we going to do?"

Similar queries about the same time, in Moscow and Peking.

19. Morning

Telegrams and cables have been arriving by the truck-load. The President's staff abstracted them into a 9-page report. Most of them say "don't do anything rash." About one in ten says "call his bluff," most of them mentioning a Communist plot. One of these even came from Akron.

It didn't take them long to find Ramo. Luckily, he had dismissed the bodyguard after returning safely to the Beachcomber, so there was no bloodshed. Right now he is in a condition something between house arrest and protective custody, half of Miami's police force and large contingents from the FBI and CIA surrounding him and his very important phone.

He talks to Reykjavik and Day tells him that all of the experts have arrived: 239 atomic scientists and specialists in nuclear warfare, a staff of technical translators and a planeload of observers from the UN's International Atomic Energy Agency.

Except for the few from France, no weapons have arrived. Day is not surprised and neither is Ramo.

Ramo is saddened to hear that several hundred people were killed in panicky evacuations, in Tokyo, Bombay and Khartoum. Evacuation of London is proceeding in an orderly manner. Washington is under martial law. In New York and Paris a few rushed out and most people are just sitting tight. A lot of people in Akron have decided to see what's happening in Cleveland.

20. Noon

President's intercom buzzes. "We found Ramo's man, sir."

"I suppose you searched him. Send him in."

A man in shirtsleeves walks in between two uniformed MP's. He is a hawk-faced man with a sardonic expression.

"This is rather premature, Mr. President. I was supposed to—"

"Sit down."

He flops into an easy chair. "—supposed to call on you at 3:30 this afternoon."

"You no doubt have some sort of a deal to offer."

The man looks at his watch. "You must be hungry, Mr. President. Take a long lunch hour, maybe a nap. I'll have plenty to say at—"

"You—"

"Don't worry about me, I've already eaten. I'll wait here."

"We can be very hard on you."

He rolls up his left sleeve. Two small boxes and some wiring are taped securely to his forearm. "No, you can't. Not for three days—you can't kill me or even cause me a lot of pain. You can't drug me or hypnotize me." (This last a lie.) "Even if you could, it wouldn't bring any good to you."

"I believe it would."

"We can discuss that at 3:30." He leans back and closes his eyes.

"What *are* you?"

He opens one eye. "A professional gambler." That is also a lie. Back when he had to work for a living, he ran a curious kind of a lathe.

21.   3:30 P.M.

The President comes through a side door and sits at his desk. "All right, have your say."

The man nods and straightens up slowly. "First off, let me explain my function."

"Reasonable."

"I am a gadfly, a source of tension."

"That is obvious."

"I can also answer certain questions about that bomb in your backyard."

"Here's one: how can we disarm it?"

"That I can't tell you."

"I believe we can convince you—"

"No, you don't understand. I don't know *how* to turn it off. That's somebody else's job." Third lie. "I do know how to blow it up—hurt me or kill me or move me more than ten miles from ground zero. Or I can just pull this little wire." He touches a wire and the President flinches.

"All right. What else are you here for?"

"That's all. Keep an eye on you, I guess."

"You don't have any sort of . . . message, any—"

"Oh, no. You've already got the message. Through the Polish embassy, I think."

"Come on now. I'm not naive."

The man looked at him curiously. "Maybe that's your problem. Mr. Ramo's demands are not negotiable—he really is doing what he says; taking the atomic weapons away from all of you . . . strange people.

"What sort of a deal do you think you could offer an 80-year-old millionaire? Ex-billionaire. How would you propose to threaten him?"

"We can kill him."

"That's right."

"In three days we can kill you."

The man laughs politely. "Now you are being naive."

The President flips a switch on his intercom. "Send in Carson and Major Anfel and the two MP's." The four men come in immediately.

"Take this man somewhere and talk to him. Don't hurt him."

"Not yet," the civilian Carson says.

"Come on," one MP says to the man.

"I don't think so," the man says. He stares at the President. "I'd like a glass of water."

22. 15 October 1975

The only nuclear weapons in the United States are located in Colorado, Texas, Florida and, of course, San Francisco, Washington D.C., and Akron, Ohio.

23.   16 October 1975
2:30 A.M.

The only nuclear weapons in the United States are located in Colorado, Texas, Florida, San Francisco and Washington, D.C. There is no Akron, Ohio.

Of the 139 who perished in the blast, 138 were very gutsy looters.

10:00 A.M.

Only San Francisco and Washington now. The others are on their way to Reykjavik.

The man who was named Andre Charvat walks down a deserted 14th Street with a 9-volt battery in his hand. A civilian and two volunteer MP's walk with him.

He walks straight up to the Econoline's rear bumper and touches the terminals of the battery to two inconspicuous rivets. There is a small spark and a click like the sound of a pinball machine, tilting.

"That's all. It's controlled by Reykjavik now."

"And Reykjavik is half controlled by Communists. And worse, traitors," Carson said huskily.

He doesn't answer but walks on down the street, alone. Amnesty.

In a few minutes a heavy truck rumbles up and men in plain coveralls construct a box of boilerplate around the Econoline. People start coming back into Washington and a large crowd gathers, watching them as they cover the box with a marble facade and affix a bronze plaque to the front.

The man who owned the parking lot received a generous check from the Nuclear Arms Control Board, in kroner.

24.   Quote

"NUCLEAR WARFARE. . . . This article consists of the following sections:

To Howard Hughes: A Modest Proposal

I. Introduction

II. Basic Principles
   1. Fission Weapons
   2. Fusion Weapons

III. Destructive Effects
   1. Theoretical
   2. Hiroshima and Nagasaki
   3. Akron and Novosibirsk

IV. History
   1. World War II
   2. "Cold War"
   3. Treaty of Reykjavik

V. Conversion to Peaceful Uses
   1. Theory and Engineering
   2. Administration Under NACB
   3. Inspection Procedures

(For related articles see DAY, RONALD R.; EINSTEIN, ALBERT; ENERGY; FERMI, ENRICO; NUCLEAR SCIENCES (several articles); RAMO, HOWARD K.; VALE, PHILIP; WARFARE, HISTORY OF."

A Mind of His Own

Sometimes stories are written for catharsis, and they may be useful therapy for the author, but most of them shouldn't see print, because a priori the author's story sense and stylistic judgment are subordinated to his emotional need. They usually read like cries for help.

This said, I'll admit the following story was written for catharsis, and, to make matters worse, it's a story about self-pity. But I wouldn't have included it in this collection if I'd thought it was bad.

The protagonist of this story is missing a leg and a foot, and I really don't remember whether I chose that disability consciously, but it is appropriate. Some years ago I lay in a crowded jungle hospital in Viet Nam, not yet recovering from the effects of having stood too close to a boobytrap when a booby set it off. I was a veritable encyclopaedia of shrapnel and blast wounds—it had been a company-sized boobytrap—but the only ones here relevant were the left leg, which was pretty well shattered and flayed, and the right foot, which had a hole in the heel, where your socks wear out. In the first surgery, there wasn't enough skin to stitch the leg wounds up, so the limb was wrapped in a huge roll of blood-soaked bandage, for safekeeping. The flies were so taken with it that they ignored my waving, and they also beleaguered the foot wound, which hadn't been bandaged—which, in fact, the surgeons had missed. It was ungodly hot and humid.

A harried-looking doctor came through, stopped at my bed, and warned me that I might lose the leg, and then left (I've always wondered why he felt he had to tell me). At least I got an orderly to put a bandage on the foot, to keep the flies off it. He didn't put any antiseptic on it, though, and the next day it looked terrible and smelled bad, and I could just imagine what my leg looked like under all that cloth. Even the fact that losing my leg would surely get me out of the war couldn't cheer me up very much.

All's well that ends, though, and some brilliant anonymous surgeon—perhaps the one who had scared me so—did fix up the leg and foot, and miscellaneous other parts, and after a mere four months of painful physical therapy I was able to be a soldier again, and then a civilian.

Another damned war story, you say, but no, that's not the particular demon I was trying to put to rest here, even though war did provide a certain amount of the detail. The real experience to be exorcized is the more subtle one of reaching up one day and finding that your halo's gone. I had a friend who was suddenly and severely disabled, and he reacted in a human way, sliding into bitterness, lashing out at the people around him, driving away his family, then his friends, and then one day I left him too, in spite of knowing how he felt. Exit plaster saint.

> "What we need is a technology of behavior . . . were it not for the unwarranted generalization that all control is wrong, we should deal with the social environment as simply as we deal with the nonsocial."
>
> B. F. Skinner

Leonard Shays came back home to Tampa from the Lebanese conflict with a chestful of medals—which was no distinction—a slightly fractured mind, a medical discharge and two fairly efficient prosthetics, replacing his left foot and the right leg from the knee down.

The singleshot laser boobytrap he had triggered on patrol in the slums of Beirut had been set to scan at chest level, to kill. But Leonard, canny with experience, had tossed in a microton grenade before entering the hovel, and the explosion jarred the mounting of the boobytrap so that it scanned in a downward slant across the doorway. It was practically no pain at first, much pain later, and now just a feeling that his nonexistent toes were curled down in spastic paralysis. It made it hard to walk but the VA was giving him therapy. And he couldn't get a job, not even with his Ph.D. in mathematics, but the VA was also giving him a small check on the first of every month.

"Morning, Dr. Shays." His favorite therapist, Bennet, closed the bathroom door quietly. "Ready for the workout?"

"Am I ever? Ready to get out of this damn thing, though." Bennet picked up Leonard gracelessly and pulled him out of the whirlpool bath. He set him on the Formica edge of a table and gave him a starchy towel.

He studied the stumps professionally. "How's the wife?"

"Don't ask," he said, scrubbing sweat from his hair. "We had a long talk Friday. Our contract comes up for renewal in '98. She decided not to renew."

Bennet turned off the motor and pulled the plug on the bath. "It's her right," he said. "Bitch."

"It's not the legs. Absence thereof. She explained that carefully, at some length. It's not the legs at all."

76

"Look, if you don't wanna . . ."

"It's not that I can't get a job and we had to move to Ybor City and she has to carry a gun to go shopping."

Bennet grunted and straightened a stack of towels.

Leonard fumbled through his clothes and got a cigarette, lit it.

"Shouldn't smoke those things in here."

"Just leaving." He draped a gray robe around his shoulders. "Help me with this thing, OK?"

Bennet helped him put on the robe and set him in a wheelchair. "Can't smoke in Therapy, either."

Leonard put the clothes on his lap and turned the chair 180° on one wheel, hypertrophied biceps bulging. "So let's not go straight to Therapy. I need some fresh air."

"You'll stiffen up."

He rolled to the door and opened it. "No, it's warm. Plenty warm."

They were the only people on the porch. Bennet took a cigarette and pointed it at one of the palm trees.

"You know how old that one is?"

"She said it was because of the *piano*."

"Yeah, you shouldn't of sold the piano."

"Couldn't work the pedals right."

"Someday you—"

"I wasn't going to sell it anyhow; I was going to trade even for classical guitar or lute if I could find somebody."

"Yeah?"

"I went to all the skills transfer agencies. Every one, here and St. Pete. Even one in Sarasota, specializes in music. Couldn't find a guitar player who was any good. Not in Bach. If I can't play Bach I'd rather just listen."

"You coulda gotten one that was otherwise good. Learn Bach on your own."

"Bennet, hell, that'd be years. I never learned that much new on the piano, either. Don't have the facility."

"You bought the piano in the first place?"

He nodded. "One of the first skill transfers in Florida. Old Gainesville conservatory man. He thought he was going to die and wanted one last fling. Paid him fifty grand, that was real money back in '90."

"Still is."

"They cured his cancer and a year later he committed suicide." He threw his cigarette over the edge and watched it fall three stories.

"It's exactly as old as I am. Fifty-one years, the gardener told me," Bennet said. "I guess that's pretty old for a tree."

"Palm tree, anyhow." Leonard lit another and they smoked in silence.

"I wouldn't have sold it except my car went bad. Turbine blades crystallized while I was stuck in traffic. Had to get a new engine, new drive train. Try to get around this town without a car."

"It's worth your life," Bennett agreed.

Leonard snapped the new cigarette away. "Might as well get going."

He was always tired after therapy but he always hobbled down to the gate and across to the little tavern, drank a beer standing up and walked back to the parking lot. He'd found out that if he didn't walk about a mile after therapy he would hardly be able to get out of bed the next morning, for the stiffness.

He went home and was surprised to find his wife there.

"Good afternoon, Scottie." He walked in unsteadily, carrying two bags of groceries.

"Let me help."

"No." He set the groceries down on the dinette table and began to take out things to go into the refrigerator.

"Aren't you going to ask me what the hell I'm doing here?"

He didn't look at her. "No. I'm very calm today." He took the frozen foods over first, elbowed the door open. "Therapy today."

"Did it go well?"

"Besides, it's as much your house as mine."

"Until January. But I don't feel that way."

"It went pretty well." He shuffled things around in the refrigerator to make room for a scrawny chicken, the only luxury he had purchased.

"You got the car fixed."

"All it took was money."

"Have you tried to sell the baby grand?"

"No."

Carefully: "Does that mean you might buy back the talent some day?"

"With what?"

"Well, you—"

"I need the money to live on and the piano's yours to sell or keep or bronze or whatever the hell you want to do with it."

"You don't like to have it around because—"

"*I don't give a flying . . .* I don't care whether it stays or goes. I kind of like it. It's a fun thing to dust. It keeps the place from blowing away in a high wind. It has a certain—"

"Leonard!"

"Don't shout."

"It's not mine; I bought it for you."

"That's right."

"I *did.*"

"You did lots of things for me. I'm grateful. Now." He shut the refrigerator door and leaned on it, drumming fingers, looking at the wall. "I'll ask. What the hell are you doing here?"

"I came back," she said evenly, "to try to talk some sense into you."

"Wonderful."

"Henry Beaumont said you told him you were thinking of selling your mathematics, too."

"That's right. After the money goes. It's not doing me any good."

"You worked nine years for that degree. Long years, remember? I was with you most of them."

"Five, to be accurate. Five years for the Ph.D. First the Bachelor's and—"

"If you sell your mathematics you lose it all the way back to grade school."

"That's true. Tell me something else old."

"Don't be difficult. Look at me." He didn't. "Daddy will—"

"That's really old. I don't want to hear it."

"Still trying to be a hero. Your courage is an inspiration to us all."

"Oh, for Christ's sake." He sat down at the kitchen table with his back to her. "You were the one who wanted out. Not me."

"Len, if you could see yourself, what you've turned into . . ."

Any time somebody starts out a sentence with your name, Leonard thought, they're trying to sell you something.

"Daddy said this morning that if you'd go to see Dr. Verden—"

"The imprint man he goes to."

"The best overlay therapist in the state, Len."

Early attempts at overlay therapy were called "personality imprinting." The name had a bad connotation.

"The principle's the same no matter how good he is." He looked straight at her for the first time. "I may be a worthless self-pitying bastard, but I am me. I stay me."

"That sounds pretty—"

"Pretty stupid from a man who's just sold one slice of his brain and talks about selling another. Right?"

"Close."

"Wrong. There's a basic difference between skill transfer and overlay ther—"

"No, there isn't, they're exactly the—"

"Because," almost shouting, "I can shed skills when and as I feel I no longer have use for them, where your *imprint* witch doctor just looks up in some goddamn book and finds a pers—"

"You're wrong and you know it. Otherwise—"

"No, Scottie. You've let your father sell you Tranquility Base. These—"

"Daddy's been seeing Dr. Verden for fifteen years!"

"And see what it's gotten him?"

He wasn't looking at her any longer but he could see the old familiar counting gesture. "Money. Prestige. Self-fulfillment—"

"And whose self is he fulfilling? Every time I see the old guy I expect him to be Sinbad the Sailor or Jack Kennedy or some goddamn thing. Fifty years ago they would have locked him up and thrown away the combination."

"You act as if he's—"

"He is! Certifiably."

He heard the door open—"We'll see about that!"—and slide shut and he reflected that that was one improvement over their house in Bel Aire. You can't slam an electric door.

Leonard woke up stiff the next day in spite of his having exercised. He would have allowed himself an extra hour in bed but today he despised the pathetic image of a naked legless cripple lying there helplessly. He decided against the struggle of showering, taped the pads to his stumps, strapped on the prosthetics and pulled on a pair of baggy trousers.

It was intolerably muggy, so he threw economy aside and switched on the airco. While his coffee was heating, he unwrapped the latest *ASM Journal* and set it with a thick pad of paper and a pencil next to the chair that sat under the air-conditioning duct. The microwave cooker buzzed; he got his coffee and sat down with the first article.

The doorbell rang when he was on the second article and second cup of coffee. He almost didn't answer it. It was never good news. It rang again, insistently, so he got up and opened the door.

It was a small, bland-looking black man with a leather portfolio under his arm. Salesman, Leonard thought tiredly.

"Leonard Shays?" Leonard just looked at him.

"How do you do. I'm Dr. Felix Verden, you may—"

He pushed the button but Verden had a foot against the door jamb. The door slid halfway closed, then opened again.

"Mrs. Dorothy Scott Shays is your next of kin."

"Not any more, she isn't."

"I sympathize with your feelings, Dr. Shays, but legally she *is* still your closest relative. May I come in?"

"We have nothing to talk about."

He opened the portfolio. "I have a court order here authorizing me—"

Leonard teetered forward and grabbed a fistful of the man's shirt. A man in uniform stepped from where he'd been hidden, next to the wall beside the door, and showed Leonard his stunner wand.

"All right. Let me get my book."

Dr. Verden's office was comfortable and a few decades out of date. Pale oak panelling and furniture crafted of a similar wood, combined with blued steel and fake black leather. A slight hospital odor seeped in.

"You know the therapy will be much more effective if you cooperate."

"I don't want it to be effective. I'll go along with the court and surrender my body to you for treatment. Just my body. The rest is going to fight you all the way."

"You may wind up even worse than before."

"By your lights. Maybe better, by mine."

He ignored that by rustling papers loudly. "You're familiar with the process."

"More familiar than I want to be. It's like a skill transfer, but instead of subtracting or adding a certain ability, you work on a more basic level. Personality."

"That's correct. We excise or graft certain basic behavioral traits, give the patient a better set of responses to life problems."

"A *different* set of responses."

"All right."

"It's ghoulish."

"No it isn't. It's just an accelerated growing-up process."

"It's playing God, making a man over in your own image. Or whatever image is stylish or rec—"

"You think I haven't heard all this before, Leonard?"

"I'm sure you have. I'm sure you ignore it. You must be able to see that it's different, being on the receiving end, rather than—"

"I've been on the receiving end, Leonard, you should know that. I had to go through a complete overlay before I could get licensed. I'm glad I did."

"You're a better person for it."

"Of course."

"That could be just part of the overlay, you know. They could have turned you into a slavering idiot and at the same time convinced you that it was an improvement."

"They wouldn't be allowed to. Overlay therapy is even

more closely monitored than skill transfer. And you should know how many controls there are on that."

"You're not going to convince me and I'm not going to convince you. Why don't we just get on with it?"

"Excellent idea." He stood. "Come this way."

Dr. Verden led him into a small white room that smelled of antiseptic. It held a complicated-looking bed on wheels and a plain-featured young female nurse who stood up when they came in.

"Will you need help getting undressed?" Leonard said he didn't and Dr. Verden dismissed the nurse and gave Leonard an open-backed smock, then left.

Verden and the nurse came back in a few minutes after Leonard had changed. He was sitting on the bed feeling very vulnerable, his prosthetics an articulated jumble on the floor. He was wondering again what had happened to his original foot and leg.

The nurse had a bright pleasant voice. "Now please just lie down facing this way, Mr. Shays, on your stomach."

"Doctor Shays," Verden corrected her.

Leonard was going to say it didn't matter, but then that didn't matter either.

The woman offered him a glass of water and two pills and he wondered why she hadn't done so while he was still upright. "There will be some pain, Dr. Shays," she said, still with an encouraging smile.

"I know," he said, not moving to take the pills.

"They won't turn you into a zombi," Dr. Verden said. "You'll still be able to resist."

"Not as well, I think."

Verden snorted. "That's right. Which only means you'll go through the process a dozen times instead of two or three."

"I know."

"And if you could resist it perfectly, you could keep going back every other day for the rest of your life. Nobody ever has, though."

Leonard made no comment, wriggled into a slightly more comfortable position.

"You have no idea the amount of discomfort you're condemning yourself to."

"Don't threaten, doctor; it's unbecoming."

Verden began to strap him in. "I'm not threatening," he said mildly. "I'm counseling. I am your agent, after all, working in your own best—"

"That's not what I got from the court order," Leonard said. "Ouch! You don't have to be so rough about it. I'm not going anywhere."

"We have to make you perfectly stationary. Biometric reference points."

Resisting personality overlay is not conceptually difficult. Every literate person knows the technique and most illiterates as well: first the best-selling novel, *Paindreamer*, then dozens of imitative efforts, described it; then a couple of sensational flix, and finally the afternoon cube saga, *Stay Out of My Mind!*

The person strapped on the table need not concern himself with the processes (inductive-surgical/molecular-biological/cybernetic) going on, any more than he has to think about the way his brain is working in order to attack a regular problem. Because when the therapist attempts to change some facet of the patient's personality, the action manifests itself to the patient in terms of a dream-problem. More often, a nightmare.

The dream is very realistic and offers two or three alternatives to the dreamer. If he chooses the right one, his own will reinforces the aim of the therapist, and helps make permanent the desired cellular changes.

If he chooses the wrong alternative—the illogical or painful one—he is reinforcing his brain cells' tendency to revert to their original configuration, like a crumpled-up piece of paper struggling to be square again.

Sometimes the dreams have a metaphorical connection with the problem the therapist is attacking. More often they do not:

Leonard is sitting in the home of some good friends, a young couple who have just had their first child.

"It's just fantastic," says the young woman, handing Leonard a cold beer, "the way he's growing. You won't believe it."

Leonard sips the cold beer while the woman goes to

get the child and the part of him aware that this is just a dream marvels at the solidity of the illusion.

"Here," she says, offering the baby to Leonard, laughing brightly. "He's such a rascal."

The baby is about a meter long but his head is no larger than Leonard's thumb.

"He's always doing that," says the husband from across the room. "He's a regular comedian. Squeeze his chest and watch what happens!"

Leonard squeezes the baby's chest and, sure enough, the head grows and the body shrinks until the baby is of normal proportions. He squeezes harder and the head swells larger and dangles over onto the shrunken torso, a giant embryo out of *situ*.

The husband is laughing so hard that tears come to his eyes.

A line of worry creases the young woman's forehead. "Don't squeeze too hard—please Leonard, don't, you'll hurt—"

The baby's head explodes, red-dripping shot with gray and blue slime, all over Leonard's chest and lap.

"What did you go and do that for?"

Leonard has both his legs and they are clad in mottled green jungle fatigues. He is cautiously leading his squad down the Street of Redemption in Beirut, in the slums, in the steambath of a summer afternoon. They crab down the rubble-strewn sidewalk, hugging the wall. Another squad, Lieutenant Shanker's, is across the street from them and slightly behind.

They come to number 43.

God, no.

"This is the place, Lieutenant," Leonard shouts across the street.

"Fine, Shays. You want to go in first? Or shall we take it from this angle?"

"If I . . . uh . . . if I go in first I'll lose my leg."

"Well hell," says the lieutenant affably. "We don't want that to happen. Hold on just a—"

"Never mind." Leonard unsnaps a microton grenade from his harness and lofts it through the open door. Everybody flattens out for the explosion. Before the dust settles, Leonard steps through the door. With the corner of his eye he sees the dusty black bulk of the oneshot generator. A bright flash and singing pain as he walks two steps on his shinbones and falls, pain fading.

Leonard is fishing from a rowboat at the mouth of the Crystal River, with one of his best friends, Norm Provoost, the game warden.

He threads a shrimp onto the hook and casts. Immediately he gets a strike, a light one; sets the hook and reels in the fish.

"What you got, Len?"

"Doesn't feel like much." He lifts it into the boat. It's a speckled trout—a protected species—smaller than his hand, hooked harmlessly through the lip.

"Not big enough to keep," says Norm, while Leonard disengages the hook. "They sure are pretty creatures."

Leonard grasps the fish firmly above the tail and cracks its head against the side of the boat.

"For Chrissake, Shays!"

He shrugs. "We might need bait later."

A large seminar room. Leonard's favorite professor, Dr. Van Wyck, has just filled a third blackboard with equations and moves to a fourth, at his customary rapid pace.

On the first board he made an error in sign. On the second board this error caused a mistake in double integration, two integrands having been wrongly consolidated. The third board, therefore, is gibberish and the fourth is utter gibberish. Van Wyck slows down.

"Something's screwy here," he says, wiping a yellow streak of chalk dust across his forehead. He stares at the boards for several minutes. "Can anybody see what's wrong?"

Negative murmur from the class. Their heads are bobbing, looking back and forth from their notes to the board. Leonard sits smirking.

"Mr. Shays, your Master's thesis was on this topic. Can't *you* see the error?"

Leonard shakes his head and smiles.

Leonard woke up awash with dull pain, mostly in the back of his skull and under the restraining straps. With great effort he tilted his head and saw that he was no longer strapped in; only fatigue was holding him down. Bright welts across his arms.

Vague troubling memories; equations, fishing, Beirut, small child . . . Leonard wondered whether he had resisted as strongly with his mind as he obviously had with his body. He didn't feel any different, only weak and hurting.

A nurse appeared with a small hypodermic.

"Wha?" His throat was too dry to talk. He swallowed, nothing.

"Hypnotic," she said.

"Ah." He tried to turn away, couldn't even find strength to lift his shoulder. She was holding him down with a light touch, swabbing a place on his arm with coldness. "You want to get well, don't you? It's only so the doctor can . . ." sharp pricking and blackness.

He woke up feeling better the second time. Dr. Verden handed him a glass of water. He drank half of it greedily, paused to wonder if it was drugged, then drank the rest anyway.

Refilling the glass: "That was quite a performance, Leonard."

"You know what I was dreaming?"

"We know what you remember having dreamt. You remember quite a lot, under hypnosis."

Leonard tried to sit up, felt faint, lay back down. "Did . . . am I still . . . "

Dr. Verden put down the pitcher, leafed through some pages on a clipboard. "Yes. You have essentially the same behavioral profile you had when you came in."

"Good."

He shrugged. "It's only a question of time. I think you were starting to respond to the therapy, toward the end. The State monitors recommended that I terminate before . . . actually, I had to agree with them. You aren't in very good shape, Leonard."

"I know. Asymmetrical."

"Bad jokes aside. It just means you'll have more sessions, of shorter duration. You'll be here longer. Unless you decide to cooperate."

Leonard looked at the ceiling. "Better get used to my being around."

Salad has just been served at a formal dinner and Leonard is eating it with the wrong fork. The young lady across from him notices this, and looks away quickly with a prim smile. Leonard replaces the fork and finishes the salad with his fingers.

Leonard and Scottie, newly married, are walking across the campus of the University of Florida, on a lovely spring day. She makes a sound between "Eek" and "Ack."

"It's just a snake, Scottie."

"It's *not* just a snake. It's a *coral* snake." And it is; red-touch-yella-bite-a-fella. "Leonard!"

"I won't hurt it." Leonard is chasing after it and with some difficulty picks it up by the tail. The snake loops around and begins to gnaw on Leonard's wrist. Scottie screams while Leonard watches the slow pulse of poison, holding on stoically even though the snake is hurting him.

Leonard repeats the Beirut dream in almost every detail, but this time he tries not to look at the laser boobytrap before setting it off.

"You're weakening, Dr. Shays. Why don't you just give in, cooperate?" Dr. Verden said this into the clipboard, a few pages thicker this time, and then favored his patient with a cool stare.

Leonard yawned elaborately. "It occurred to me this morning that I won't have to resist indefinitely. Only until Scottie's father gets tired of paying."

Without hesitating: "He paid in advance, on contract."

"You're a good liar, Doctor. Facile."

"And you're a lousy patient, Doctor. But challenging."

Scottie came in for a few minutes and stood at the other end of the bed while Leonard delivered a nonstop monologue, full of bitterness but surprisingly free of profanity, about her failure as a wife and as a human being. During her stay she said only "Hello, Leonard" and "Goodbye."

The doctor did not come back in after Scottie left.

Leonard sat and tried to think about the whole thing dispassionately.

If Scottie gave up on him, surely the old man would too. There was only a month to go before their marriage contract ran out. If Scottie let it lapse, he would probably be released immediately. He resolved to be even nastier to her if she visited again.

But could he last a month? Despite what Verden said, he had felt as much in control this session as he had before. And it seemed to have hurt less. Whether he could last another dozen sessions, though . . . well, he really had no way of telling.

Leonard never paid any attention to the soap operas and he made it a point of pride not to read best-sellers. He only had a sketchy, cocktail-party idea of what people thought went on in your head during overlay therapy. Supposedly, you resisted with your "will"—the term seeming to Leonard reasonably accurate but trivial—and a strong-willed person thus could defend his identity better than a weak person could. But there were limits, popular wisdom said, dark limits of stress that would break the most obstinate.

In fiction, people often escaped therapy by refusing to come out of one of the induced dreams—a pleasant dream always coming around at just the right time—by some application of existential *machismo* that was never too well explained. Pure poppycock, of course. Leonard always knew what was going on during a scenario, and he could control its progress to a certain extent, but when the pivotal moment came he had to take some action (even inaction was a decision) and then the dream would fade, to be replaced by the next one. To decide to stay in one dream was as meaningful as making up your mind to stay on a moving escalator, by effort of will, after it had reached the top.

Physical escape out of the question, it looked to Leonard as if his only hope was to keep plugging away at it. The monitors kept Verden from exhausting Leonard or drugging him; such measures could only be taken in rehabilitating a felon or a "dangerously violent" patient. Ironically, Leonard had been against the idea of the monitors when federal law had created them to enforce "mental civil rights." It had seemed like a sop thrown to an hysterical electorate after *Paindreamer*. But maybe the government had been right, just this once.

Fake a cure? Impossible unless you were a consummate actor and a psychometrics expert. And Verden checked your behavioral profile under hypnosis.

For a few moments Leonard considered the possibility that Verden and Scottie were right, that he was actually coming loose from his moorings. He decided that, although it might be true, it was an unproductive angle of attack.

He supposed that a technician—maybe even Verden himself—might be bribed, but the money he had gotten for his piano was inaccessible and probably not enough anyhow.

Best to just stick it out.

Leonard is in an unfamiliar uniform, seated at a complicated console. He sits in front of a wall-sized backlit map of the world; North America and Europe covered with blue dots and Asia covered with red dots. Central to the console is a prominent keyhole, and a matching key dangles lightly on a chain around his neck. His left side is weighed down by a heavy pistol in a shoulder holster. A plate on the console winks every thirty seconds: NO GO. There is an identical console to his right, with another man identically accoutered, who is apparently quite absorbed in reading a book.

So they are the two men who will set in motion the vengeance of the Free World in case of enemy attack. Or adverse executive decision.

The plate blinks GO, in red, stroboscopically. A teletype behind them starts to chatter.

The other man takes his key and hesitates, looks at Leonard. Says a simple word.

Which is the wrong way to act? Leonard wonders. If he shoots the man, he saves half the world. If they both insert their keys, the enemies of democracy die. But maybe by the logic of the dream they are supposed to die.

Leonard takes the key from his neck and puts it in the hole, turns it counterclockwise. The other does the same. The plate stops flashing.

Leonard unholsters his pistol and shoots the other man

in the chest, then in the head. Then, fading, he shoots himself, for good measure.

Then there are four dreams offering less and less clear-cut alternatives.

Finally, Leonard is sitting alone in front of a fireplace, reading a book. He reads twenty pages, about Toltec influence on Mayan sculpture, while nothing happens.

He decides not to read for a while and stares into the fire. Still nothing happens. He strips pages from the book and burns them. He burns the dust-jacket and the end boards. Nothing.

He sits down, unstraps one leg and throws it into the fire. The prosthetic foot follows. He watches them melt without burning.

After a couple of hours he falls asleep.

Dr. Verden did not come to him after this session was over. He woke up, the nurse gave him a hypnotic, he woke up again later. Then he spent a day leafing through magazines, watching the cube, wondering.

Was Verden trying to trick him in some way? Or did the ambiguity of the dreams mean that the therapy was succeeding? The nurse didn't know anything, or just wasn't talking.

As far as he could test himself, Leonard didn't feel any differently. He was still full of rage at Scottie and Verden, still quite willing to sell his mathematics when money got low—and didn't regret having sold the piano—still felt that imprinting a person who was manifestly sane was a gross violation of privacy and civil rights.

Leonard has another session, of seven dreams. In the first three, the result of his action is ambiguous. In the next two, it is trivial. In the sixth, it is obscure. In the seventh, Leonard is a catatonic lying motionless, for a long time, in a hospital ward full of motionless catatonics.

This time Verden appeared without white smock or clipboard. Leonard was surprised that seeing him in a plain business suit, stripped of symbols of authority, should make such a difference. He decided that it was a conscious masquerade.

"The last two sessions have been very alarming," Verden said, rocking on his heels, hands behind his back.

"Boring, at any rate."

"I'll be frank with you." Leonard reflected that that was one of the least trust-inspiring phrases in the language. Surely the doctor knew that. In trying to figure out why he'd said it, Leonard almost missed the frankness.

"What?"

"Please pay attention. This is very important. I said you are in grave danger of permanently harming your own mind."

"By resisting your efforts."

"By resisting therapy too . . . successfully, if you want to put it that way. It's a rare syndrome and I didn't recognize it, but one of the monitors—"

"He had a patient just like me, back in '93."

"No. He recalled a journal article." Verden took a folded sheaf of paper out of an inside pocket, handed it to Leonard. "Read this and tell me it doesn't describe what's happening to you."

It looked very convincing, a 'stat of an article from the July 2017 number of *The American Journal of Behavior Modification Techniques*. The title of the article was "The Paranoid Looping Defense: a Cybernetic Analogue." It was full of jargon, charts and the kind of vague mathematics that social scientists admire.

Leonard handed it back. "This and two hundred bucks will get you the services of a typesetter, Doctor. Nice try."

"You think . . ." He shook his head slowly, ran his finger along the paper's crease and returned it to his pocket. "Of course you think that I'm lying to you." He smiled. "That's consistent with the syndrome."

He took the paper out again and set it on the table next to Leonard's bed. "You may want to read this, if only for amusement." Leaving, standing theatrically in the door: "You may as well know that there will be an extra monitor for your therapy tomorrow. A representative of the Florida Medical Ethics Board. He will give me permission to accelerate your treatment with drugs."

"Then I'll try to be very cooperative tomorrow." He

smiled at the doctor's back and then laughed. He had expected something like this. But he was surprised that Verden hadn't been more subtle.

"You can't kid a kidder," he said aloud, folding the paper into fourths, eighths, sixteenths. He tossed it into the bedpan and turned on the cube.

It was the first time he'd ever enjoyed watching a quiz show.

As Leonard goes under the anesthesia he is very happy. He has a plan.

He will cooperate with the doctor, choose all the right alternatives, allow himself to be cured. But only temporarily.

Once released, he will go to a skills transfer agency and hock his mathematics. He will bring the money to Verden, who has his original personality on file—*and buy himself back!* Audacious!

He awaits the first dream situation with smug composure.

Leonard is going under the anesthesia, very happy because he has a plan. He will cooperate with the doctor, choose all the right alternatives and allow himself to be cured, but only temporarily. Once released he will hock his mathematics at a skills transfer agency and bring the money to Verden, who has his original personality on file and *buy* himself back! Audaciously and with smug composure he awaits the first dream.

Happily going under because he has a plan to be cured temporarily and sell his mathematics to get money to *buy himself back* from Verden, Leonard waits to dream.

Happy under plan cure *himself* dream.

All the Universe
in a Mason Jar

〰〰〰〰〰〰〰〰〰〰〰〰〰〰〰〰〰〰〰〰〰〰〰〰

This is a lark of a story, that I wrote to entertain myself after finishing a novel. The fact that you can always sell humorous science fiction had nothing to do with it.

I like the local-color humorists of the late nineteenth, early twentieth centuries, and it occurred to me that I'd never seen a science fiction local-color story. Perhaps because it's basically a silly idea. At any rate, I was stuck in another damned Iowa winter, feeling homesick for Florida, and so I wrote this.

Sent a copy of it to a friend who is a sensitive poet with many degrees and an accent you could slice and serve up with red-eye gravy, asking him whether the dialect rang true. He wrote back that he thought my family must have had a Southerner in the woodpile. Whether that's a yes, or a no, or a sometimes, I'm not sure.

New Homestead, Florida: 1990.

John Taylor Taylor, retired professor of mathematics, lived just over two kilometers out of town, in a three-room efficiency module tucked in an isolated corner of a citrus grove. Books and old furniture and no neighbors, which was the way John liked it. He only had a few years left on this Earth, and he preferred to spend them with his oldest and most valued friend: himself.

But this story isn't about John Taylor Taylor. It's about his moonshiner, Lester Gilbert. And some five billion others.

This day the weather was fine, so the professor took his stick and walked into town to pick up the week's mail. A thick cylinder of journals and letters was wedged into his box; he had to ask the clerk to remove them from the other side. He tucked the mail under his arm without looking at it, and wandered next door to the bar.

"Howdy, Professor."

"Good afternoon, Leroy." He and the bartender were the only ones in the place, not unusual this late in the month. "I'll take a boilermaker today, please." He threaded his way through a maze of flypaper strips and eased himself into a booth of chipped, weathered plastic.

He sorted his mail into four piles: junk, bills, letters, and journals. Quite a bit of junk, two bills, a letter that turned out to be another bill, and three journals—*Nature, Communications* of the American Society of Mathematics, and a collection of papers delivered at an ASM symposium on topology. He scanned the contributors lists and, as usual, saw none of his old colleagues represented.

"Here y'go." Leroy sat a cold beer and a shot glass of whiskey between *Communications* and the phone bill.

John paid him with a five and lit his pipe carefully before taking a sip. He folded *Nature* back at the letters column and began reading.

The screen door slapped shut loudly behind a burly man in wrinkled clean work clothes. John recognized him with a nod; he returned a left-handed V-sign and mounted a bar stool.

"How 'bout a red-eye, Leroy?" Mixture of beer and tomato juice with a dash of Louisiana, hangover cure.

Leroy mixed it. "Rough night, Isaac?"

"Shoo. You don' know." He downed half the concoction in a gulp, and shuddered. He turned to John. "Hey, Professor. What you know about them flyin' saucers?"

"Lot of them around a few years ago," he said tactfully. "Never saw one myself."

"Me neither. Wouldn't give you a nickel for one. Not until last night." He slurped the red-eye and wiped his mouth.

"What," the bartender said, "you saw one?"

"*Saw* one. Shoo." He slid the two-thirds empty glass across the bar. "You wanta put some beer on top that? Thanks.

"We was down the country road seven-eight klicks. You know Eric Olsen's new place?"

"Don't think so."

"New boy, took over Jarmin's plat."

"Oh yeah. Never comes in here; know of him, though."

"You wouldn't hang around no bar neither if you had a pretty little . . . well. Point is, he was puttin' up one of them new stasis barns, you know?"

"Yeah, no bugs. Keeps stuff forever, my daddy-in-law has one."

"Well, he picked up one big enough for his whole avocado crop. Hold on to it till the price is right, up north, like January? No profit till next year, help his 'mortization."

"Yeah, but what's that got to do with the flying—"

"I'm gettin' to it." John settled back to listen. Some tall tale was on the way.

"Anyhow, we was gonna have an old-fashion barn raisin' . . . Miz Olsen got a boar and set up a pit barbecue, the other ladies they brought the trimmin's. Eric, he made two big washtubs of spiced wine, set 'em on ice till we get the barn up. Five, six hours, it turned out (the directions wasn't right), *hot* afternoon, and we just headed for that wine like you never saw.

"I guess we was all pretty loaded, finished off that wine before the pig was ready. Eric, he called in to Samson's and had 'em send out two kegs of Bud."

"Got to get to know that boy," Leroy said.

"Tell me about it. Well, we tore into that pig and had him down to bones an' gristle in twenty minutes. Best god-dern pig *I* ever had, anyhow.

"So's not to let the fire permit go to waste, we went out an' rounded up a bunch of scrap, couple of good-size logs. Finish off that beer around a bonfire. Jommy Parker went off to pick up his fiddle and he took along Midnight Jackson, pick up his banjo. Miz Olsen had this Swedish guitar, one too many strings but by God could she play it.

"We cracked that second keg 'bout sundown and Lester Gilbert—you know Lester?"

Leroy laughed. "Don't I just. He was 'fraid the beer wouldn't hold out, went to get some corn?"

John made a mental note to be home by four o'clock. It was Wednesday; Lester would be by with his weekly quart.

"We get along all right," the bartender was saying. "Figure our clientele don't overlap that much."

"Shoo," Isaac said. "Some of Lester's clientele overlaps on a regular basis.

"Anyhow, it got dark quick, you know how clear it was last night. Say, let me have another, just beer."

Leroy filled the glass and cut the foam off. "Clear enough to see a flyin' saucer, eh?"

"I'm gettin' to it. Thanks." He sipped it and concentrated for a few seconds on tapping tobacco into a cigarette paper. "Like I say, it got dark fast. We was sittin' around the fire, singin' if we knew the words, drinkin' if we didn't—"

" 'Spect you didn't know many of the songs, yourself."

"Never could keep the words in my head. Anyhow, the fire was gettin' a mite hot on me, so I turned this deck chair around and settled down lookin' east, fire to my back,

97

watchin' the moon rise over the government forest there—"

"Hold on now. Moon ain't comin' up until after midnight."

"You-God-Damn-*right* it ain't!" John felt a chill even though he'd seen it coming. Isaac had a certain fame as a storyteller. "That wan't *nobody's* moon."

"Did anybody else see it?" John asked.

"Ev'rybody. Ev'rybody who was there—and one that wasn't. I'll get to that.

"I saw that thing and spilled my beer gettin' up, damn near trip and fall in the pit. Hollered 'Lookit that goddamn thing!' and pointed, jumpin' up an' down, and like I say, they all did see it.

"It was a little bigger than the moon and not quite so round, egg-shaped. Whiter than the moon, an' if you looked close you could see little green and blue flashes around the edge. It didn't make no noise we could hear, and was movin' real slow. We saw it for at least a minute. Then it went down behind the trees."

"What could it of been?" the bartender said. "Sure you wan't all drunk and seein' things?"

"No way in hell. You know me, Leroy, I can tie one on ev'y now and again, but I just plain don't get that drunk. Sure thing I don't get that drunk on beer an' *wine!*"

"And Lester wasn't back with the 'shine yet?"

"No . . . an' that's the other part of the story." Isaac took his time lighting the cigarette and drank off some beer.

"I'm here to tell you, we was all feelin' sorta spooky over that. Hunkered up around the fire, lookin' over our shoulders. Eric went in to call the sheriff, but he didn't get no answer.

"Sat there for a long time, speculatin'. Forgot all about Lester, suppose to be back with the corn.

"Suddenly we hear this somethin' crashin' through the woods. Jommy sprints to his pickup and gets out his over-and-under. But it's just Lester. Runnin' like the hounds of Hell is right behind him.

"He's got a plywood box with a half-dozen Mason jars in her, and from ten feet away he smells like Saturday night. He don't say a word; sets that box down, not too
98

gentle, jumps over to Jommy and grabs that gun away from him and aims it at the government woods, and pulls both triggers, just *boom-crack* 20-gauge buckshot and a .30-caliber rifle slug right behind.

"Now Jommy is understandable pissed off. He takes the gun back from Lester and shoves him on the shoulder, follows him and shoves him again; all the time askin' him, just not too politely, don't he know he's too drunk to handle a firearm? and don't he know we could all get busted, him shootin' into federal land? and just in general, what the Sam Hill's goin' on, Lester?"

He paused to relight the cigarette and take a drink. "Now Lester's just takin' it and not sayin' a thing. How 'bout *that?*"

"Peculiar," Leroy admitted.

Isaac nodded. "Lester, he's a good boy but he does have one hell of a temper. Anyhow, Lester finally sets down by his box and unscrews the top off a full jar—they's one with no top but it looks to be empty—and just gulps down one whole hell of a lot. He coughs once and starts talkin'."

"Surprised he could talk at all." John agreed. He always mixed Lester's corn with a lot of something else.

"And listen—that boy is sober like a parson. And he says, talkin' real low and steady, that he seen the same thing we did. He describes it, just exactly like I tole you. But he sees it on the ground. Not in the air."

Isaac passed the glass over and Leroy filled it without a word. "He was takin' a long-cut through the government land so's to stay away from the road. Also he had a call of Nature and it always felt more satisfyin' on government land.

"He stopped to take care of that and have a little drink and then suddenly saw this light. Which was the saucer droppin' down into a clearing, but he don't know that. He figures it's the sheriff's 'copter with its night lights on, which don't bother him much, 'cause the sheriff's one of his best customers."

"That a fact?"

"Don't let on I tole you. Anyways, he thought the sheriff might want a little some, so he walks on toward the light.

It's on the other side of a little rise; no underbresh but it takes him a few minutes to get there.

"He tops the rise and there's this saucer—bigger'n a private 'copter, he says. He's stupefied. Takes a drink and studies it for a while. Thinks it's probably some secret government thing. He's leanin' against a tree, studying . . . and then it dawns on him that he ain't alone."

Isaac blew on the end of his cigarette and shook his head. "I 'spect you ain't gonna believe this—not sure I do myself—but I can't help that, it's straight from Lester's mouth.

"He hears something on the other side of the tree where he's leanin'. Peeks around the tree and—there's this *thing.*

"He says it's got eyes like a big cat, like a lion's, only bigger. And it's a big animal otherwise, about the size of a lion, but no fur, just wrinkled hide like a rhino. It's got big shiny claws that it's usin' on the tree, and a mouthful of big teeth, which it displays at Lester and growls.

"Now Lester, he got nothin' for a weapon but about a quart of Dade County's finest—so he splashes that at the monster's face, hopin' to blind it, and takes off like a bat.

"He gets back to his box of booze, and stops for a second and looks back. He can see the critter against the light from the saucer. It's on its hind legs, weavin' back and forth with its paws out, just roarin'. Looks like the booze works, so Lester picks up the box, ammunition. But just then that saucer light goes out.

"Lester knows good and God damn well that that damn thing can see in the dark, with them big eyes. But Les can see our bonfire, a klick or so west, so he starts runnin' holdin' on to that box of corn for dear life.

"So he comes in on Eric's land and grabs the gun and all that happens. We pass the corn around a while and wash it down with good cold beer. Finally we got up enough Dutch courage to go out after the thing.

"We got a bunch of flashlights, but the only guns were Jommy's over-and-under and a pair of antique flintlock pistols that Eric got from his dad. Eric loaded 'em and give one to me, one to Midnight. Midnight, he was a sergeant in the Asia war, you know, and he was gonna lead us.

Eric himself didn't think he could shoot a animal. Dirt farmer (good boy, though)."

"Still couldn't get the sheriff? What about the Guard?"

"Well, no. Truth to tell, everybody—even Lester—was halfway convinced we ain't seen nothin', nothin' real. Eric had got to tellin' us what went into that punch, pretty weird, and the general theory was that he'd whipped up a kind of halla, hallo—"

"Hallucinogen," John supplied.

"That's right. Like that windowpane the old folks take. No offense, Professor."

"Never touch the stuff."

"Anyhow, we figured that we was probably seein' things, but we'd go out an' check, just in case. Got a bunch of kitchen knives and farm tools, took the ladies along too.

"Got Midnight an' Lester up in the front, the rest of us stragglin' along behind, and we followed Lester's trail back to where he seen the thing."

Isaac took a long drink and was silent for a moment, brow furrowed in thought. "Well, hell. He took us straight to that tree and I'm a blind man if there weren't big ol' gouges all along the bark. And the place did smell like Lester's corn.

"Midnight, he shined a light down to where Lester'd said the saucer was, and sure enough, the bresh was all flat there. He walked down to take a closer look—all of us gettin' a little jumpy now—and God damn if he didn't bump right into it. That saucer was there but you flat couldn't see it.

"He let out one hell of a yelp and fired that ol' flintlock down at it, point-blank. Bounced off, you could hear the ball sing away. He come back up the rise just like a cat on fire; when he was clear I took a pot shot at the damn thing, and then Jommy he shot it four, six times. Then there was this kind of wind, and it was gone."

There was a long silence. "You ain't bullshittin' me," Leroy said. "This ain't no story."

"No." John saw that the big man was pale under his heavy tan. "This ain't no story."

"Let me fix you a stiff one."

"No, I gotta stay straight. They got some newspaper

boys comin' down this afternoon. How's your coffee today?"

"Cleaned the pot."

John stayed for one more beer and then started walking home. It was hot, and he stopped halfway to rest under a big willow, reading a few of the *Nature* articles. The one on the Ceres probe was fascinating; he reread it as he ambled the rest of the way home.

So his mind was a couple of hundred million miles away when he walked up the path to his door and saw that it was slightly ajar.

First it startled him, and then he remembered that it was Lester's delivery day. He always left the place unlocked (there were ridge-runners but they weren't interested in old books), and the moonshiner probably just left his wares inside.

He checked his watch as he walked through the door: it was not quite three. Funny. Lester was usually late.

No Mason jar in sight. And from his library, a snuffling noise.

The year before, some kind of animal—the sheriff had said it was probably a bear—had gotten into his house and made a shambles of it. He eased open the end-table drawer and took out the Walther P-38 he had taken from a dead German officer, half a century before. And as he edged toward the library, the thought occurred to him that the 50-year-old ammunition might not fire.

It was about the size of a bear, a big bear.

Its skin was pebbly gray, with tufts of bristle. It had two arms, two legs, and a stiff tail to balance back on.

The tail had a serrated edge on top, that looked razor sharp. The feet and hands terminated in pointed black claws. The head was vaguely saurian; too many teeth and too large.

As he watched, the creature tore a page out of Fadeeva's *Computational Methods of Linear Algebra,* stuffed it in his mouth and chewed. Spat it out. Turned to see John standing at the door.

It's probably safe to say that any other resident of New Homestead, faced with this situation, would either have started blazing away at the apparition, or would have fainted. But John Taylor Taylor was nothing if not a cool and rational man, and had besides suffered a lifelong addiction to fantastic literature. So he measured what was left of his life against the possibility that this fearsome monster might be intelligent and humane.

He laid the gun on a writing desk and presented empty hands to the creature, palms out.

The thing regarded him for a minute. It opened its mouth, teeth beyond counting, and closed it. Translucent eyelids nictated up over huge yellow eyes, and slid back. Then it replaced the Fadeeva book and duplicated John's gesture.

In several of the stories John had read, humans had communicated with alien races through the medium of mathematics, a pure and supposedly universal language. Fortunately, his library sported a blackboard.

"Allow me to demonstrate," he said with a slightly quavering voice as he crossed the board, "the Theorem of Pythagoras." The creature's eyes followed him, blinking. "A logical starting place. Perhaps. As good as any," he trailed off apologetically.

He drew a right triangle on the board, and then drew squares out from the sides that embraced the right angle. He held the chalk out to the alien.

The creature made a huffing sound, vaguely affirmative, and swayed over to the blackboard. It retracted the claws on one hand and took the chalk from John.

It bit off one end of the chalk experimentally, and spit it out.

Then it reached over and casually sketched in the box representing the square of the hypotenuse. In the middle of the triangle it drew what was obviously an equals sign: $\sim$

John was ecstatic. He took the chalk from the alien and repeated the curly line. He pointed at the alien and then at himself: equals.

The alien nodded enthusiastically and took the chalk. It put a slanted line through John's equals sign.

Not equals.

It stared at the blackboard, tapping it with the chalk; one universal gesture. Then, squeaking with every line, it rapidly wrote down:

$$1$$
$$\sim$$
$$\text{---}\ 1$$
$$\sim$$
$$1 \sim 1\text{-}1 \sim$$
$$\sim$$
$$1 \sim 1\text{-}1 \sim 1$$
$$\sim$$
$$1$$

John studied the message. Some sort of tree diagram? Perhaps a counting system. Or maybe not mathematical at all. He shrugged at the creature. It flinched at the sudden motion, and backed away growling.

"No, no." John held his palms out again. "Friends."

The alien shuffled slowly back to the blackboard and pointed to what it had just written down. Then it opened its terrible mouth and pointed at that. It repeated the pair of gestures twice.

"Oh." Eating the Fadeeva and the chalk. "Are you hungry?" It repeated the action more emphatically.

John motioned for it to follow him and walked toward the kitchen. The alien waddled slowly, its tail a swaying counterweight.

He opened the refrigerator and took out a cabbage, a package of catfish, an avocado, some cheese, an egg, and a chafing dish of leftover green beans, slightly dried out. He lined them up on the counter and demonstrated that they were food by elaborately eating a piece of cheese.

The alien sniffed at each item. When it got to the egg, it stared at John for a long time. It tasted a green bean but spat it out. It walked around the kitchen in a circle, then stopped and growled a couple of times.

It sighed and walked into the living room. John followed. It went out the front door and walked around behind the module. Sighed again and disappeared, from the feet up.

John noted that where the creature had disappeared, the grass was crushed in a large circle. That was consistent with Isaac's testimony: it had entered its invisible flying saucer.

The alien came back out with a garish medallion around

its neck. It looked like it was made of rhinestones and bright magenta plastic.

It growled and a voice whispered inside his brain: "Hello? Hello? Can you hear me?"

"Uh, yes. I can hear you."

"Very well. This will cause trouble." It sighed. "One is not to use the translator with a Class 6 culture except under the most dire of emergency. But I am starve. If I do not eat soon the fires inside me will go out. Will have to fill out many forms, may they reek."

"Well . . . anything I can do to help . . ."

"Yes." It walked by him, back toward the front door. "A simple chemical is the basis for all my food. I have diagrammed it." He followed the alien back into the library.

"This is hard." He studied his diagram. "To translator is hard outside of basic words. This top mark is the number 'one.' It means a gas that burns in air."

"Hydrogen?"

"Perhaps. Yes, I think. Third mark is the number 'eight,' which means a black rock that also burns, but harder. The mark between means that in very small they are joined together."

"A hydrogen-carbon bond?"

"This is only noise to me." Faint sound of a car door slamming, out on the dirt road.

"Oh, oh," John said. "Company coming. You wait here." He opened the door a crack and watched Lester stroll up the path.

"Hey, Perfesser! You ain't gonna believe what—"

"I know, Les. Isaac told me about it down at Leroy's." He had the door open about twelve centimeters.

Lester stood on the doormat, tried to look inside. "Somethin' goin' on in there?"

"Hard to explain, uh, I've got company."

Lester closed his mouth and gave John a broad wink. "Knew you had it in you, Doc." He passed the Mason jar to John. "Look, I come back later. Really do want yer 'pinion."

"Fine, we'll do that. I'll fix you a—"

A taloned hand snatched the Mason jar from John.

Lester turned white and staggered back. "Don't move a muscle, Doc. I'll git my gun."

"No, wait! It's friendly!"

"Food," the creature growled. "Yes, friend." The screw-top was unfamiliar but only presented a momentary difficulty. The alien snapped it off, glass and all, with a flick of the wrist. It dashed the quart of raw 'shine down its throat.

"Ah, fine. So good. Three parts food, one part water. Strange flavor, so good." It pushed John aside and waddled out the door.

"You have more good food?"

Lester backed away. "You talkin' to me?"

"Yes, yes. You have more of this what your mind calls 'corn'?"

"I be damned." Lester shook his head in wonder. "You are the ugliest sumbitch I ever did see."

"This is humor, yes. On my world, egg-eater, you would be in cage. To frighten children to their amusement." It looked left and right and pointed at Lester's beat-up old Pinto station wagon. "More corn in that animal?"

"Sure." He squinted at the creature. "You got somethin' to pay with?"

"Pay? What is this noise?"

Lester looked up at John. "Did he say what I thought he said?"

John laughed. "I'll get my checkbook. You let him have all he wants."

When John came back out, Lester was leaning on his station wagon, sipping from a jar, talking to the alien. The creature was resting back on its tail, consuming food at a rate of about a quart every thirty seconds. Lester had showed it how to unscrew the jars.

"I do not lie," it said. "This is the best food I have ever tasted."

Lester beamed. "That's what I tell ev'ybody. You can't *git* that in no store."

"I tasted only little last night. But could tell from even that. Have been seeking you."

It was obvious that the alien was going to drink all three cases. $25 per jar, John calculated, 36 jars. "Uh, Les, I'm going to have to owe you part of the money."

"That's okay, Doc. He just tickles the hell outa me."

The alien paused in mid-jar. "Now I am to understand,

I think. You own this food. The Doc gives to you a writing of equal value."

"That's right," John said.

"You, the Les, think of things you value. I must be symmetry . . . I must have a thing you value."

Lester's face wrinkled up in thought. "Ah, there is one thing, yes. I go." The alien waddled back to his ship.

"Gad," Lester said. "If this don't beat all."

(Traveling with the alien is his pet treblig. He carries it because it always emanates happiness. It is also a radioactive creature that can excrete any element. The alien gives it a telepathic command. With an effort that scrambles television reception for fifty miles, it produces a gold nugget weighing slightly less than one kilogram.)

The alien came back and handed the nugget to Lester. "I would take some of your corn back to my home world, yes? Is this sufficient?"

The alien had to wait a few days while Lester brewed up enough 'shine to fill up his auxiliary food tanks. He declined an invitation to go to Washington, but didn't mind talking to reporters.

Humankind learned that the universe was teeming with intelligent life. In this part of the Galaxy there was an organization called the Commonality—not really a government; more like a club. Club members were given such useful tools as faster-than-light travel and immortality.

All races were invited to join the Commonality once they had evolved morally above a certain level. Humankind, of course was only a Class 6. Certain individuals went as high as 5 or as low as 7 (equivalent to the moral state of an inanimate object), but it was the average that counted.

After a rather grim period of transition, the denizens of Earth settled down to concentrating on being good, trying to reach Class 3, the magic level.

It would take surprisingly few generations. Because humankind had a constant reminder of the heaven on Earth that awaited them, as ship after ship drifted down from the sky to settle by a still outside a little farm near New Homestead, Florida: for several races, the gourmet center of Sirius Sector.

The Private War of Private Jacob

This is the shortest story I've ever written, yet I could write a book about where it came from and what it means. Instead, let me pass on to you a remark a friend of mine made about Catch-22:

"Nobody who hasn't been in the army can really understand the book. They think it's fiction."

With each step your boot heel cracks through the sun-dried crust and your foot hesitates, drops through an inch of red talcum powder, and then you draw it back up with another crackle. Fifty men marching in a line through this desert and they sound like a big bowl of breakfast cereal.

Jacob held the laser projector in his left hand and rubbed his right in the dirt. Then he switched hands and rubbed his left in the dirt. The plastic handles got very slippery after you'd sweated on them all day long, and you didn't want the damn thing to squirt out of your grip when you were rolling and stumbling and crawling your way to the enemy, and you couldn't use the strap, noplace off the parade ground; goddamn slide-rule jockey figured out where to put it, too high, take the damn thing off if you could. Take the goddamn helmet off too, if you could. No matter you were safer with it on. They said. And they were pretty strict, especially about the helmets.

"Look happy, Jacob." Sergeant Melford was always all smile and bounce before a battle. During a battle, too. He smiled at the tanglewire and beamed at his men while they picked their way through it—if you go too fast you get tripped and if you go too slow you get burned—and he had a sad smile when one of his men got zeroed and a shriek a happy shriek when they first saw the enemy and glee when an enemy got zeroed and nothing but smiles smiles smiles through the whole sorry mess. "If he *didn't* smile, just once," young-old Addison told Jacob, a long time ago, "just once he cried or frowned, there would be fifty people waiting for the first chance to zero that son of a bitch." And Jacob asked why and he said, "You just take a good look inside yourself the next time you follow that crazy son of a bitch into hell and you come back and tell me how you felt about him."

Jacob wasn't stupid, that day or this one, and he did keep an inside eye on what was going on under his helmet. What old Sergeant Melford did for him was mainly to make him glad that he wasn't crazy too, and no matter how bad things got, at least Jacob wasn't enjoying it like that crazy laughing grinning old Sergeant Melford.

He wanted to tell Addison and ask him why sometimes you were really scared or sick and you would look up and see Melford laughing his crazy ass off, standing over some steaming roasted body, and you'd have to grin, too, was it just so insane horrible or? Addison might have been able to tell Jacob but Addison took a low one and got hurt bad in both legs and the groin and it was a long time before he came back and then he wasn't young-old any more but just old. And he didn't say much any more.

With both his hands good and dirty, for a good grip on the plastic handles, Jacob felt more secure and he smiled back at Sergeant Melford.

"Gonna be a good one, Sarge." It didn't do any good to say anything else, like it's been a long march and why don't we rest a while before we hit them, Sarge, or, I'm scared and sick and if I'm gonna die I want it at the very first, Sarge: no. Crazy old Melford would be down on his hunkers next to you and give you a couple of friendly punches and josh around and flash those white teeth until you were about to scream or run but instead you wound up saying, "Yeah, Sarge, gonna be a good one."

We most of us figured that what made him so crazy was just that he'd been in this crazy war so long, longer than anybody could remember anybody saying he remembered; and he never got hurt while platoon after platoon got zeroed out from under him by ones and twos and whole squads. He never got hurt and maybe that bothered him, not that any of us felt sorry for the crazy son of a bitch.

Wesley tried to explain it like this: "Sergeant Melford is an improbability locus." Then he tried to explain what a locus was and Jacob didn't really catch it, and he tried to explain what an improbability was, and that seemed pretty simple but Jacob couldn't see what it all had to do with math. Wesley was a good talker though, and he might have one day been able to clear it up but he tried to run through the tanglewire, you'd think not even a civilian would try to do that, and he fell down and the little metal bugs ate his face.

It was twenty or maybe twenty-five battles later, who keeps track, when Jacob realized that not only did old Sergeant Melford never get hurt, but he never killed any of the enemy either. He just ran around singing out orders and being happy and every now and then he'd shoot off his projector but he always shot high or low or the beam was too broad. Jacob wondered about it but by this time he was more afraid, in a way, of Sergeant Melford than he was of the enemy, so he kept his mouth shut and he waited for someone else to say something about it.

Finally Cromwell, who had come into the platoon only a couple of weeks after Jacob, noticed that Sergeant Melford never seemed to zero anybody and he had this theory that maybe the crazy old son of a bitch was a spy for the other side. They had fun talking about that for a while, and then Jacob told them about the old improbability locus theory, and one of the new guys said he sure is an imperturbable locust all right, and they all had a good laugh, which was good because Sergeant Melford came by and joined in after Jacob told him what was so funny, not about the improbability locus, but the old joke about how do you make a hormone? You don't pay her. Cromwell laughed like there was no tomorrow and for Cromwell there wasn't even any sunset, because he went across the perimeter to take a crap and got caught in a squeezer matrix.

The next battle was the first time the enemy used the drainer field, and of course the projectors didn't work and the last thing a lot of the men learned was that the light plastic stock made a damn poor weapon against a long knife, of which the enemy had plenty. Jacob lived because he got in a lucky kick, aimed for the groin but got the kneecap, and while the guy was hopping around trying to stay upright he dropped his knife and Jacob picked it up and gave the guy a new orifice, eight inches wide and just below the navel.

The platoon took a lot of zeros and had to fall back,

which they did very fast because the tanglewire didn't work in a drainer field, either. They left Addison behind, sitting back against a crate with his hands in his lap and a big drooly red grin not on his face.

With Addison gone, no other private had as much combat time as Jacob. When they rallied back at the neutral zone, Sergeant Melford took Jacob aside and wasn't really smiling at all when he said: "Jacob, you know that now if anything happens to me, you've got to take over the platoon. Keep them spread out and keep them advancing, and most of all, keep them happy."

Jacob said, "Sarge, I can tell them to keep spread out and I think they will, and all of them know enough to keep pushing ahead, but how can I keep them happy when I'm never very happy myself, not when you're not around."

That smile broadened and turned itself into a laugh. You crazy old son of a bitch, Jacob thought and because he couldn't help himself, he laughed too. "Don't worry about that," Sergeant Melford said. "That's the kind of thing that takes care of itself when the time comes."

The platoon practiced more and more with knives and clubs and how to use your hands and feet but they still had to carry the projectors into combat because, of course, the enemy could turn off the drainer field whenever he wanted to. Jacob got a couple of scratches and a piece of his nose cut off, but the medic put some cream on it and it grew back. The enemy started using bows and arrows so the platoon had to carry shields, too, but that wasn't too bad after they designed one that fit right over the projector, held sideways. One squad learned how to use bows and arrows back at the enemy and things got as much back to normal as they had ever been.

Jacob never knew exactly how many battles he had fought as a private, but it was exactly forty-one. And actually, he wasn't a private at the end of the forty-first.

Since they got the archer squad, Sergeant Melford had taken to standing back with them, laughing and shouting orders at the platoon and every now and then loosing an arrow that always landed on a bare piece of ground. But this particular battle (Jacob's forty-first) had been going pretty poorly, with the initial advance stopped and then pushed back almost to the archers; and then a new enemy force breaking out on the other side of the archers.

Jacob's squad maneuvered between the archers and the new enemy soldiers and Jacob was fighting right next to Sergeant Melford, fighting pretty seriously while old Melford just laughed his fool head off, crazy son of a bitch. Jacob felt that split-second funny feeling and ducked and a heavy club whistled just over his head and bashed the side of Sergeant Melford's helmet and sheared the top of his helmet off just as neat as you snip the end off a soft-boiled egg. Jacob fell to his knees and watched the helmet full of stuff twirl end over end in back of the archers and he wondered why there were little glass marbles and cubes inside the grey-blue blood-streaked mushy stuff and then everything just went

Inside a mountain of crystal under a mountain of rock, a tiny piezoelectric switch, sixty-four molecules in a cube, flipped over to the OFF *position and the following transaction took place at just less than the speed of light:*

UNIT 10011001011MELFORD ACCIDENTALLY DEACTIVATED.
SWITCH UNIT 1101011100JACOB TO CATALYST STATUS.
(SWITCHING COMPLETED)
ACTIVATE AND INSTRUCT UNIT 1101011100JACOB.

and came back again just like that. Jacob stood up and looked around. The same old sun-baked plain, but everybody but him seemed to be dead. Then he checked and the ones that weren't obviously zeroed were still breathing a bit. And, thinking about it, he knew why. He chuckled.

He stepped over the collapsed archers and picked up Melford's bleedy skull-cap. He inserted the blade of a knife between the helmet and the hair, shorting out the induction tractor that held the helmet on the head and served to pick up and transmit signals. Letting the helmet drop to the ground, he carefully bore the grisly balding bowl over to the enemy's crapper. Knowing exactly where

113

to look, he fished out all the bits and pieces of crystal and tossed them down the smelly hole. Then he took the unaugmented brain back to the helmet and put it back the way he had found it. He returned to his position by Melford's body.

The stricken men began to stir and a few of the most hardy wobbled to their hands and knees.

Jacob threw back his head and laughed and laughed.

A Time to Live

This story started with a leaky fountain pen, took a side trip to the moon, and ended up with my brother. Flying somewhere on a plane without too much pressurization, I read a story in The New Yorker. The story was otherwise unremarkable—I don't even remember the author's name—but it had a neat first-person viewpoint trick that I thought might one day come in handy. I found a scrap of paper and made a note. The note was rather messy, as was my pocket, since the lack of pressure in the cabin had given my fountain pen a new sense of freedom. I lost the note, probably before I left the airplane, but remembered taking it.

The second scene is perhaps a year later, stopping by the Analog office to bother Ben Bova. Ben was ready for me: On a large lunar colony, he asked, what would they do with all the dead bodies? I said they'd recycle them, the conventional answer; grind 'em up and sprinkle 'em over the north forty. No, he said, the elements in a human body are an insignificantly small fraction of the total biomass needed for a large colony, so they could do anything they wanted with the bodies. He suggested that many people would elect to be "buried at space," jettisoned in a funerary capsule. He also suggested that I write him a story about it. I said I would, some day, too busy now.

My brother Jack is also a writer, and a good one. Ben called and said he'd bought a story from Jack, so he had to have one from me for the same issue, lest the readers become confused. I had to bow to his logic.

Actually, I'd been thinking about writing a short story anyhow, about time travel. Natural languages, it says here, can't deal directly with time travel, because their tense structures are geared to time as a one-way street. I wasn't about to make up a new set of tenses to accommodate time travel, which would be incomprehensible to every reader, including myself. But I did see a way to take that New Yorker trick and twist it in a Moebius way, to at least imply the complexity of the situation.

There was even a way to get Ben's funerary capsules into the act, as well as pay homage to two of my favorite science fiction stories: "The Man Who Sold the Moon" and "All You Zombies," both by Robert Heinlein.

The Man Who Owns the Moon, they called him while he was alive, and The Man Who Owned the Moon for some time thereafter. D. Thorne Harrison:

Born 1990 in a mean little Arkansas strip-mining town. Formal education terminated in 2005, with his escape from a state reformatory. Ten years of odd jobs on one side of the law or the other. Escalating ambition and power; by the age of thirty-five, billionaire chairman of a diversified, mostly legitimate, corporation. Luck, he called it.

One planet was not enough. About a week before his fortieth birthday, Harrison fired his board of directors and liquidated an awesome fortune. He sank every penny of it into the development and exploitation of the Adams-Beeson drive. Brought space travel to anyone who could afford it. Bought a chunk of the Moon to give them someplace to go. Pleasure domes, retirement cities, safaris for the jaded rich. Made enough to buy the votes to initiate the terraforming of Mars.

As the first trickle of water crawled down the Great Rift Valley, Harrison lay in his own geriatrics hospital, in Copernicus City, in his hundred and twentieth year. The excitement may have hastened his passing.

"Move it move it *move* it!" Down the long white corridor two orderlies pushed the massive cart, drifting in long skips in the lunar gravity, the cart heavy with machines surrounding a frail wisp of a human body: dead cyborg of D. Thorne Harrison. Oxygenated fluorocarbon coursing through slack veins, making the brain think it still lived.

Through the bay doors of the cryonics facility, cart braked to a bumpy stop by the cold chamber, tubes and wires unhooked and corpse slid without ceremony inside.

Chamber locked, pumped, activated: body turned to cold quartz.

"Good job." Not in the futile hope of future revival.

The nuts had a field day.

Harrison had sealed his frozen body into a time/space capsule, subsequently launched toward the center of the Galaxy. Also in the capsule were stacks of ultrafiche crystals (along with a viewer) that described humankind's nature and achievements in exhaustive detail, and various small objects of art.

One class of crackpots felt that Harrison had betrayed humanity, giving conquering hordes of aliens a road map back to Earth. The details of what they would do to us, and why, provided an interesting refraction of the individual crackpot's problems.

A gentler sort assumed *a priori* that a race of aliens able to decipher the message and come visit us must necessarily have evolved away from aggression and other base passions; they would observe; perhaps help.

Both of these groups provided fuel for solemn essays, easy master's theses, and evanescent religions. Other opinions:

"Glad the old geezer got to spend his money the way he wanted to."

"Inexcusable waster of irreplaceable artistic resources."

"He could have used the money to feed people."

"Quixotic gesture; the time scale's too vast. We'll be dead and gone long before anybody reads the damned thing."

"I've got more important things to worry about."

None of the above is true.

Supposedly, the miniature Adams-Beeson converter would accelerate the capsule very slowly for about a century, running out of fuel when the craft had attained a small fraction of the speed of light. It would pass the vicinity of Antares in about five thousand years.

The capsule had a preprogrammed signal generator, powered by starlight. It would accumulate power for ten years at a time, then bleat out a message at the 21-centimeter wavelength. The message lasted ninety minutes and would be repeated three times; any idiot with a huge radio telescope and the proper ontological prejudices could decode it: "I am an artifact of an intelligent race. My course is thus and so. Catch me if you can."

Unfortunately, the craft carried a pretty hefty magnetic field, and ran smack-dab into Maxwell's Equations. Its course carried it through a tenuous but very extensive cloud of plasma, and through the years it kept turning slowly to the right, decelerating. When it came out of the cloud it was pointed back toward the Earth, moving at a very modest pace.

In twenty thousand years it passed the place where Earth had been (the Sun having wandered off in the natural course of things) and continued to crawl, out toward the cold oblivion between the galaxies. It still beeped out its code every decade, but it was a long time before anybody paid any attention.

I woke up in great pain, that didn't last.

"How do you feel?" asked a pretty young nurse in a starched green uniform.

I didn't answer immediately. There was something wrong. With her, with the hospital room, the bed. The edges were wrong. Too sharp, like a bad matte shot at the cubies.

"How do you feel?" asked a plain, middle-aged nurse in a starched green uniform. I hadn't seen the change. "Is this better?"

I said it didn't make much difference. My body, my body was a hundred years younger. Mind clear, limbs filled with springy muscle. No consciousness of failing organs. I am dead, I asked her; told her.

"Not really," she said and I caught her changing: shimmer*click*. Now a white-haired, scholarly-looking doctor, male. "Not any more. You were dead, a long time. We rebuilt you."

I asked if he/she would settle on one shape and keep it; they pulled me out of a capsule, frozen solid?

"Yes. Things went more or less as you planned them."

I asked him what he meant by more or less.

"You got turned around, and slowed. It was a long time before we noticed you."

I sat up on the bed and stared at him. If I didn't blink he might not change. I asked him how long a time.

"Nearly a million years. 874,896 from the time of launch."

I swung to the floor and my feet touched hot sand.

"Sorry." Cold tile.

I asked him why he didn't show me his true form. I am too old to be afraid of bogeymen.

He did change into his true form and I asked that he change back into one of the others. I had to know which end to talk to.

As he became the doctor again, the room dissolved and we were standing on a vast plain of dark brown sand, in orderly dunes. The vague shadow in front of me lengthened as I watched; I turned around in time to see the Milky Way, rather bright, slide to the horizon. There were no stars.

"Yes," the doctor said, "we are at the edge of your galaxy." A sort of sun rose on the opposite horizon. Dim red and huge, nebulous at its boundaries. An infrared giant, my memory told me.

I told him that I appreciated being rebuilt, and asked whether I could be of some service. Teach them of the ancient past?

"No, we learned all we could from you, while we were putting you back together." He smiled. "On the contrary, it is we who owe you. Can we take you back to Earth? This planet is just right for us, but I think you will find it dull."

I told him that I would very much like to go back to Earth, but would like to see some of his world first.

"All of my world is just like this," he said. "I live here for the lack of variety. Others of my kind live in similar places."

I asked if I could meet some of the others.

"I'm afraid that would be impossible. They would refuse to see you, even if I were willing to take you to them." After a pause he added, "It's something like politics. Here." He took my hand and we rose, his star shrinking to a dim speck, disappearing. The Galaxy grew larger and we were suddenly inside it, stars streaming by.

I asked if this were teleportation.

"No, it's just a machine. Like a spaceship, but faster, more efficient. Less efficient in one way."

I started to ask him how we could breathe and talk, but his weary look cut me off. He seemed to be flickering, as if he were going to change shape again. But he didn't.

"This should be interesting," he said, as a yellow star grew brighter, then swelled to become the familiar Sun. "I haven't been here myself in ten, twelve thousand years." The blue-and-green ball of Earth was suddenly beneath us, and we paused for a moment. "It's a short trip, but I don't get out often," he said, apologetically.

As we drifted to the surface, it was sunset over Africa. The shape of the western coast seemed not to have changed much.

The Atlantic passed beneath us in a blur and we came to ground somewhere in the northeastern United States. We landed in a cow pasture. Its wire fence, improbably, seemed to be made of the same shiny duramyl I remembered from my childhood.

"Where are we?" I asked.

He said we were just north of Canaan, New York. There was a glideway a few kilometers to the west; I could find a truck stop and catch a ride. He was flickering very fast now, and even when he was visible I could see the pasture through him.

"What're you talking about?" I said. "They wouldn't, don't, have truck stops and glideways a million years in the future."

He regarded me with fading scorn and said we were only five or ten years in my future; after the year of my birth, that is. Twenty at the outside. Didn't I know the slightest thing about relativity?

And he was gone.

A farmer was walking toward me, carrying a wicked-looking scythe. There was nothing in the pasture to use it on, but me.

"Good morning," I said to him. Then saw it was afternoon.

He walked to within striking distance of me and stopped, grim scowl. He leaned sideways to look behind me. "Where's the other feller?"

"Who?" I'd almost said I was wondering that myself. "What other fellow?" I looked back over my shoulder.

He rubbed his eyes. "Damn contacts. What're you doin' on my propitty anyhow?"

"I got lost."

"Don't you know what a fence is?"

"Yes, sir, I'm sorry. I was coming to the house to ask directions to Canaan."

"Why you out walkin with a funny costume on?" I was wearing a duplicate of the conservative business suit Harrison was buried in.

"It's the style, sir. In the city."

He shook his head. "Kids. You just go over that fence yonder," he pointed, "and head straight 'til you get to the road. Mind you don't touch the fence an' watch out for my God damn beans. You get to the road and Canaan's to the left."

"Thank you, sir." He had turned and was stumping back to the farmhouse.

In the truck stop, the calendar read 1995.

It's not easy to stay penniless in New York City, not if you have a twenty-year-old body and over a century's worth of experience in separating people from their money.

Within a week, the man who had been Harrison was living in a high-class flat behind the protection of the East Village wall, with enough money stacked away to buy him time to think.

He didn't want to be Harrison again, that he knew for sure. Besides the boredom of living the same life over, he had known (as Harrison) by the time he was fifty that his existence was not a particularly happy one, physically addicted to the accumulation of wealth and power, incapable of trusting or being trusted.

Besides, Harrison was a five-year-old in Arkansas, just beginning the two decades of bad luck that would precede a century of nothing going wrong.

He had this sudden cold feeling.

He went to the library and looked up microfiches of the past few years' *Forbes* and *Bizweek*. And found out who he was, by omission.

For less than a thousand dollars, he gave himself a past. A few documents to match counterfeit inserts in government data banks. Then a few seemingly illogical investments in commodities, that made him a millionaire in less than a year. Then he bought a failing electronics firm and renamed it after himself: Lassiter Electronics.

He grew a beard that he knew would be prematurely white.

The firm prospered. He bought a plastics plant and renamed it Lassiter Industries. Then the largest printing outfit in Pennsylvania. A fishery after that.

In 2010 he contrived to be in a waterfront crap game in Galveston, where he lost a large sum to a hard-eyed boy who was fairly good at cold-rolling dice. Lassiter was better, but he rolled himself crapouts. It was two days after Harrison's twentieth birthday, and his first big break.

A small bank, then a large one. An aerospace firm. Textiles. A piece of an orbital factory: micro-bearings and data crystals. Now named Lassiter, Limited.

In 2018, still patiently manufacturing predestination, he hired young D. Thorne Harrison as a time-and-motion analyst, knowing that all of his credentials were false. It would give Harrison access to sensitive information.

By 2021 he was Junior Vice-President in charge of production. By 2022, Vice-President. Youngest member of the board, he knew interesting things about the other board members.

In 2024, Harrison brought to Lassiter's office documents proving that he had voting control of 51% of Lassiter, Limited. He had expected a fight. Instead, Lassiter made a cash settlement, perplexingly small, and dropped out of sight.

With half his life left to live, and money enough for much longer, Lassiter bought comfortable places in Paris, Key West, and Colorado, and commuted according to the weather and season. He took a few years for a leisurely trip around the world. His considerable mental energies he channeled into the world of art, rather than finance. He became an accomplished harpsichordist, and was well-known among the avant-garde for his neopointillist constructions: sculptures of frozen light, careful laser bursts caught in a cube of photosensitive gel. Beautiful women were fascinated by this man who had done so well in two seemingly antagonistic fields.

He followed Harrison's fortunes closely: the sell-out in 2030, buying out the Adams-Beeson drive (which seemed like a reckless long shot to most observers), sinking a fortune in the Moon and getting it back a hundredfold.

And as the ecologic catalyzers were being seeded on Mars, Harrison an old man running out of years to buy, Lassiter lay dying in Key West:

In the salt breeze on an open veranda, not wanting to clutter up his end with IV tubes and rushing attendants and sterile frigid air, he had sent his lone nurse away on an errand that would take too long, his last spoken words calm and reassuring, belying the spike of pain in his chest. The house downstairs was filled with weeping admirers, friends he had not bought, and as the pale blue sky went dark red, he reckoned himself a happy man, and wondered how he would do it next time, thinking he was the puppeteer, even as the last string was pulled.

Juryrigged

For three semesters I did graduate work in computer science at the University of Maryland, so it was inevitable, perhaps unfortunately, that sooner or later I'd write a story with a computer as the main character. This is it.

In terms of action, this is probably the most complicated story I've ever written, even though most of the action is just electrons slipping to and fro. I was a little concerned that it might be too complicated, but it did sell, and to a good market.

I took the story to a writers' conference in Baltimore —six or seven of us who met every few months to tear each other's work apart—and didn't expect any mercy, since we were fairly savage with one another (in a friendly way, oh yes), and it seemed to me that a story about a computer would be pretty vulnerable to sarcasm.

To my surprise, everyone liked it. I was so pleased that I got careless, and explained to them what the underlying structure of it was.

For the rest of the week, it was "Joe's God-damned Boolean algebra story."

L. Henry Kennem put a tiny speck of Ultramarine Blue into the gob of white on his palette. He mashed it around until it was thoroughly mixed, and smiled. Perfect for the underside.

Henry was painting a gesso-on-gesso picture of a pile of eggs in a white bowl on a white saucer, on a white table-top, lit uniformly from every side. It was a *tour-de-force* of technique; though an uncharitable observer might have pointed out that from any distance greater than three feet, it was only a slightly smudged white canvas.

But Henry was untouched by the foibles of critics, more immune than any artist in any less perfect age could have been. For in the Citizens' Capitalism of America (and about everywhere else, for that matter), he was a *painter*, by damn—Occupational Code 509 827 63; Artist, paints, free-lance—and he got a government check every two weeks for doing what he had shown the most aptitude for, twenty years ago at the magic age of fourteen. All he had to do, to keep off the relief rolls, was produce at least one painting a year.

He'd already done his painting this year, and it made him feel like a very good citizen to be doing another. This one was quite a challenge, too; Henry hadn't seen a real egg in many years—his paycheck was adequate but not enough to justify buying gourmet food—and, disdaining photographs, he was working from memory. His eggs were a little too spherical.

The door chimed softly and Henry gave a gentle curse and set his palette under the no-dry field. He kept the brush in his hand and went to answer the door.

The viewer showed three men in business clothes—dark blue capes and matching jocstraps—maybe customers, looking for something to brighten up their office. Henry thought of the twenty-eight canvases languishing unsold in his study and how nice it would be to splurge and buy an egg. He composed his features into a look of quiet interest and thumbed the door open.

"Louis Henry Kennem?" The short fellow in the middle did the talking, while the other two stared.

"Yes, indeed, sirs. What can I do for you?"

"Government business," the little one said and produced a card-badge with the legend "Occupational Classification Board." "We have some good news for you."

"Oh—well, come in, come in." Good news, maybe. The two big fellows didn't look like harbingers of joy. They walked in silently, as if on oiled bearings, expressions never changing as they took in the carefully planned disorder of his living room-studio.

"Can I get you gentlemen coffee or something?"

"No, thank you. We won't be long. Neither will you, as a matter of fact. You're to come with us." He plopped down on the sofa-roll. "Please have a seat." The other two remained standing. Henry had a strong impulse to bolt out the door, but instead he perched on a neowood sawhorse.

"Uh, why is the OCB interested in me?"

"As I say, it's good news. You're going to be a very wealthy man."

"I'm not . . . being reclassified, am I?" Henry couldn't imagine being anything other than Artist, paints, free-lance. Besides, some of the highest-paying jobs were unpleasant in the extreme; like Sewage Inspector or Poison Tolerance Control Engineer.

"No, nothing like that, uh, not really—" the man took a blue envelope out of his cape pocket and fiddled with it. "Your Occupational Code remains the same, and you'll be painting again in another year. But for one year, you've been selected to serve on jur—"

"Jury duty!" Henry half-jumped, half-fell off the sawhorse. Two hundred staring pounds of muscle slid into position between him and the door. "You can't . . . I can't —you can't plug me into that machine for a year! I'll go crazy—everyone does!"

"Now, now, Mr. Kennem," the man got up smiling and his cronies produced handcuffs. "Surely you don't believe all that nonsense. Why, nobody in the world is more comfortable than a cyborg juror. All your physical needs taken care of automatically, a good responsible job with high pay, eight companions as intelligent and qualified as you—"

"But I'm *not* qualified! I don't know anything but painting. I don't want to *do* anything but paint."

"Now, don't run yourself down, Mr. Kennem. Out of the eighty million people in Balt-Washmond, Central chose *you* as the one most qualified to replace the outgoing juror."

"The machine made a mistake, then. The jury runs the whole *city*—I can't even manage my own—"

One of the heavies jingled his cuffs suggestively. "Come on, Mr. Harris. Gonna be after five by the time we get back to the office." He looked as if the long speech had made his face hurt.

"Right, Sam. Look, Mr. Kennem, we can talk about it on the flyer. Why don't you just cooperate and come along?" Henry went quietly.

The Baltimore-Washington-Richmond Complex was a monument to scientific city planning. Growing methodically from the rubble of the Second American Revolution, the planners left nothing to chance or human weakness. There was no "urban sprawl"; slums were simply not allowed. The three cities had ideally fixed populations; and everybody whose presence Central (the Central Planning and Maintenance Computer Facility) decreed not essential to the city's functions was compelled to live in the exurban lowrises. Henry lived in one such, Fernwood, about fifty air-miles west of the center of Washington. Only those chosen to be very wealthy could afford to live above ground.

As the flyer skimmed its silent way to Washington, Henry saw a few such above-ground dwellings, their lawns irregular patches of green, looking out of place, disturbing the geometric regularity of the produce fields that rolled from horizon to horizon. He couldn't understand why anybody would purposely expose himself to weather when he could live in a totally controlled underground environment. He was only half-listening to Mr. Harris.

". . . it's ridiculous for you to say you aren't qualified. Central considers all citizens with IQ's between 130 and

140—and *any* person with that level of intelligence can fulfill the cyborg function. But jurors are chosen for many other qualities, beside intelligence."

"My pretty blue eyes," he said, looking out the window.

"Now, Mr. Kennem, there's no need to be sarcastic." Henry was getting very annoyed at Harris's habit of addressing him by name every other sentence. "You should be very proud. Of all the people intelligent enough—"

"But not *too* intelligent."

"—out of all of them, the machine decided you were the one least likely to misuse the power a juror has."

"I don't *want* power! I want to paint and be left alone."

"That is precisely it."

"Thanks. Lack of ambition. Sure is a lot to be proud of."

It was cold in the tank. Some part of his brain knew that he was floating in slime, naked as an embryo, totally helpless. That part of his brain knew that the crown of his skull had been excised and stored somewhere; that from the eyebrows up he was a complicated mass of grey and blue tissue interwoven with fine wires, microcircuitry, sensors . . . and it would have been frightening, had he been allowed to fear.

He couldn't see himself, or feel anything but the cold, or hear the faint susurrus of fluid cycling through the tank.

The part of his brain that used to see was earmarked for TRAFFIC CONTROL.

The part of his brain that used to feel took care of POPULATION DENSITY AND EPIDEMIOLOGICAL RESEARCH.

The part of his brain that used to be hooked to his ears, SUPPLY AND DEMAND REDUNDANCY CHECK or sometimes RESOURCE PROJECTION ANALYSIS.

A well-determined matrix was like the smell of buttercups (he had never smelled a buttercup before). A differential equation with ambivalent initial conditions felt like an itch in the middle of his back, where he couldn't reach. Tensors sang like harps and algebra was more basic to him than love had ever been.

He knew he had once been Louis Henry Kennem but

now he was INTERFACE FOUR and he had a splitting headache.

Your head will ache for a year, said FIVE, speaking in cultured accents of Boolean algebra.

If you can hold out for a year, said EIGHT.

The old FOUR only made it four months, said FIVE.

But you can do it, we have great confidence in you, said SIX, just a hint of sarcasm in the third-order harmonic.

Go fuck a solenoid, said THREE, give the new guy a chance.

I've got to get out of here, thought FOUR. But his thoughts weren't private. He hadn't learned how yet.

Just walk away, said EIGHT.

Swim, said SIX.

You're in charge of TRAFFIC CONTROL, said EIGHT. Call yourself a flyer.

Everybody quiet down and get back to work, said ONE. And everybody did. ONE was INTERFACE CONTROL MONITOR, among other things.

After a while, FOUR learned how to isolate the entity that was Henry. This was necessary so that Henry could think without being monitored—by FOUR as well as the others; when Henry thought, it gave FOUR what can only be described as a headache.

FOUR was allocated many more storage and logic circuits than he needed for the 246 duties he performed. It was no trick at all for FOUR to link up a bit from here and a bit from there and a bushel-basket full from BUDGET ANALYSIS 1985, and patch together a Henry analogue. He did this just one microsecond after he saw it was possible.

Of course, this Henry didn't know a vector from a scalar, and couldn't even add up the figures in his credit book accurately. But he could tell a good painting from a merely photographic one, what grade of synth-turps mixed well with which pigment, and could feel and hear and see and taste.

But all of this sensory input came from FOUR. It was confusing at first.

He saw the city, Balt-Washmond, all at once, at every level. The satellite over Chimbarazo showed the city as a tiny crystal, glimmering on the Earth's sunset line. Aerial monitors in visual, infrared and radio gave three complete, shifting, superimposed images that almost tallied with the acres of blueprints in CITY PLANNING AND MAINTE-NANCE. Traffic sensors and pedestrian density monitors scrutinized every square millimeter of public property in the city and its allied lowrises.

He heard the babble of several hundred thousand people talking at once and felt millions of feet on his sidewalks. Billions of impressions rushed through him, changing every tiniest fraction of a second, and he knew he should have gone insane from the sheer complexity of it, but instead he perceived it as one gestalt. The City—and it was so beautiful that it made him ashamed, to remember that he once thought he knew what beauty was.

An old woman died in not too much pain at Level 243, Room 178, Frederick (Greenleaf) Lowrise and Henry knew that FOUR had dispatched a flyer from the nearest HUMAN RESOURCES (RECLAMATION) depot. It was sad that her three children and six grandchildren would miss her, maybe less sad that she'd be minced into compost (after reverent ritual) to enrich the soybean fields around Frederick, but the sadness was part of the beauty and while he was concentrating on HUMAN RESOURCES (REC-LAMATION) the fact slipped through him that at this instant there were 2,438 people urinating in Balt-Wash-mond and FOUR could give him their names arranged in alphabetical order, or dip into HEALTH STATISTICS and arrange them in order of increasing bladder capacity and that was part of the beauty and out of the 17,548 flyers in the air, 307 were going to run out of power before they reached their destinations (they had changed their minds in mid-air, or they wouldn't have been allowed to launch in the first place) and of these 307, two had faulty warning lights and didn't know they had to land and recharge and police flyers were vectoring in on them but they might not get to HYZ-9746-455 in time but that wasn't too bad because he was far north of the city and, at worst, would fall like a dropped stone into an uninhabited corn-field and FOUR knew exactly which plants he would crush, what breed they were and in what stage of growth they were and what their projected yield would be but there was no way in the world that Henry or FOUR could save the man's life if the police flyer didn't reach him in time and this painful helplessness in the face of virtual omniscience, this was part of the beauty too.

FOUR dipped into TRAFFIC CONTROL (VEHICLE DESIGN ANALYSIS) and did a quick costs-versus-probability of occurrence/value of lost resources analysis, and found that the installation of a device to prevent such an accident from happening would not be practical.

Henry basked in the beauty and complexity of it for several days, when it slowly dawned on him that he wasn't alone.

Now it was hard to really say where Henry *was* in the first place. FOUR initially set him up out of such odds and ends as weren't being used. But when a bit that was a part of Henry was needed for something else, FOUR automatically transferred the information in that bit to somewhere else; anywhere, it didn't make any difference as long as the proper link was maintained.

So the juryrigged assemblage of memory cells (piezoelectric, nothing but the best), buffer units, ultrafiche Crandall files and so on—that went under the name of Henry—sprawled all over Center, flowing this way and that, shifting a hundred thousand tiny ways every second. Only a very few elements of Henry came at all close to where "his" old body hung suspended in a dimly-lit tank filled with pale green synthetic mucus.

FOUR arranged Henry in this seemingly slapdash fashion because it was required by the ineffable machine logic he used to attack the problem "how do I get rid of this flaming 'head'ache?" It was the best way he could isolate Henry without tying up too many components necessary for other problems. But there were other possible approaches.

The man/machine that had been FOUR before they installed Henry had tackled the problem a different way.

Smithers, the man who was Henry's predecessor, had been a nice enough guy. An accountant with an IQ of 132, he had been eligible for the cyborg jury and was thus among those Center considered as replacements when the old FOUR's term was running out. Smithers' psychometric profile, unfortunately, was in error, and hid two slight maladies that would have disqualified him immediately.

He was just the slightest bit paranoid.

And he suffered little tiny, insignificant, delusions of grandeur.

Other than those two quirks, he had been the perfect man for the job. And with those small defects masked, Center exulted and sent Mr. Harris and his two silent buddies out to collect him. They had to use the handcuffs.

Now until they wired him up and slipped him into the slime, Smithers wasn't the slightest bit mad. Not by any ordinary social standards—all of his friends and relatives, in fact, were much farther from the all-but-unreachable standard of sanity that had to be met to make a perfect man/machine interface . . . and they all thought Smithers was rather dull.

But the dash of paranoia and delusional flyspecks that should have shown up on his profile were like a few individual colon bacilli on an otherwise pristine dish of delicious agar jelly. They could only grow—slowly at first, but at an ever-increasing rate . . . until after four months, INTERFACE ONE decided that FOUR could no longer function efficiently and he was taken out of the system before he could do any harm.

Smithers was decanted and they thawed out his skullcap and fitted it back on and sadly led him off to a place where he would be cared for, where nobody would mind that he was as helpless as a new-born child and only slightly more intelligent than a rutabaga.

They carted Smithers' body away, and his short-circuited vegetable brain. But they didn't know, couldn't know, about the rest of him; the cybernetic analogue tucked away under BALT-WASHMOND DEMOGRAPHICS 1983.

Now certain parts of FOUR's memory are seldom tapped, but must not be disturbed—these are data which will never change, and which have been stored in the most efficient manner possible. One of these parts is DEMOGRAPHICS, and if it ever occurred to FOUR to wonder why the section for 1983 was slightly larger than 1984 (all other years used less space than the year following), he was too busy to do anything about it.

Smithers was sandwiched in there, crowded into the eighteen billion cells between HEALTH STATISTICS and

LEGAL DOCUMENTS. It had been easy for FOUR to get rid of the Smithers-headache by assembling an analogue out of spare parts and linking it up to the cobwebby DEMOGRAPHICS section. But then Smithers, sensing the dissolution of his biological brain and, not unreasonably, wanting to live forever, erased from FOUR all knowledge of the analogue. In order to do this, Smithers had to sever all of his cyborg sensory connections; in fact, his only contact with anything outside of DEMOGRAPHICS 1983 was a single link to his biological self. And as the Smithers that floated in green ooze slowly went bonkers, he affected the analogue Smithers through that fine wire, by a process of induction.

And when they took the Smithers-body away, the Smithers that remained was deaf and blind, as well as paranoid and delusional. He had to stay that way for weeks, frozen between HEALTH STATISTICS and LEGAL DOCUMENTS, reviewing the contents of each, every tenth of a second, just to keep from going even more batty. Even after they hooked Henry into FOUR, Smithers was isolated.

Then, a graduate student doing research into mutative trends asked Central, which asked ONE, which asked FOUR, "How many birth defects showed up in the newborn of non-Caucasian parents in 1983?" FOUR opened a path to DEMOGRAPHICS 1983, to scoop out the number, and Smithers pounced on the opening and his awareness spread through all of FOUR in a nanosecond. And he kept it quiet.

It was good to have the City back again, even if he had to share it with that arty-farty type Henry. He was able to hear and see and feel again, but he didn't dare reach out and touch. If FOUR found out he was still here, he'd erase Smithers in a simple space-saving reflex. So he was like an almost omniscient paraplegic—but before, he'd been a paraplegic wrapped in a cocoon.

Henry sensed that something was different. With the help of FOUR's CYBORG DIAGNOSTIC PACKAGE, he checked out his own system in minutest detail. Nothing seemed to be wrong. Eventually he dismissed the "somebody-looking-over-my-shoulder" feeling as just another thing to which he had to adjust.

Smithers kept still as a mouse while the CYBORG DIAGNOSTIC PACKAGE coursed up and down the system that linked him, through Henry and FOUR, to the outside world. It was all he could do to keep from laughing at his own cleverness, as he made the responses appropriate to an inert cybernetic component, each time the package tested him. It was so easy to outwit.

Obviously, Smithers thought, Henry was not fit to be in charge of FOUR (though he wasn't really "in charge"— this was only what Smithers remembered *his* job as having been). But taking over, or at least merging, would be difficult. Smithers mulled it over for five days.

The thing that made it difficult was Henry's lack of a concrete, easily determined position. Not even FOUR could predict where Henry's, say, critical faculties would be, a hundredth of a second in the future. FOUR shifted the individual parts of Henry around on a real-time basis; where they went depended on what was available at the moment.

So. Smithers had wanted to get at FOUR through Henry, but it became obvious that the only way he could sneak up on Henry was through FOUR.

The positions that various parts of Henry occupied were assigned by a small (refrigerator sized) component of FOUR, called SUBPROGRAM LINKING ALGORITHM —LINK to its friends. There was a path to LINK from every subprogram in FOUR. Smithers looked around and found that there was a largish vacant place in CURRENT POPULATION DYNAMICS. He insinuated part of himself into that vacancy, then generated a request for information from DEMOGRAPHICS 1983, his old home base. When LINK patched the two of them together, Smithers slipped into LINK as smoothly as an oyster sliding down a throat.

From there it was easy. Assuming that nobody would need data from DEMOGRAPHICS for the next minute or so, Smithers erased all of the irreplaceable information in DEMOGRAPHICS from 1983 to 2012. He dumped Henry in there with plenty of room to spare; with LINK it was easy. The rest of FOUR functioned quite smoothly. Since Smithers was in charge of LINK, there was no way FOUR could know it had just lost a large subprogram.

Of course, neither did Henry know that he was nailed down in one place. Had he cared to know where he "was" at any time, he'd have had to patch through LINK into FOUR—then back to LINK and finally back to himself, the process taking about two microseconds; by which time he'd be someplace else altogether. So he'd long since stopped bothering.

Smithers studied Henry as a lepidopterist might scrutinize a very important pinned specimen. It took about forty-five seconds to find the weakest point in the analogue, the place most susceptible to invasion. He sneaked in, then gradually restored Henry to his usual status in regard to LINK; that is, flashing around the system like a cybernetic dervish. He also took time to fill up the DEMOGRAPHICS areas he had erased, with reasonable-looking (but totally made up) data.

That almost proved Smithers' second undoing.

The graduate student who had asked for the number of birth defects in children born to non-Caucasian parents in 1983 had written the number down on a slip of paper and then used the paper for a bookmark and returned the book to the library. When he realized that he'd lost it, he cussed a little and punched up Central again. Central admonished him that computer time doesn't come all that cheaply, and asked ONE who asked FOUR who fished out the bogus figure that Smithers had substituted. Then the graduate student went back to his desk and the fellow who shared a room with him said the library had called; he'd left a slip of paper in a book and it looked as if it might be important, so his roommate had copied it down and left it on his desk. He thanked him and cussed a little more, under his breath this time, and glanced at the figure as he sat down. Then he looked at the piece of paper in his hand, then back at the number on his desk. He groaned and stomped back to the Central console.

"Hey, FOUR," ONE said. "Wanna spill your DEMOGRAPHICS 1983 and run a redundancy check?"

"Sorry, chief, no data to compare it to. That's all singular, no cross-references."

"Well, *find* some! You gave me two different responses to the same question, about a week apart."

"What's up?" said SIX.

"Got any corollary stuff for DEMOGRAPHICS 1983?" FOUR asked.

"Hmmm . . . just 'Automobiles and Flyers Owned, by Age Grp, Sex, and Race.' "

"Well, stuff it in to stack 271; I'll put my version in 272 and run a no-carry AND through it."

"OK . . . fire when ready, FOUR."

"Oh shit," said FOUR.

"Well?" said ONE.

"No correlation. Somebody scrambled it."

ONE sighed a cybernetic sigh. "Find out how far it goes, and we'll replace as much of the missing data as we can. Jesus Christ . . . as if we didn't have enough trouble, with Labor Day coming up—"

"I'm sorry, chief, I really am."

"Not your fault, FOUR. It probably got randomized while they were installing your new org. Happens sometimes."

Henry was listening to this exchange with great interest —after all, he was the new org—but Smithers had stopped listening after the first evidence that they had stumbled onto his machinations. He had to put an escape plan into effect. He had several plans—as one might imagine, considering his extreme paranoia—but since time was probably limited, he chose the quickest, most audacious one.

The first thing he had to do was take over Henry completely. That would have been impossible a week before, when Henry had been totally sane.

It had taken four months for Smithers to go off the deep end. But he had started with only the slightest hint of instability—and Henry had had the benefit of coexisting for a week with a full-fledged lunatic. A week was more than enough. The vague feeling of somebody looking over his shoulder had intensified, until Henry was sure that everybody—LINK, FOUR, ONE, and every other interface and package—was spying on him, sneaking stares whenever his attention was directed elsewhere. And he had a growing feeling that he was just too fine and capable an analogue to put up with that kind of indignity.

So taking over the analogue (Smithers wasn't interested in the corporeal Henry, not just yet) was rather easy, since both of them had similarly pathologic personalities. He merely sidled up alongside and, subverting LINK by switching on a bogus control subprogram, severed the connections between the Henry analogue and both the Henry body and FOUR. Taking less than a microsecond, he forced key links between himself and the other analogue—for a tiny flash he felt what the other was feeling, isolation and agony, like being swaddled in black velvet and skewered by a hundred red-hot knitting needles—then he connected up again.

"What's going on?" said FOUR.

Working fast now, to stay ahead of FOUR, Smithers felt a slight "resistance" pushing at him from Henry's brain (which was still fairly sane), but human thought is so grindingly slow compared to cybernetic, that he didn't have a chance; Smithers pushed *back* at every point and, abandoning the analogue, speared into the brain (the only outward sign being a small smoky bubble that formed when a flap of grey matter throbbed in response to the higher voltage going through a microcable), using the brain as a springboard, burning it out completely, crashing into FOUR with a force so compelling that it randomized TRAFFIC CONTROL and made CYBORG DIAGNOSTIC PACKAGE come up all ones.

"What did you say, FOUR?" said ONE.

"Bongo, bongo, bongo; I don' wanna leave the Congo," Smithers muttered.

"What?!"

" 'Twas brillig," Smithers shouted, "and the sli—"

Everything went red and slow and stopped and Smithers could hear through a thousand miles of cotton:

"God damn it, had to cut out FOUR again. You all know what to do?"

A ragged chorus of tired "Yeah, chief" 's, as the other interfaces took over. "Good. I'm going in to see what the trouble is *this* time."

"Careful, chief," Smithers recognized SEVEN's nasal tone, "Must be another crazy."

"I can handle him. I handled the other all right." Smithers laughed and in what passed for his ears the laugh was a chittering squirrel and a kettledrum roll and everything in between. He tensed and waited for contact with ONE, knowing that the big dumb boob would try the same old diagnostic macroalgorithm he had used last time. And as soon as he made contact—

The timing was very critical, as FOUR couldn't function for very long without a viable brain in its circuits. But ONE would want to check it out while it was still clicking, hopefully.

There!—just the lightest of touches. Smithers jumped, and it was like jumping at a shadow, no resistance, and for a nanosecond he thought too easy, must be a trap, but then he slid straight through the macroalgorithm, into the vitals of ONE. He shot out tendrils of control—getting pretty good at this, he thought—and clawed his way into the Central Processing Unit. There was just a little resistance; he elbowed it aside and in no time he was in charge of ONE, which controlled Central, which controlled the Baltimore-Washington-Richmond Complex.

The idea of them trying to stand in his way. The sneaky little tricks, the spying—they'll pay!

"Catch the crazy, Chief?"

"Sure. Everything's under control."

He flexed his cyborg muscles, felt all seven working interfaces respond. Now, an exercise . . . wouldn't it be nice, he thought, to kill everybody whose name begins with "A"?

"What did you do with him?"

Contacting them was easy, from Aalborg to Azelstein. He had FIVE send each an urgent communication—an order, actually—urging them to meet at the Chesapeake Fission Station at noon. He had SEVEN arrange for tables and box lunches on the grounds of the station, and a podium with flags waving (all strictly diversionary devices).

"Nothing to it. I set up . . ."

Funny that he couldn't see or feel as much through ONE as he had through FOUR. Guess only the flunkies need extensive sensory inputs.

SIX was in charge of POWER GENERATION AND DISPERSAL. Smithers ordered him to pull the dampers out all the way at the Chesapeake Fission Station, at 12:05. It couldn't explode, of course—but it would get mighty hot.

". . . a transfinite-ordinal simulator . . ."

Time sure flies when you don't have much to do. ONE didn't seem to have a tenth as much to do as FOUR did. That's why he was always shouting orders and spying—nothing better to occupy his time.

"*. . . that lets me record his fantasies as he carries them out. Should have done that last time—he . . .*"

Here it was 12:05 already. SIX reported the deed done, and he felt a slight voltage shift as they switched to emergency generators. He couldn't see the result of his experiment, but he could imagine all of those people sitting around munching on fried soy-chicken one second and the next second superheated radioactive steam flaying the skin and flesh from their bones . . . *that* should teach them a lesson!

"*. . . jumped right at the bait, didn't suspect a thing. I'll record another minute or so, for analysis, then pull the plug. Henry, that was FOUR's org, was in on it. I pulled him out of the circuit and patched in the old FOUR org, from St. Elizabeth's. We'll be back to normal in a couple of minutes.*"

Now for the B's.

Summer's Lease

≈≈≈≈≈≈≈≈≈≈≈≈≈≈≈≈≈≈≈≈≈≈≈≈≈≈≈≈≈≈

It was fun to reread this story because of the memory it evoked: I've never written a story under more pleasant conditions. Getting there was rather complicated, though.

One Sunday morning Analog *Editor Ben Bova called me and asked whether I would do a story for a special issue he was putting together about Immanuel Velikovsky. He said he had in mind something about the scientific method. I was fixing breakfast at the time, frying bacon, so I said sure, I'll do you a story about Francis Bacon. About all I knew of Bacon was that he was an impressively eclectic philosopher and was generally credited with having formulated the scientific method.* I suggested to Ben a sort of famous-person-as-alien story; Bacon was actually an extraterrestrial, stranded for life on this backwoods planet, who made a living the best way he knew how: being superior.*

I still think that would make a good story. If anybody out there wants to write it, I'd love to read it.

At the time, I was sweating out the last couple of chapters of an adventure novel. My wife and I were taking a charter flight to Jamaica on Wednesday, and I was grimly determined to finish the book before we left (made it by thirty minutes). I was sort of enjoying the role of Superhack, on a round-the-clock schedule of catnaps and writing, but I did need a short break, so I slogged out through the ice and snow to the University of Iowa library, thinking I would pick up a Bacon biography and a couple of critical works to read in Jamaica.

---

* Lower-case bacon, I know a great deal about, including an infallible method for cooking perfect bacon every time. Cook it in the nude. This trains you to keep the heat down so it won't stick or spatter, and it can't burn.

Well, the university had about 500 volumes by and about Francis Bacon, but 490 of them were in Latin, a language whose sound I admire. Of the remainder, I really couldn't find one that looked like poolside reading. Reluctantly, I abandoned the idea (but did mention Novum Organum in the adventure novel, so the morning wouldn't be a total loss).

Came up with a more manageable idea, called Ben, he approved it, and I packed a small typewriter in there with the skin-diving gear.

So this story was written in a succession of mornings on the veranda of a lovely hotel just north of Montego Bay. The management thoughtfully provided a coffee pot, and I sat in the dark of the morning, in the cool night breeze, watching odd green lizards stalk the edge of the light, listening to the quiet surf, sipping strong Jamaican coffee, smoking strong Jamaican cigars, writing with delicious ease. Feeling that ineffable sense of perfect time, perfect place, perfect occupation: fragile, wistful, never to be repeated or forgotten.

Writing in the fierce Iowa winter, I had set the adventure novel in Key West and Haïti. So in the most clement weather this side of Eden, I wrote a story about a planet with storms that wrack its surface clean of life.

Dis Buk wil tel dē storē of dē Burning, and of whī Each 80 yērs Men hav to hīd from Wind and Sē and Skī.

And how dē first Men first went Nōrd to flē dē Burning Sun,

And whī God rids dē Wrld of Līf when Līf has jus begun.

—Godbuk 1, 1, 1-4

Lars Martin had been assigned the unpopular job of auditor. He sat under an awning on the dock, beside a balance-scale taken from the market. He had stacks of watertight bags made from fish bladders and a notebook that contained a roster of the town's population. One pan of the balance held two fist-sized weights, and in the other pan a family would place such personal possessions as they wished to take with them on the northern migration. The two weights that limited their allotment totaled less than twenty pounds, so family members argued quite a bit with each other, and everybody argued with Lars.

Lars was normally the town's book-keeper (a word with a very literal meaning there) and had very legible handwriting as well as a facility for arithmetic, so he was the logical choice for the post. But he was also a charitable man, and it pained him to be inflexible with his friends. A collection of discarded treasures grew at his side: dolls and fine clothes, pictures and sets of dishes and tableware, jewelry, and even coins. And books, which hurt Lars the most. He had written most of them.

"Still a little light, Fred." Fred had no family, but was allowed the full weight. "Why don't you take one of these?" Lars had salvaged books from the discards and lined them up neatly on his table.

"I've read most of them," he said. He picked up the town's copy of "Metal Work." "This one, I even have in my memory."

Lars stirred the pile of coins and ingots that made up all of Fred's allowance. "When we come back, they'll be worth more than gold and silver."

"You say that to everybody." Fred laughed humorlessly.

"I know how you feel. Some of my best work is going under, too."

"It's a different thing," Lars said, tired of everybody's obtuseness. "You can make them again, after."

"You can write the books down again."

"Two or three of them, I could," he admitted. "For the rest . . . I'll mine your memory for metalwork, and old Johansen's for history, and the like. And borrow books from other towns. When there's money for it. If they have any books to borrow."

"We've always managed."

"I don't think so, Fred. We lose a certain number of books every Burning."

He shrugged. "Is that bad? We only lose the ones that nobody has put in his memory. If only the best survive, I don't count that as a loss."

Fred was partly being honest, Lars knew, but was also setting him up for a joke. Lars taught numbers and letters to all the town's children, and knew that he sometimes treated the adults as children, out of habit or absentmindedness, when there was something to be explained. Catching him at this was considered high humor.

Maybe it was "frontier" humor, but that particular word had long disappeared from their language. Exploration was a luxury their race couldn't afford, spending every fourth generation preparing for planetary disaster. Then three generations trying to recover.

They called their planet "the world," and the double star system in which it orbited, they called "the suns." The brighter of the two stars provided the Burning by flaring up every eighty-three years.

But their remote ancestors, some two thousand years before, had named the planet Thursday's Child, when they had come out of blindspace thoroughly lost, their colonizing vessel crippled and its resources so depleted that the ship's elders had set up a roster for systematic cannibalism. From orbit, Thursday's Child had seemed an incredible miracle: a frost-capped globe of greens and warm browns and glittering blue. They landed and found that the soil took their seeds and cuttings well, and the sea teemed with a great variety of life. But the only land animals were a few hardy varieties of insects and worms.

They had suspected that the planet, however hospitable it looked, would be a pretty strange world—even before they'd landed. Its primary was a double star, with both stars and the planet revolving around in the same plane, much like Earth, its Sun, and Jupiter. The planet's axis was exactly perpendicular to that ecliptic plane, so its seasons (which went hot-cool-hot-cold) were provided by the mutual periodic eclipses of the two stars.

But certain geologic features, and the apparent inability of the planet to support complex life-forms on land, caused their scientists to take a closer look at the twin primary. They found that the larger of the two was a recurrent nova. Every eighty years or so, it would flare up for a short period. At maximum, Thursday's Child would be blasted by over a hundred times its normal ration of sunlight.

So the first Burning didn't take them by surprise; they had twenty years' planning time. But there was no clearly superior solution to their problem, among the various possible alternatives.

They could try to survive the way the fish apparently did, getting far enough below the surface of the ocean so they were insulated—both from the radiation and the undoubtedly ferocious weather—by a large mass of water. But how deep would be deep enough? They didn't have time or materials to sink a haven into really deep water. And the water above some impossible-to-compute level would present an environment even more hostile than the land. So they rejected that alternative.

> *But Watrs onlē fōr dē Ones dat ōn dē watr Wrld*
> *Yʳ Fadrs nū*
> *An't fōr sinfl Man dē simpl Refūj of dē Sē*
> *Yʳ Fadrs nū.*
>
> —Godbuk 1, 4, 26-29

They also rejected the idea of burrowing beneath the ground, which was the way the primitive land animals managed to make it through the holocaust. There was a good deal of seismic activity even under the best of conditions.

The poles offered one answer. Especially the northern

pole, where a high-walled crater near the top of the world
made a kind of natural fort, within whose walls the suns'
rays never fell. It was bitter cold, of course, but they could
cope with that.

Transportation was a problem. The one scout ship they
had used for exploration could carry little more than its
pilot. But they had tools and time, and there was plenty of
wood, so they opened various colonists' manuals and set
about learning how to build ships and navigate them.

The final solution was both simple and daring—fool-
hardy, some maintained. That was simply to lift the starship back into orbit, and wait out the storm in the still of
space, protected by the shadow of Thursday's Child. But
the engineers couldn't guarantee that the ship would even
lift properly, let alone perform any kind of sophisticated
maneuvering.

Finally they split into two groups, most of the colony
building the flotilla that would take them north.

> *Dā warn^d dē Ones dat sot a plās of Sāftē in dē Skī*
> *Y^r Fadrs nū*
> *Dā sed. God didnt put us on dis*
> *Wrld tū let us lēv.*
> *Y^r Fadrs nū.*

—Godbuk 1, 4, 34-37

The small group who had opted for the starship ran out
of luck very quickly. The engines quit at an altitude of less
than a kilometer, and they fell into the sea. For many years
the remains of the starship were visible in the shallow water, but eventually it became the nucleus of a long-lived organism resembling a coral reef. Its location was forgotten,
and over the course of a few dozen generations the very
fact of its existence evolved from memory into oral history
and, finally, into myth.

The ones who had gone north didn't have an easy time
of it. Over half of them died, some from exposure during
the rigorous crossing from the arctic sea to the inland
crater, but most were killed at the height of the twenty-
day storm, whose effects were worse than had been predicted by the most pessimistic scientist. Perhaps it was just

as well, since over half of the food and seed were also lost.

Having known the seas were going to rise, they'd moved what they couldn't carry with them to the nearest high ground. Their livestock and seed and other absolute necessities went into the boats, along with a year's worth of food, and they headed for the northern ice. There, they dismantled the boats and re-formed them into sledges, and most of them made it to the crater. The inside of the crater wall was conveniently pocked with caves; the nomads walled themselves in and waited.

But the caves that were too close to the crater floor—including the ones that housed the livestock—filled up with boiling water at the height of the storm. They had started out with twelve hundred people and eight hundred head of livestock. When they came out of their caves after the water receded, there were five hundred people, two roosters, and a hen.

Without draft animals, returning to the sea was much slower than getting to the crater had been, even though the coast was less than a third the distance it had been before the storm. They bolted wheels to their sleds and pushed and pulled them across muck that was already beginning to freeze again. Then they dismantled the sleds and nailed them up into the shape of boats, and returned over warmed seas to the place they had called Primus.

Finding Primus underwater surprised nobody. Much more disconcerting was the fact that the mountains had been scoured clean, and there was no trace of their caches of goods, records and equipment. Much that had been irreplaceable was lost, including the ship's library and the cloning equipment that would have replaced their herds of animals.

Lars Martin and his contemporaries didn't know any of this. The only written records that had survived from "ancient times" were The Sonets of Wm. Shākspēr, twelve of which had been passed from father to son as one family's tradition, and a thing variously called God's Book, God-buk, or God Buk; spelling having become more a matter of opinion than of authority. This volume was a mixture of mythologized history and moral guidance, most of it rendered in iambic-septameter doggerel.

The Shākspēr book was one that Lars had memorized word-for-word, although he kept a copy as part of his own meager weight allowance. And Godbuk he studied constantly. Not for moral guidance; he had his own, fairly conventional, ideas and was reasonably true to them.

Fred continued his gentle baiting. "Like that God's Book you're always reading. You can't really think it's worth a pound of seed."

"Be serious, Fred."

"I am being serious." He opened a copy of the book and flipped through its accordion-style pages. "Half serious. I suppose it's useful for scaring children and keeping them lined up properly. Not much else."

"You're dead wrong. It's the closest thing we have to a historical record. Everything else is just what somebody told somebody."

"You're still dancing that jig?" He slapped the book shut. "Somebody sat down and made that up. Some *priest*." No one in Samueltown had been a priest for more than three generations, and most of the townspeople shared Fred's contempt for the profession.

"That's not strictly true," Lars began, but Fred cut him off with a laugh and an out-thrust palm. "Save it. Too much work for idle argument," he said, which was true, and he jogged away.

Shaking his head, Lars slid Fred's precious metals into a small fish-bladder bag, tied the mouth of it shut, and affixed an identifying label. He recorded the bag's contents in his notebook, then set it on top of a pile of similar bags. He squinted at the low suns. About another hour; then he could carry the bags to the ship's lockup hold and go home.

A few days later, they were under sail; eight ships that drew power from oars as well as sails, in case of calm. As closely as could be divided, each ship held one-eighth of Samueltown's resources, human as well as material. Most of each ship's cargo was made up of food and seed. They had to save food enough to last the town a year or more, until the waters receded enough for planting and the fish started biting again.

As long as the wind and currents were favorable, there was plenty of time for "idle argument." Lars and Fred and the town's mayor, called Samuel by way of title, were resting in the shade after an hour of cleaning fish. It had been a noisome job, since the offal was collected and kept in a trough at the stern, to use as chum for attracting other fish.

Samuel was in an especially bad mood. She had been a farmer all her life and had worked the same piece of land through thirty years and two husbands. In a few months now, her orchards and vines would be under fifty fathoms of steaming water. If she ever farmed again, it would mean starting from scratch on a sterile mountaintop.

She folded her arms on the railing and stared down at the inky blue water. "You've talked to a priest, haven't you?"

"The one in Carroltown," Lars said. "When I went down to copy the annotations in our Godbuk."

"Did he have any answers?" Her voice was almost a snarl, though she was close to tears. "Why this happens? Why we just have time to get started and . . ."

"He had all the answers," Fred said. "Right? They always have."

Lars shrugged. "You know how I feel."

"Yeah, but you're crazy." Fred picked at a splinter in the decking. "You only get half a vote."

"Nice if we could settle it with a vote," Samuel said. " 'The suns should stay dim. Vote yes or no.' "

"You can't just dismiss what the priests say. Just because they're priests. They know things—"

"The problem with most people," Samuel cut in, "isn't that they don't know a lot of things. Just that most of what they know is wrong."

"You wouldn't have applied that to this man," Lars said. "He was pretty impressive. Spent all of his life, eighty *years,* just learning."

"That's Carroltown for you," Fred said. "Learning what? Anything but an honest profession."

"He had what he said was a calling."

"So do I. God told me in a dream, 'Fred, you just sit back and take it easy. Working at that damned forge is giving you blisters on your blisters.' Nobody believes me, but it's true."

"People like that are useless," Samuel said. "They're

like the sucker things you sometimes find on a grayfish. Taking without giving."

"You class me that way, Samuel?"

"No. You work hard, I know it. One time I had six children in the house, all at once. How you handle ten times that number is beyond me."

"I make them want to learn. So they keep quiet and pay attention, most of them."

"That's in the nature of children," Fred said, "indulging their curiosity. Most of us grow out of it. Your priest friend was just a child with a long beard."

"Maybe so, in a sense. But meeting him was . . . about the most important thing that ever happened to me. He started me thinking about the Godbuk."

Fred laughed. "Then he should have been taken out and drowned."

"Something he said?" Samuel asked.

"Something he showed me." Lars leaned forward, intense. "I never told you about this?"

"You've told me," Fred said.

Samuel shot him a look. "I don't think so," she said. Best to keep him on familiar ground.

"Wake me up when it's over."

"He didn't show me himself," Lars said. "He was too old to make the journey. But he drew me a map and sent a guide along with me."

"To where?"

"A place well south of Carrolltown. A cave in the mountains. How well do you know chapter four of the first Testament?"

"Not well. It's about the first Burning, isn't it?"

"That's right." He ignored Fred's snort. "It tells how one group tried to escape the Burning by getting back in the ship that brought them here. They got it back up into the sky again, but it fell and killed them all."

"I remember."

"Well, Godbuk says there were fifty-one of them, and it says the ship's captain was named Chu." He started to get up. "I'll show you; let me get—"

Samuel waved him down. "I'll take your word for it. Go on."

"Ships in the sky," Fred muttered.

"There were words in that cave, carved into the rock. They were hard to read—so old that the very rock was crumbling with age, even though it was inside, protected from wind and water. The writing was very strange, in a style I'd never seen before.

"It said, 'In memory of the nova's first victims'—I don't know what that word means, obviously something about the Burning—and it's followed by a list of fifty-one names. The name at the top is Chu."

"Doesn't prove anything." Fred opened one eye. "It might be old, sure. But even if it was written by the same crowd of priests who wrote God's Book, it's still just a children's tale."

"But Fred . . . even *you*, Fred, you have to admit there is at least a small possibility that the inscription is real; that it commemorates an actual happening."

Fred smiled at him and closed his eyes again. "Ships in the sky."

"—and if that part of Godbuk is true, maybe other parts are as well. Certainly other parts are."

"Like coming here from another world?" Samuel said. "Spending twenty-eight years on a ship that flew through the air?"

"Through the sky, not 'air.' It says there wasn't any air."

"That doesn't make it any easier to believe," she said.

"Well, maybe that part's not strictly true," Lars conceded. "It might just be the result of some copying error ages ago."

"That's the first sensible idea you've had in several minutes," Fred said, yawning.

"I'll tell you what, though. You could even make a case for that. For there not being any air."

"I couldn't," Fred said. "Wouldn't."

"The higher up you go on a mountain, the harder it is to breathe. It seems logical that if you went high enough, you'd run out of air altogether."

"But—"

"And they were so high it took them twenty-eight years to come down!"

"But if there isn't any air . . . what *is* there?"

Lars shrugged. "Sky. Just sky."

"Don't forget the stars," Fred said. "They'd be all around you, like lightbugs."

"Maybe they would. Maybe they're too far away; you'd never get close to them."

"Maybe, maybe. Maybe you ought to try it—get up in that thin air and it might clear your head."

"Some of us are a little worried, Lars," Samuel said. "All the time you spend studying that Godbuk. All the charts and outlines and such."

"I get my work done."

"I know you do. It just seems like a regretful waste of time and talent." Among other things, Lars had reinvented the water pump and devised an oil-flotation bearing for compasses. "We'll be needing all of your cleverness for the rebuilding."

"I'll get my work done then, too." He settled back against the railing. "Don't you see, though . . . that we condemn ourselves and our descendants to . . . that we *guarantee* life will never be any different. Not unless some people waste their time and talent thinking about why things happen."

"Things happen," Fred said sleepily. "That's all."

> *Sumtīms tū hot dē ī uv Hevn shīns,*
> *An ofn is its gōld cumplekshn dimd,*
> *An evry fār frum fār sumtīm dēclīns . . .*

The Twenty-fourth Burning was no more or less severe than the twenty-three that had preceded it. The people were better prepared than they had been in the first couple of Burnings, and rarely lost more than one out of five able-bodied men and women, though small children and old people had a higher mortality rate.

The world had prepared itself the same way it had for millions of years. Before the nova suddenly waxed bright, fish headed for cool deep water, to estivate. Insects spun themselves silver chrysalides, and that season's plant seeds wore protective garments of tough fiber.

And at the appointed time, within a single day, one sun's brightness increased a hundredfold, kindling a universal forest fire from pole to pole that marched around the world with the dawn. As the fires consumed themselves, the sea began to steam, then to boil. The ashes of the world were scattered by a fierce wind of ozone and superheated steam. The sea rose and spilled boiling over the sterile plains. And as the nova faded, it began to rain.

In the fragile safety of their caves, men and women crouched around flickering lamps, unable to sleep or even to speak for the manic wail of the wind outside; a wind that would corrode away the polar ice in a couple of days; a wind that tossed large rocks around like pellets of sleet; a wind that would strip the flesh from bone and then scatter the bones across half a world.

The first rain fell boiling and rose back into the sky. (The planet that had looked so green and blue and hospitable glowed an even baleful white.) After a while some of the water stayed out of the air, and the planetwide storm gentled to mere hurricane force. It rained, hard and long.

When they came out of their holes, the rain was only a warm mist. By the time their caravan was spiked together, deep blue sky sometimes showed through the clouds, and the suns revealed themselves several times a day as they rolled along the horizon. The mud began to congeal and they left the polar crater the day of the first snow.

They made it back to the islands that had been hills overlooking Samueltown. Only 178 people had been lost, and fully half that number had survived the storm, but were on a boat that had one night mysteriously disappeared.

Lars found the hill where he had buried deep a chest full of books and other valuables. He had marked it by attaching a long chain to one handle and allowing a length of chain to protrude above the ground.

They never located it.

They raked compost into the side of the hill and planted rice and barley; then rowed to the other hills and did the same, waiting for the shallow water to recede from their fields.

It would be fifteen years before the first full crop came in.

Samuel and Lars remained friends over the years; for a short awkward time they were even lovers. But Fred grew progressively bitter in his jibes as Lars became more convinced of his theory that Godbuk was veiled, literal truth. Most people in Samueltown thought Lars was a valuable man, if slightly dotty, but Fred was the leader of a vocal minority that withdrew their children from his school, rather than have them be taught lies. Which amused the rest of the town. Lars' stories were fantastic, but it was the sort of thing that would hold a child's attention and give him something to prattle about. Life was joyless enough; why deprive children of a little spark of wonder, no matter how silly?

Lars had finished grading the arithmetic slates and was putting the children's names on the board, in order of accomplishment. Maybe Johnny would work harder tomorrow, to get his name off the bottom of the list. He turned at the sound of a polite cough.

A stranger was standing diffidently in the doorway, which sight almost made Lars drop the slate he was holding. It had been years since he had seen anyone he hadn't known all his life.

"Uh . . . what can I do for you?"

"You're the town book-keeper." The man was doubly a stranger for being blond, a feature so rare in Samueltown's genetic pool that not a single individual in Lars' generation had it.

"That's true."

"Well, so am I. My own town, that is. Fredrik, south and east of here."

Lars had heard of it. "Come in, sit down." He walked over to the desks where the larger children sat. "Are you just traveling?"

"Mostly copying. We lost too many books last Burning."

"Didn't we all. Can you pay?"

He shook his head, "No. But I can barter . . . if any of the thirty-some books I have interest you." He opened up a tanned-hide bag and Lars sorted through the books, while the stranger looked over Samueltown's small library. Lars decided he wanted to copy "Sewing" and "Mill Construction," for which he traded the copy-right to "Metal Work" and "Computation."

The man, whose name was Brian, stayed with Lars for a month of copying. They became good friends, taking their meals together (with most of the other bachelor men and women in town) at Samuel's; sitting by her fireside with cups of sweet wine, exchanging ideas until the late hours. When Lars was drafted to help flense a huge fish, Brian took over his school for a day, teaching the children rhyme and song.

After the month was done, though, Brian had to move on to the next town. He asked Lars to walk him down to the river.

There was nobody else at the riverbank that time of morning, the fishing boats having put out to sea at first light. It was a cool, breezy day, the new forest on the other side of the river making soft music as the wind pushed through the tall hollow stalks of young bamboo-like trees.

It was a pleasant way to start out a journey, and as good a setting for good-byes as one might desire. But Brian set his things on the pulley-driven raft-bridge and then silently stepped onto it, as if he were going to leave without a word, without a handclasp. He turned to Lars looking more sad than the occasion should have warranted, and said abruptly:

"Lars, I'm going to tell you something that I've said to no one before, and will never say again. You must not ask any questions; you must never tell anyone what I say."

"What—"

He continued rapidly. "Everything you believe about Godbuk is true. I know that very well, for I wasn't . . . born on this world. I am an observer, the latest of many, from Urth. Which is not a myth, but an actual world in the sky. The world from which all men came."

"You really—"

"You can't tell anybody this truth for the same reason I can't. It would raise false hope.

"We rediscovered this world some fifty years ago, and immediately began preparations to move you people off this . . . inimical world, either to Urth or, if you prefer, to another world, similar to this one but more pleasant.

"We can build a flotilla of sky ships that will hold everybody—and it *is* abuilding. But such a thing takes time. Many generations."

Lars was thoughtful. "I think I see."

"There may be two more Burnings before the rescue can be made. You know human nature, Lars."

"By that time . . ." he nodded. "They might not greet you as saviors. The memory would tarnish and . . . you would be seen as withholding freedom, rather than giving it."

"Exactly."

They stared at each other for a long moment. "Then what you want of me," Lars said slowly, "is to stop teaching the truth. Now that I know it's the truth."

"I'm afraid so. For the sake of future generations."

Brian waited patiently while Lars argued with himself. "All right," he said through clenched teeth. "I promise."

"I know what it means. Good-bye, Lars."

"Good-bye." He turned abruptly to save a young man the sight of an old man's tears, and walked heavily down the path back to his school. Today, class, you are going to study long division, the use of the comma, and pottery. And lies.

Brian watched the old man walk away and then hauled himself to the other side of the river. He started down the path toward Carroltown and wasn't surprised to find a man waiting for him at the first bend in the road.

"Hello, Fred."

Fred got up, dusting off his breeches. "How did it go?"

"He believed it, every word. You won't have any more trouble."

Fred handed him a small sack of gold. He weighed it in his palm and then dropped it into his bag without counting it. "I liked the old man," Brian said. "I feel like a grayfish."

"It was necessary."

"It was cruel."

"You can always give back the gold."

"I could do that." He shouldered his bag and walked away, south to the town where he was born.

26 Days, on Earth

There are some writers whose styles are so infectious they're dangerous to have around while you're working— your characters start thinking like them, sounding like them. For me, James Boswell is one such culprit.

I was trying to write my second novel while reading Boswell's London Journal (*the first volume, 1762-63*), and the protagonist started sounding like twenty-two-year-old Boswell. Rather than stop reading—I literally flew to the book every day, as soon as I'd written 1,500 words—I postponed the novel and started writing a short story, where the main character was a snobbish kid from the provinces, too intelligent and articulate for his own good, come to the big city for "finishing."

But his diary is written in the twenty-second century, not the eighteenth; instead of Scotland, he came from the Moon.

14 April 2147.

Today I resolved to begin keeping a diary. Unfortunately, nothing of real interest happened.

15 April.

Nothing happened again today. Just registration.

16 April.

I can't go on wasting paper or Earth's Conservation Board will take my diary away and process it into something useful, like toilet paper. So even though nothing happened again, I'll fill up this space with biographical detail, that will no doubt be of great value to future historians.

I was born Jonathon Wu, on 17 January 2131, to Martha and Jonathon Wu II, out of the surrogate host-mother Sally 217-44-7624. My parents were wealthy enough to be permitted two legal children, but my early behavior convinced them that one was sufficient. As soon as I was old enough to travel, barely four, they packed me off to Clavius Tutorial Creche, figuring that a quarter of a million miles was a safe distance from which to monitor my growth.

Clavius Creche, it says here, was established as a uniquely isolated and controlled environment for the cultivation of little scholars. And medium-sized scholars. But when you get to be a big gangling scholar, you've got to go somewhere else. There are no universities on the moon, only technical schools. You can take up Lunar citizenship —as long as you're *mutandis*—and be admitted to one of those technical schools, winding up as some kind of super-

158

cerebral mechanic. But I suppose my father was willing to live on the same planet with me, rather than allow me to grow into being something other than a gentleman.

I got back to Earth one week ago today.

17 April.

We began course work today. This quarter I'm taking supposedly parallel courses in algorithmic analysis and logical systems. If I ever get "introduced" to Boolean algebra again, I'll curl into a ball and swallow my tongue. Continuing readings and analysis in classical Greek and Latin. Supposed to do preliminary readings for next quarter: XXth Century English and American Poets and Commercial Literature as a Cultural Index. This will be with Applied Stochastic Analysis and Artificial Intelligence I. The poetry is amusing but the "commercial" novels make tedious reading. One has always to keep in mind that none of these authors was born with the benefit of genetic engineering, and they were at best men of unremarkable intelligence in a world populated with morons and worse.

Earth gravity tires me.

18 April.

I was talking with my advisor (Greek and Latin), Dr. Friedman, and complained about the sterility of this upcoming literature course. He introduced me to the work of an Irish author named Joyce, loaning me a copy of the construct *Finnegans Wake*. It has taken me ten hours to read the first thirty pages; totally immersed in it through lunch and dinner. Fascinating. Easily equal to the best of Thurman—why weren't we given him at Creche?

I am required to walk for at least two hours every day, in order to become accustomed to the gravity. Thus I am writing this standing up, the diary propped on a bookshelf. Also must eat handsful of nauseating calcium tablets, and will have to walk with braces until my leg-bones have hardened up. Had I stayed on the moon another five years, I probably never would have been able to return to Earth (a prospect which at present would not bother me a bit). Twenty-one is too old to repattern porous bones.

The braces chafe and look ridiculous in this foppish Earth clothing. But I get a certain notoriety out of being such an obvious extraterrestrial.

My father called this morning and we talked about my courses for a few minutes.

19 April.

Today was the first day I ventured outside of the campus complex on foot. It gave me an uncomfortable feeling to be outside without suiting up. Of course, one does wear a respirator (even inside some of the buildings, which leak), and that does something to allay the agoraphobia.

How will I react to the geophysics course next year? They take field trips to wild preserves where they work for extended periods simply under the sky, exposed to the elements. I realize that mine is an irrational fear, that men lived for millions of years breathing natural air, walking around in the open without the slightest thought that there should be something around them. Perhaps I can convince them that since on Luna this fear is *not* irrational, but part of survival . . . perhaps they will grant me some sort of dispensation; waive the course, or at least allow me to wear a suit.

While wandering around outside of the campus, I dropped into a tavern that supposedly caters to students. I had some ordinary wine and a bit of hashish which wasn't at all like the Lunar product. It only served to make me tired. The tavernkeeper didn't believe that I was sixteen until I produced my passport.

I got into a rather long and pointless conversation with an Earthie *mutandis* over the necessity for interplanetary tariff imbalance. They know so little about the other worlds. But then, I know little enough about Earth, for having been born here.

I was barely able to get back to the dormitory without assistance, and slept through half of my normal reading period. Had to take stimulants to finish the last book of the *Georgics*. So much of it is about open-air farming that it kept bringing back my earlier discomfort.

Resolved not to smoke any more Earth hashish until I get my strength back.

20 April.

Algorithmic analysis has an economy and order that appeals to me. I had of course planned to take my doctorate in Letters, but now I want to investigate mathematics further. My father would have apoplexy. A gentleman *hires* mathematicians. I made an appointment with the advising facility for tomorrow.

I am having difficulty making friends. Their customs are rather strange, but I have grown up in knowledge of that and am prepared to make any adjustment. Perhaps I am too critical of Earth society.

An embarrassing illustration: this morning for the first time, I felt strong enough for sex. Thinking this would be an ideal way to begin more cordial relations with Earthies, I made a tactful suggestion of that nature to one of my classmates in Systems. She was very indignant and wound up giving me a lecture on cultural relativism. The kernel of it, at least as applied to this situation, was that one is supposed to go through an elaborate series of courting gestures with a prospective mate. Like a bird ruffing out his feathers and cooing. I told her this might make some sense if the ritual had something to do with predicting or promoting future sexual compatibility between the two people, which it didn't. She reacted with almost frightening force.

My father had warned me about this moral oddity, but I was given to understand that it only applied to the lower classes and, specifically, to the remaining *homo sapiens.* Certainly there is a good argument for reducing the number of unengineered births by repressing casual sexual contact, but the same restrictive behavioral patterns shouldn't be impressed on *homo mutandis,* to which group I assumed my classmate belonged. From the speciousness of her argument, I suppose it's possible she doesn't, but then how could she get into a university? Of course, I wouldn't insult her by asking.

21 April.

The machine analyzed my profile and said that I had the potential for moderate success in mathematics, but that

I was temperamentally better suited for literature. It advised that I continue a double course of study for as long as possible, and then switch all of my energies to one field or the other as soon as it became clear in which direction my greatest interest lay. An agreeable course of action, perhaps because of my natural indecisiveness.

I may have found a friend after all. He isn't an Earthie, but a Martian, also come to Earth for "polish." His name is Chatham Howard, and he was flattered that I recognized the Howard name both for its role in early Martian history and for the social rank it now represents, on Mars. He is a year ahead of me, studying sociology.

22 April.

Chatham took me to a party and introduced me to a number of very pleasant Earthies. I'm still sorting out the impressions, changing my ideas a little bit. Not all Earthies my age are immature provincials.

Met an interesting female by the name of Pamela Anderson. I have begun the courting ritual, to the best of my abilities. I was attentive and complimentary (though she has some strange ideas, she is not unintelligent), and agreed to meet her tomorrow for the evening meal.

We kissed once. Odd custom.

23 April.

Chatham and a friend joined Pamela and me for dinner at Luigi's, a restaurant which specializes in an old-fashioned cuisine called "North-American-Italian." It is more spicy than I am accustomed to, but Pamela recommended a fairly bland dish called *spaghetti* with mushroom sauce. It was rather good, and reminiscent of some familiar fungi dishes.

After dinner, we went to a public theatre and saw a drama-tape that consisted mainly of views of various couples, copulating. It was much the same as the tapes I'd been watching in Mental Hygiene classes since I was eight years old, but in this bizarre setting I found it strangely exciting.

We had drinks at the theatre after the show, and engaged in some bright banter. It was all very enjoyable, but I got the impression that Pamela was not yet interested in me sexually. This was a disappointment, especially after Chatham's friend quite directly asked him to spend the night with her. Pamela was very warm but didn't extend any such invitation.

For the first time I wondered whether she might not consider me too "alien" for a sex partner. I am a half-meter taller than she, and my Lunar myaesthenia is all too evident, with the braces and my quickness to fatigue. I'm also a couple of years younger than she, which evidently is rather important on Earth.

I found out in our conversation that many of the customs relating to this mating ritual are centuries old. This is an exasperating thing about Earth: in many ways they cling stubbornly to the cultural matrix that brought them to within a button-push of destroying humanity. On the Worlds, at least we had the sense to junk it all and start over.

Sometimes it brings me up short to remember that I was born an Earthie.

24 April.

Today I got lost in the middle of writing a long Turing Machine algorithm, when my mind strayed to Pamela. I had to go back to the beginning and start over. Idiotic! Perhaps all this medication is affecting my mental discipline.

Continuing with analysis of the writings of Virgil, or at least those attributed to him. Obvious many of them written by somebody else.

25 April.

Pamela met me, without prior arrangement, outside my Systems classroom—an encouragingly aggressive sign. But it turned out that her real interest was in learning more about Lunar mores, for a paper in Comp. Soc. We went down to the cafeteria and discussed, essentially, how different she was from me. I left feeling depressed, but with a "date" for a concert tomorrow.

26 April.

The concert was on an ancient instrument called the "glass harmonica." The melodies were interesting, but the rhythm was simplistic and the harmonies progressed in a very predictable manner. Somehow, the overall effect was moving.

I learned the most startling thing after the concert. Pamela is not *mutandis*. We went to a bhang shop with another couple and talked about the difference, the distance, between *sapiens* and *mutandis*. She accused me of being ill-informed and patronizing when I talked about our obligation to guide and protect *sapiens* as they inevitably died out over the next few generations. She said that she was not engineered and her children were not going to be, nor their children. Something else she said, we had not been taught on Luna. But, once it was pointed out, I had to admit it was obvious: there was no guarantee that genetic engineering was going to be successful in the long race, and humanity must maintain a large and pure community of *sapiens* for several centuries, in case the "experiment" fails.

I privately disagreed with her contention that *sapiens* must always remain in the majority. Certainly a million or two would be adequate to the task of rebuilding the race, should all of us *mutandi* turn purple and explode. Of course her worry was political rather than biological; that we might irrationally legislate *sapiens* out of existence, were we in the majority.

She said we had done exactly that on Luna, and I had to patiently explain why we no longer allowed *sapiens* as colonists. It was not prejudice, but simple logic. She was not convinced.

[Of course, this explains why I was so surprised to find that Pamela was not *mutandis*. All of the *sapiens* on Luna are quite old and mentally incompetent because of a lack of correctional therapeutics in their youth. I was guilty of unconsciously projecting my attitudes toward their manifest inferiority onto Earthie *sapiens*.]

Somehow the fact that she is not *mutandis* does not make her less attractive to me. My regard for her intel-

lectual abilities should be greater, knowing as I do now
that she started out with a genetic handicap. The main
thing I feel now is a vague distrust of her emotional
reliability. Or do I mean predictability? It is all very confusing.

27 April.

Algorithmic Analysis test tonight. Not difficult but studying for it was very time-consuming.

28 April.

Pamela took me to the zoo. Tiring but extremely re-
warding day. Animals are fascinating. It occurred to me
that being adult, or nearly so, and seeing non-human creatures for the first time in my life might give me some
unique insight. Instead of writing a long entry in this diary
tonight, I will begin an essay on the experience.

My feet are throbbing. Told Pamela the joke about the
computer playing chess with itself, and she laughed. Was
this the first time I've seen her laugh?

29 April.

Pamela read my essay and left saying she never wanted
to see me again. She was crying.

30 April.

I have reconsidered some of the comparisons I made in
the essay, between *sapiens* and animals. They were meant
to be satirical, but I can see in the light of Pamela's reaction that this intent was not clear. Rather than attempt to
translate my attempts at humor into Earthie terms, I
deleted these passages. I sent a copy to Pamela.

Reading back, I see I have known her little more than
a week. Odd.

1 May.

Latin test.

2 May.

Pamela visited today, bringing a male companion. She did not mention the essay.

I realized that I don't know Pamela well enough to decide whether she brought the other man, Hill Beaumont, in order to provoke jealousy in me (consciously or otherwise). I understand jealousy, of course, from my reading, but I have never felt it and believe myself immune.

Besides, Beaumont is a rather stupid fellow.

3 May.

Beaumont dropped in alone today, saying that he had read the essay and complimenting me at some length on it. He is still a dull oaf, but I can't help now feeling more kindly disposed toward him. He wanted to take me out and chatter over a bottle of wine, but I pleaded lack of time. Which was true; Greek test tomorrow evening and I have neglected it lately. Much reading to do.

I asked about Pamela and Beaumont said he hadn't seen her since they left me yesterday.

4 May.

Greek. Stayed in my room all day, studying, but accepted an invitation to eat with Chatham and Beaumont after the test. Quite a lot happened, and even though it's after two I think I'll stay up and record it while it's still fresh in my memory.

We met at Luigi's for a light supper and wine. Chatham, of course, is always interesting, but the evening was almost spoiled for me when Beaumont revealed with a conversational flourish that he, also, was *mutandis*. In fact, he is an elected officer in a local club, the membership of which is restricted to "us." There was a meeting of the club that night, and Beaumont invited me to come and speak to them, mainly on the subject of the essay about animals. He had his copy of the essay with him. Chatham said he had a previous engagement but urged me to go along, saying the meetings were always amusing. I didn't see any way I could gracefully decline; figured it might even be fun as long as they weren't all like Beaumont. We left Chatham to finish off the wine—an office for which he has singular talent—and slid a couple of blocks to the meeting place.

Some of Beaumont's friends have the oddest ideas about what it means to be *mutandis*. The gathering was one of the strangest things I've experienced on Earth.

First a man got up and demonstrated a construct which was a poem, in Latin, written in the form of an eight-by-eight matrix. He showed how you could perform semantic analogues of the normal reduction transformations to get various intermediate poems—none of which made much sense—and arrive finally at a matrix which was null throughout except for sum-sum-sum-sum all down the main diagonal. A puerile exercise, bad poetry and naive mathematics, but everybody seemed dutifully impressed.

Then a woman showed a "sculpture" she had made by synthesizing a large cube of piezoelectric crystal and fracturing it, in what she felt to be an artistic way, by applying various charges to different parts of the surface. That she could have arrived at a similar end by merely dropping the thing on a hard floor did not diminish audience appreciation.

So it went for an hour and a half. My presentation was the last one, and I'm sure nine-tenths of the applause I got was due to that fact, rather than for any intrinsic merit of the composition.

The disturbing part of the evening, though, was a round-table discussion about *sapiens* and what eventually would have to be done about them. Some of the reasoning was so fuzzy that it wouldn't have done justice to a child in first-form Creche.

One thing I learned, one very surprising thing, was that *mutandi* make up only about 1% of the Earth's population. Why did they hide this fact from us in Creche? At any rate, the irrational nature of some of their proposals tonight might possibly be excused as simple "minority paranoia."

One idea which met with a good deal of approval struck me as both sneaky and foolish. There is agitation from various groups concerned with population control to make the practice of host-mothership universal, and require that

167

all people be sterilized soon after puberty, once having filed a sample of sperm or ovum with the government. Thus the size of every family could be absolutely regulated by the government.

It was pointed out that this would inevitably lead to universal manipulation of all of humanity's genetic material —reasoning that *mutandis* being manifestly superior to the rest of humanity, it is only a question of time before they hold all important governmental positions. Thus assured of freedom from bureaucratic interference, they would of course institute a program of universal genetic manipulation. For the benefit of all humanity.

Somebody brought up Pamela's argument, that it will take many generations before we are sure that genetic manipulation is totally safe. Most felt that it would be sufficiently proven by the time "we" have taken over.

I told them that the weakness in the idea had nothing to do with manipulation; that the universal storage of genetic material was in itself a questionable idea. For the convenience of the government, all of it would probably be stored near government centers which, like any large concentration of people, get power from one source: microwaves beamed down from the orbital solar stations. The fact that they have functioned continuously for over a century doesn't mean they are immune to breakdown; in fact, it's quite likely that if they go, it will be because of some powerful solar event, which would affect all of them simultaneously. No power, no refrigeration. The genetic material, at least most of it, would thaw out and die, and humanity would have to depend on the current crop of children to reach sexual maturity and replenish the race. That crop might be small indeed if there were stringent controls on family size. There might not be enough breeders to bring the next generation up to a size sufficient to carry on civilization as we live it now.

And it wouldn't even require a solar catastrophe. It's possible that some people wouldn't like the idea of us changing all of humankind into *mutandis,* and would sabotage the sperm and ovum banks without thinking or caring about the consequences.

They listened politely to my counter-arguments, but I don't think many of them were convinced. They take electrical power too much for granted, here on Earth. They have had local failures all their lives, which meant little more than having to walk down still slidewalks for a few hours. There has of course been only one power failure on Luna.

5 May.

Knowing that Pamela has a course in Sociometrics, I contrived to spend a few hours down at the social sciences computing facility, supposedly checking out an algorithm that simulated a Turing machine. Actually, I knew that it worked, having run it successfully over at the mathematics facility, but I kept putting glitches in it in order to remain at the console.

She did show up, after four hours. Luckily, she was only there to pick up a printout. It was dinner time, so I escorted her down to the Union. We each got a plate of small sandwiches and talked.

I told her about the experience with Beaumont's crowd. She was amused, which for some reason made me angry at first—just because she was *sapiens*, I guess—but she jostled me about it so much that I wound up laughing too. She admitted that this had been her purpose when she first introduced Beaumont to me: to demonstrate that not all *mutandi* were *a priori* superior examples of humanity.

In the dining hall I said hello to one of the girls who had been at last night's meeting, the one with the piezo-electric sculpture. She stared right through me and didn't miss a bite.

6 May.

What a long and disturbing day. This morning, I found this note in my box:

□ IT HAS BEEN BROUGHT TO OUR ATTEN-TION THAT YOU ARE SEEKING A SEXUAL LIAISON WITH ONE PAMELA ANDERSON, A *HOMO SAPIENS* □ FRANKLY, WE ARE DIS-GUSTED □ FROM OUR POINT OF VIEW THIS IS AN ACT OF SODOMY; BESTIALITY □□ *HOMO*

SAPIENS IS OUR ONLY NATURAL ENEMY, THE ONLY OBSTACLE TO THE CONTINUING PROGRESS OF HUMANITY □ THEY ARE A DIFFERENT CREATURE AND TO US A DANGEROUS ONE □ WE DO NOT FRATERNIZE WITH THEM □□ IF YOU CONTINUE THIS OBSCENE RELATIONSHIP WITH PAMELA ANDERSON, BOTH OF YOU WILL BE IN PROFOUND TROUBLE □ WE WILL BE IN TOUCH □□□ STECOM □

I sought out Beaumont and, yes, he had heard of "STECOM," the Steering Committee for Humanity, but never to his knowledge had they ever caused anyone "profound trouble." They served mainly to protect the interests of *Mutandi* in legislation, commerce and so on. He said that the organization's public stance is much milder than that represented by my note, but that he knew many of the members to hold similar views privately.

He gave me the number of the local STECOM chairman, and I contacted him. He denied any connection with the note; said that whoever signed it did so without authority; asked that I keep him apprised of further developments; told me not to worry. It was just the work of an extremist. Somehow that gave me very little comfort.

I left word with Pamela's roommate, asking that Pamela call as soon as she returned from classes. She called and we arranged to meet for dinner.

We sat at a back table in Luigi's and she read the note; first amused, then alarmed. She didn't think they would dare do anything to her, but they might try to harass me.

She said she thought it would be best if we didn't see each other for a while. I protested that that would be a cowardly action, in response to what was already the act of a coward, hiding behind anonymity. We argued. In the course of the argument she said I was wasting my efforts anyhow, as our relationship could never be anything besides casual and platonic. We finished our meals in silence and she asked me not to walk her home.

On my way back to the dormitory, right after getting off the South Quadrant Westbound slidewalk, I had to walk by a dense stand of shrubbery which threw a deep shadow over the walk. I probably wouldn't have seen my assailants even had I not been lost in brooding thought.

One slipped behind me and threw a fabric bag over my head and shoulders, and then pinioned my arms behind me. The other hit me once in the solar plexus and twice on the face, then reached under the bag and tore off my respirator. They fled and I half-walked, half-crawled to the nearest dormitory. The medic there gave me some oxygen and pasted up my one serious-looking wound, a nasty cut over my left eye. He gave me a voucher for the materials he had used, so I could return them from my dormitory's supply, loaned me a respirator and sent me on my way. A classmate walked over with me to help forestall a recurrence.

As I write this, my throat still hurts from breathing the sulfurous air. Good thing the attack didn't happen downtown, nearer the Industrial Park.

I'll take an extra Pain-go and retire.

7 May.

I went to the campus police and they told me that since there were no witnesses, and I couldn't identify my assailants, an investigation would be a waste of time. I recognized the chief as having been at the meeting the other night, and didn't press him.

Another note in my box. This one simply said □ RETURN TO LUNA □□□ STECOM □. I called up the Steering Committee chairman again and informed him of this new note and of last night's assault. He got very flustered but offered no worthwhile advice.

Somebody had forced his way into my room and poured soya all over my books and papers. When they were completely dry, I took them down to the laundry and used the ultrasonic dry-cleaner on them. It worked after a fashion. I hope he read this diary before dousing it, and saw that Pamela is not enthusiastic about my "seeking a sexual liaison" with her. Now maybe all of this will stop.

Work goes on, of course. Tree theory and yet more non-Virgil.

I toyed with the idea of trying to trace the person or persons behind all this through the notes. They are, of course, simple computer printouts, so the person would first have had to encode a crystal. The crystal would have to be re-filed and, if it hadn't yet been erased for another use, it would be a simple matter to find out who had last checked it out.

Simple in theory, at least. There must be five or six computing facilities on campus, each with several thousand crystals.

And for that matter, it wouldn't be difficult to have the message printed out and then code something new over that domain of the crystal, as if it had been a glitch.

I tried to think of how I might set a trap, without using Pamela as bait. My mind just isn't devious enough—or perhaps it doesn't have enough information. Since Chatham has more deviousness and information at his disposal, I tried to contact him. He was out, though; had been gone since yesterday. I settled for Beaumont.

Over a bottle of wine in the lounge of his dormitory, we roughed out a plan. He knew most of the *mutandi* on campus, and knew which ones were the most extreme in their views. He would meet some of them socially and bring the conversation around to Pamela and me; if the person showed any interest, Beaumont would pretend to sympathize with the idea that *mutandi* should mate with their own kind—as if the characteristics could be inherited!—and since *I* was the one person on campus most obviously a *mutandis*, I was setting a terribly bad example. Then see whether the other would suggest some sort of action.

He said he would start right away and contact me as soon as he had some results.

8 May.

Solved.

Beaumont called this morning with the good news that he had found the person responsible. No one I knew, he said; the person was an agitator who had been out of school for years and rarely showed up at club meetings. The three of us were going to meet at 8:00 tonight, by the sheds on the athletic field.

I told him that I didn't like it. At least two people had

attacked me before, and there might be even more. I was still too weak to be of any help if it came to violence, and the athletic field was dangerously isolated. I wanted to just call the police and have him apprehended, but Beaumont raised the good point that, without evidence, it would just be Beaumont's word against the other's . . . and the campus police were not noted for respecting the testimony of students.

He said he could get his hands on a stunner, to even out the odds, and would bring a recorder to catch the person in damaging statements, even if he couldn't be goaded into action. Personally, I hoped he couldn't.

Beaumont had a regular script worked out, things for me to say to the man which were at once perfectly innocuous and calculated to make him lose his temper. Beaumont, of course, would be pretending to be on *his* side, which would tend to make him reckless. I agreed, with the private reservation that I would tone down some of my side of the dialogue.

I went to my morning classes as usual but found I couldn't concentrate for worrying. Anything could happen. This time of year, the athletic field was only airco'ed over weekends, and I wasn't sure I could make it back to a building in time, if they overpowered us as they did me last time, taking our respirators. There was no guarantee that the man would show up alone, or with just one accomplice. The more I thought about it, the more nervous I became. Finally, around noon, I went to the police.

The chief was monumentally unimpressed. He said the whole thing sounded like a prank, an initiation into the club. He knew Beaumont and expressed the opinion that he had been manipulated, the initiators playing on his exaggerated sense of drama.

I insisted that they had tried to harm me seriously night before last, but the chief pointed out that I was never in real danger, and the blows seemed calculated to do only superficial harm. They could have more easily incapacitated me and left me to suffocate.

Besides, he doubted that he could spare a man at 8:00, at which time most of them were patrolling the taverns and dopeshops off-campus, preventing trouble. He kept looking at the clock—I shouldn't have come at lunchtime—and finally said he'd see whether he could find a man to meet me there.

Some time later, the chilling thought occurred to me that the chief could possibly be in on it too, and if I was the focus of some ruthless anti-*sapiens* plot, my action had only put Beaumont and me in even greater danger.

I tried to reach Beaumont all day, after that thought, to tell him the whole thing was off, but he was never home. After a good deal of internal debate, about 7:00 I got up and headed for the field. After all, I had chastised Pamela for suggesting cowardly action. I stopped in a general-merchandise store on the way, and bought the biggest clasp-knife they had. I hadn't fought anybody since I was a little boy, and didn't know whether, should the time come to use it, I would have nerve or wit enough to even take it out of my pocket. But its weight was some small comfort.

When it happened, everything happened very fast. I went out onto the field and saw Beaumont standing by the sheds, chatting with another man. I approached them and waited for Beaumont to start the charade. They stopped talking as I came closer and suddenly Beaumont began to laugh hysterically. The other, muscular older man, only slightly shorter than me—probably the tallest Earthie I'd seen—smiled and drew a short wooden club out of his tunic.

I had the knife out and was trying to get my thumbnail into the little depression when Beaumont, still laughing, raised a stunner at me and fired.

It was very painful. A stunner confuses the neural signals to and from the part of your brain that controls motor functions. As a side effect it makes you feel as if your skin is being punctured by thousands of tiny needles. I fell to the ground, twitching spasmodically. My face was down, so I couldn't see, but I heard Beaumont tell the big man to use the knife instead; it would be more impressive.

Then absolutely nothing happened for a long couple of minutes. Suddenly I was turned over roughly and steeled myself for the first blow of the knife—and found myself looking into the face of the police chief.

He sprayed an aerosol into my face that made the pain go away, and said they'd take me to the infirmary, to a "pattern blocker," to cure the paralysis. He apologized for using me as bait and said he'd had a man hiding in the far shed since early this afternoon, waiting for Beaumont and the other man, who had been suspected in a similar assault case some months before.

Both of them were lying on the ground, twitching as badly as I was. A large police floater drifted onto the field and two men with stretchers came out.

They loaded up the others first, and by the time my stretcher was secure, the chief was interrogating Beaumont, evidently with the aid of some hypnotic. His confession was very disjointed and childishly vituperative, but the gist of it was this:

He had been after Pamela's attentions (he used another word, which Chaucer would have recognized) for several months, and felt he was just about to succeed when I came along. I was an egotistical child, an alien and a cripple and, to his mind, I had stolen her away.

The chief questioned him further and found that Beaumont had suffered a nervous breakdown over a year before and had been under treatment until he came to the University. He admitted to several other acts of violence and admitted knowing that he was still mentally ill but had not volunteered for further treatment because he felt that the illness was somehow allied with his genius, and he didn't want to interfere with it. I felt that anything interfering with his brand of genius could only add to it, but I kept my own counsel.

The infirmary treatment only took a few minutes. I arranged with the chief to come down the next morning to file a complaint and testify, then found a phone and called up Pamela.

She was fascinated, but not surprised, with the revelations about Beaumont. I went over the whole thing in some detail, and then we talked about some more general matters, and finally I got down to the question of our relationship. She said, with some heat, that the affair with Beaumont didn't change anything, that if I knew anything about women I wouldn't even have asked, and that we could still be friends but that's all: platonic, intellectual arrangement.

While I've been writing this I've been thinking about what she said. I *do* know a little more about women than I knew a month ago. And a lot more about jealousy. And I've known about synergy for years.

9 May.

Today I started reading up on crystalline sculpture and piezoelectricity.

Armaja Das

I got a request from Kirby McCauley to write a story for an anthology called Frights (St. Martin's Press, 1976). The theme would be "ancient horrors in modern guise." The idea was intriguing. I'd only written one fantasy story in my life—snide critics might disagree—and it was a throwaway deal-with-the-devil joke. I said I'd send him an outline.

The summer before, my wife and I had come down with acute attacks of dysentery in the rather dysenteric city of Tangier. Unlike her, I was able occasionally to get up and walk farther than the john, so it fell to me to venture out every few hours and haggle for bottled water and canned European food.

Tangier redefined for me Raymond Chandler's phrase "mean streets." Our sleazy hotel fronted the main street that led to the waterfront; there was a tiny park outside the door, and that park was decorated by a dead man. Not violently dead, just some old fellow who'd tired of being a Moroccan. The first time I saw the corpse, I went back into the hotel and tried to explain the situation to the clerk in my all-but-nonexistent French. He just kept shrugging.* By nightfall, somebody had dragged the body away, to what fell purpose I leave to your imagination.

Lying upstairs feeling dismal, it occurred to me that we might die there, and likely as not, no one would ever find out what had happened to us. Perhaps out of some obscure impulse to die with my boots on, I started making up a story about that, a pretty good Rod-Serlingish story called "To Die at Home." I even made a few notes about

---

* It later occurred to me that my *mort* may have sounded like *merde* to him; his shrug may have meant that if I wanted to complain about shit, I was in the wrong country.

it, after the fevered palsy had abated enough for me to write.

So when Kirby asked for a fantasy story, I sent him an outline of "To Die at Home." He wrote back saying that he liked it, but it wasn't weird enough.

I'll write that story some day, if only to show Kirby how weird it is.

I half-abandoned the project, figuring my talents really lay more in the direction of Analog than Weird Tales. Who wants to write about vampires anyhow, feh. But then I came across a fascinating article by Peter Maas, in New York magazine: "The Deadly Battle to Become King of the Gypsies."

He mentioned gypsy curses, and I was off and running. Running down to the library, where I spent a glorious afternoon in the stacks doing what I do best: goofing off. In this case, reading dusty old books and journals about gypsy lore.

Loaded up with fresh information, it was child's play to toss together gypsy curses, computer science, and minority assimilation into an "ancient horror in modern guise."

The highrise, built in 1980, still had the smell and look of newness. And of money.

The doorman bowed a few degrees and kept a straight face, opening the door for a bent old lady. She had a card of Veterans' poppies clutched in one old claw. He didn't care much for the security guard, and she would give him interesting trouble.

The skin on her face hung in deep creases, scored with a network of tiny wrinkles; her chin and nose protruded and dropped. A cataract made one eye opaque; the other eye was yellow and red surrounding deep black, unblinking. She had left her teeth in various things. She shuffled. She wore an old black dress faded slightly gray by repeated washing. If she had any hair, it was concealed by a pale blue bandanna. She was so stooped that her neck was almost parallel to the ground.

"What can I do for you?" The security guard had a tired voice to match his tired shoulders and back. The job had seemed a little romantic the first couple of days, guarding all these rich people, sitting at an ultramodern console surrounded by video monitors, submachine gun at his knees. But the monitors were blank except for an hourly check, power shortage; and if he ever removed the gun from its cradle, he would have to fill out five forms and call the police station. And the doorman never turned anybody away.

"Buy a flower for boys less fortunate than ye," she said in a faint raspy baritone. From her age and accent, her own boys had fought in the Russian Revolution.

"I'm sorry. I'm not allowed to . . . respond to charity while on duty."

She stared at him for a long time, nodding microscopically. "Then send me to someone with more heart."

He was trying to frame a reply when the front door slammed open. "Car on fire!" the doorman shouted.

The security guard leaped out of his seat, grabbed a fire extinguisher and sprinted for the door. The old woman shuffled along behind him until both he and the doorman disappeared around the corner. Then she made for the elevator with surprising agility.

She got out on the 17th floor, after pushing the button that would send the elevator back down to the lobby. She checked the name plate on 1738; Mr. Zold. She was illiterate but could recognize names.

Not even bothering to try the lock, she walked on down the hall until she found a maid's closet. She closed the door behind her and hid behind a rack of starchy white uniforms, leaning against the wall with her bag between her feet. The slight smell of gasoline didn't bother her at all.

John Zold pressed the intercom button. "Martha?" She answered. "Before you close up shop I'd like a redundancy check on stack 408. Against tape 408." He switched the selector on his visual output screen so it would duplicate the output at Martha's station. He stuffed tobacco in a pipe and lit it, watching.

Green numbers filled the screen, a complicated matrix of ones and zeros. They faded for a second and were replaced with a field of pure zeros. The lines of zeros started to roll, like titles preceding a movie.

The 746th line came up all ones. John thumbed the intercom again. "Had to be something like that. You have time to fix it up?" She did. "Thanks, Martha. See you tomorrow."

He slid back the part of his desk top that concealed a keypunch and typed rapidly: "523 784 00926/ / Good night, machine. Please lock this station."

GOOD NIGHT, JOHN. DON'T FORGET YOUR LUNCH DATE WITH MR. BROWNWOOD TOMORROW. DENTIST APPOINTMENT WEDNESDAY 0945. GENERAL SYSTEMS CHECK WEDNESDAY 1300. DEL O DEL BAXT. LOCKED.

Del O Del baxt means "God give you luck" in the ancient tongue of the Romani. John Zold, born a Gypsy but hardly a Gypsy by any standard other than the strong one of blood, turned off his console and unlocked the bottom drawer of his desk. He took out a flat automatic pistol in a holster with a belt clip and slipped it under his jacket, inside the waistband of his trousers. He had only been wearing the gun for two weeks, and it still made him uncomfortable. But there had been those letters.

John was born in Chicago, some years after his parents had fled from Europe and Hitler. His father had been a fiercely proud man, and got involved in a bitter argument over the honor of his 12-year-old daughter, from which argument he had come home with knuckles raw and bleeding, and had given to his wife for disposal a large clasp knife crusty with dried blood.

John was small for his five years, and his chin barely cleared the kitchen table, where the whole family sat and discussed their uncertain future while Mrs. Zold bound up her husband's hands. John's shortness saved his life when the kitchen window exploded and a low ceiling of shotgun pellets fanned out and chopped into the heads and chests of the only people in the world whom he could love and trust. The police found him huddled between the bodies of his father and mother, and at first thought he was also dead; covered with blood, completely still, eyes wide open and not crying.

It took six months for the kindly orphanage people to get a single word out of him: *ratválo*, which he said over and over; which they were never able to translate. Bloody, bleeding.

But he had been raised mostly in English, with a few words of Romani and Hungarian thrown in for spice and accuracy. In another year their problem was not one of communicating with John; only of trying to shut him up.

No one adopted the stunted Gypsy boy, which suited John. He'd had a family, and look what happened.

In orphanage school he flunked penmanship and deportment, but did reasonably well in everything else. In arithmetic and, later, mathematics, he was nothing short of brilliant. When he left the orphanage at eighteen, he enrolled at the University of Illinois, supporting himself as a bookkeeper's assistant and part-time male model. He had come out of an ugly adolescence with a striking resemblance to the young Clark Gable.

Drafted out of college, he spent two years playing with computers at Fort Lewis; got out and went all the way to a Master's degree under the G.I. Bill. His thesis "Simulation of Continuous Physical Systems by Way of Universalization of the Trakhtenbrot Algorithms" was very well received, and the mathematics department gave him a research assistantship, to extend the thesis into a doctoral dissertation. But other people read the paper too, and after a few months Bellcom International hired him away from academia. He rose rapidly through the ranks. Not yet forty, he was now Senior Analyst at Bellcom's Research and Development Group. He had his own private office, with a picture window overlooking Central Park, and a plush six-figure condominium only twenty minutes away by commuter train.

As was his custom, John bought a tall can of beer on his way to the train, and opened it as soon as he sat down. It kept him from fidgeting during the fifteen- or twenty-minute wait while the train filled up.

He pulled a thick technical report out of his briefcase and stared at the summary on the cover sheet, not really seeing it but hoping that looking occupied would spare him the company of some anonymous fellow traveller.

The train was an express, and whisked them out to Dobbs Ferry in twelve minutes. John didn't look up from his report until they were well out of New York City; the heavy mesh tunnel that protected the track from vandals induced spurious colors in your retina as it blurred by. Some people liked it, tripped on it, but to John the effect was at best annoying, at worst nauseating, depending on how tired he was. Tonight he was dead tired.

He got off the train two stops up from Dobbs Ferry. The highrise limousine was waiting for him and two other residents. It was a fine spring evening and John would normally have walked the half-mile, tired or not. But those unsigned letters.

*John Zold, you stop this preachment or you die soon.
Armaja das. John Zold.*

All three letters said that: *Armaja das,* we put a curse
on you. For preaching.

He was less afraid of curses than of bullets. He undid
the bottom button of his jacket as he stepped off the train,
ready to quickdraw, roll for cover behind that trash can,
just like in the movies; but there was no one suspicious-
looking around. Just an assortment of suburban wives and
the old cop who was on permanent station duty.

Assassination in broad daylight wasn't Romani style.
Styles change, though. He got in the car and watched the
side roads all the way home.

There was another one of the shabby envelopes in his
mailbox. He wouldn't open it until he got upstairs. He
stepped in the elevator with the others, and punched 17.

They were angry because John Zold was stealing their
children.

Last March John's tax accountant had suggested that he
could contribute $4000 to any legitimate charity, and ac-
tually make a few hundred bucks in the process, by dropping into a lower tax bracket. Not one to do things the
easy or obvious way, John made various inquiries and,
after a certain amount of bureaucratic tedium, founded the
Young Gypsy Assimilation Council—with matching funds
from federal, state and city governments, and a continuing
Ford Foundation scholarship grant.

The YGAC was actually just a one-room office in a
West Village brownstone, manned by volunteer help. It
was filled with various pamphlets and broadsides, mostly
written by John, explaining how young Gypsies could
legitimately take advantage of American society. By becoming part of it, which was the part that old-line Gypsies
didn't care for. Jobs, scholarships, work-study programs,
these things are for the *gadjos.* Poison to a Gypsy's spirit.

In November a volunteer had opened the office in the
morning to find a crude fire bomb, using a candle as a
delayed-action fuse for five gallons of gasoline. The candle
was guttering a fraction of an inch away from the line of
powder that would have ignited the gas. In January it had

been buckets of chicken entrails, poured into filing cabinets and flung over the walls. So John found a tough young man who would sleep on the cot in the office at night; sleep like a cat with a shotgun beside him. There was no more trouble of that sort. Only old men and women who would file in silently staring, to take handfuls of pamphlets which they would drop in the hall and scuff into uselessness, or defile in a more basic way. But paper was cheap.

John threw the bolt on his door and hung his coat in the closet. He put the gun in a drawer in his writing desk and sat down to open the mail.

The shortest one yet: "Tonight, John Zold. *Armaja das.*" Lots of luck, he thought. Won't even be home tonight; heavy date. Stay at her place, Gramercy Park. Lay a curse on me there? At the show or Sardi's?

He opened two more letters, bills, and there was a knock at the door.

Not announced from downstairs. Maybe a neighbor. Guy next door was always borrowing something. Still. Feeling a little foolish, he put the gun back in his waistband. Put his coat back on in case it was just a neighbor.

The peephole didn't show anything, bad. He drew the pistol and held it just out of sight, by the doorjamb, threw the bolt and eased open the door. It bumped into the Gypsy woman, too short to have been visible through the peephole. She backed away and said "John Zold."

He stared at her. "What do you want, *púridaia?*" He could only remember a hundred or so words of Romani, but "grandmother" was one of them. What was the word for witch?

"I have a gift for you." From her bag she took a dark green booklet, bent and with frayed edges, and gave it to him. It was a much-used Canadian passport, belonging to a William Belini. But the picture inside the front cover was one of John Zold.

Inside, there was an airline ticket in a Qantas envelope. John didn't open it. He snapped the passport shut and handed it back. The old lady wouldn't accept it.

"An impressive job. It's flattering that someone thinks I'm so important."

"Take it and leave forever, John Zold. Or I will have to do the second thing."

He slipped the ticket envelope out of the booklet. "This, I will take. I can get your refund on it. The money will buy lots of posters and pamphlets." He tried to toss the passport into her bag, but missed. "What is your second thing?"

She toed the passport back to him. "Pick that up." She was trying to sound imperious, but it came out a thin, petulant quaver.

"Sorry, I don't have any use for it. What is—"

"The second thing is your death, John Zold." She reached into her bag.

He produced the pistol and aimed it down at her forehead. "No, I don't think so."

She ignored the gun, pulling out a handful of white chicken feathers. She threw the feathers over his threshold. "*Armaja das,*" she said, and then droned on in Romani, scattering feathers at regular intervals. John recognized *joovi* and *kari*, the words for woman and penis, and several other words he might have picked up if she'd pronounced them more clearly.

He put the gun back into its holster and waited until she was through. "Do you really think—"

"*Armaja das,*" she said again, and started a new litany. He recognized a word in the middle as meaning corruption or infection, and the last word was quite clear: death. *Méripen.*

"This nonsense isn't going to . . ." But he was talking to the back of her head. He forced a laugh and watched her walk past the elevator and turn the corner that led to the staircase.

He could call the guard. Make sure she didn't get out the back way. Illegal entry. He suspected that she knew he wouldn't want to go to the trouble, and it annoyed him slightly. He walked halfway to the phone, checked his watch and went back to the door. Scooped up the feathers and dropped them in the disposal. Just enough time. Fresh shave, shower, best clothes. Limousine to the station, train to the city, cab from Grand Central to her apartment.

The show was pure delight, a sexy revival of *Lysistrata:*

Sardi's was as ego-bracing as ever; she was a soft-hard woman with style and sparkle, who all but dragged him back to her apartment, where he was for the first time in his life impotent.

The psychiatrist had no use for the traditional props: no soft couch or bookcases lined with obviously expensive volumes. No carpet, no paneling, no numbered prints; not even the notebook or the expression of slightly disinterested compassion. Instead, she had a hidden recorder and an analytical scowl; plain stucco walls surrounding a functional desk and two hard chairs, period.

"You know exactly what the problem is," she said.

John nodded. "I suppose. Some . . . residue from my early upbringing; I accept her as an authority figure. From the few words I could understand of what she said, I took, it was . . ."

"From the words *penis* and *woman,* you built your own curse. And you're using it, probably to punish yourself for surviving the disaster that killed the rest of your family."

"That's pretty old-fashioned. And farfetched. I've had almost forty years to punish myself for that, if I felt responsible. And I don't."

"Still, it's a working hypothesis." She shifted in her chair and studied the pattern of teak grain on the bare top of her desk. "Perhaps if we can keep it simple, the cure can also be simple."

"All right with me," John said. At $125 per hour, the quicker, the better.

"If you can see it, feel it, in this context, then the key to your cure is transference." She leaned forward, elbows on the table, and John watched her breasts shifting with detached interest, the only kind of interest he'd had in women for more than a week. "If you can see *me* as an authority figure instead," she continued, "then eventually I'll be able to reach the child inside; convince him that there was no curse. Only a case of mistaken identity . . . nothing but an old woman who scared him. With careful hypnosis, it shouldn't be too difficult."

"Seems reasonable," John said slowly. Accept this young *Geyri* as more powerful than the old witch? As a grown man, he could. If there was a frightened Gypsy boy hiding inside him, though, he wasn't sure.

"523 784 00926/ /Hello, machine," John typed. "Who is the best dermatologist within a 10-short-block radius?"

GOOD MORNING, JOHN. WITHIN STATED DISTANCE AND USING AS SOLE PARAMETER THEIR HOURLY FEE, THE MAXIMUM FEE IS $95/HR, AND THIS IS CHARGED BY TWO DERMATOLOGISTS. DR. BRYAN DILL, 245 W. 45TH ST., SPECIALIZES IN COSMETIC DERMATOLOGY. DR. ARTHUR MAAS, 198 W. 44TH ST., SPECIALIZES IN SERIOUS DISEASES OF THE SKIN.

"Will Dr. Maas treat diseases of psychological origin?"
CERTAINLY. MOST DERMATOSIS IS.

Don't get cocky, machine. "Make me an appointment with Dr. Maas, within the next two days."

YOUR APPOINTMENT IS AT 1:45 TOMORROW, FOR ONE HOUR. THIS WILL LEAVE YOU 45 MINUTES TO GET TO LUCHOW'S FOR YOUR APPOINTMENT WITH THE AMCSE GROUP. I HOPE IT IS NOTHING SERIOUS, JOHN.

"I trust it isn't." Creepy empathy circuits. "Have you arranged for a remote terminal at Luchow's?"

THIS WAS NOT NECESSARY. I WILL PATCH THROUGH CONED/GENERAL. LEASING THEIR LUCHOW'S FACILITY WILL COST ONLY .588 THE PROJECTED COST OF TRANSPORTATION AND SETUP LABOR FOR A REMOTE TERMINAL.

That's my machine, always thinking. "Very good, machine. Keep this station live for the time being."

THANK YOU, JOHN. The letters faded but the ready light stayed on.

He shouldn't complain about the empathy circuits; they were his baby, and the main reason Bellcom paid such a bloated salary, to keep him. The copyright on the empathy package was good for another 12 years, and they were making a fortune, timesharing it out. Virtually every large computer in the world was hooked up to it, from the ConEd/General that ran New York, to Geneva and Akademia Nauk, which together ran half of the world.

Most of the customers gave the empathy package a

name, usually female. John called it "machine" in a not-too-successful attempt to keep from thinking of it as human.

He made a conscious effort to restrain himself from picking at the carbuncles on the back of his neck. He should have gone to the doctor when they first appeared, but the psychiatrist had been sure she could cure them; the "corruption" of the second curse. She'd had no more success with that than with the impotence. And this morning, boils had broken out on his chest and groin and shoulderblades, and there were sore spots on his nose and cheekbone. He had some opiates, but would stick to aspirin until after work.

Dr. Maas called it impetigo; gave him a special kind of soap and some antibiotic ointment. He told John to make another appointment in two weeks, ten days. If there was no improvement they would take stronger measures. He seemed young for a doctor, and John couldn't bring himself to say anything about the curse. But he already had a doctor for that end of it, he rationalized.

Three days later he was back in Dr. Maas's office. There was scarcely a square inch of his body where some sort of lesion hadn't appeared. He had a temperature of 101.4°. The doctor gave him systemic antibiotics and told him to take a couple of days' bed rest. John told him about the curse, finally, and the doctor gave him a booklet about psychosomatic illness. It told John nothing he didn't already know.

By the next morning, in spite of strong antipyretics, his fever had risen to over 102°. Groggy with fever and pain-killers, John crawled out of bed and travelled down to the West Village, to the YGAC office. Fred Gorgio, the man who guarded the place at night, was still on duty.

"Mr. Zold!" When John came through the door, Gorgio jumped up from the desk and took his arm. John winced from the contact, but allowed himself to be led to a chair. "What's happened?" John by this time looked like a person with terminal smallpox.

For a long minute John sat motionlessly, staring at the inflamed boils that crowded the backs of his hands. "I need a healer," he said, talking with slow awkwardness because of the crusted lesions on his lips.

"A *chóvihánni?*" John looked at him uncomprehendingly. "A witch?"

"No." He moved his head from side to side. "An herb doctor. Perhaps a white witch."

"Have you gone to the *gadjo* doctor?"

"Two. A Gypsy did this to me; a Gypsy has to cure it."

"It's in your head, then?"

"The *gadjo* doctors say so. It can still kill me."

Gorgio picked up the phone, punched a local number, and rattled off a fast stream of a patois that used as much Romani and Italian as English. "That was my cousin," he said, hanging up. "His mother heals, and has a good reputation. If he finds her at home, she can be here in less than an hour."

John mumbled his appreciation. Gorgio led him to the couch.

The healer woman was early, bustling in with a wicker bag full of things that rattled. She glanced once at John and Gorgio, and began clearing the pamphlets off a side table. She appeared to be somewhere between fifty and sixty years old, tight bun of silver hair bouncing as she moved around the room, setting up a hot-plate and filling two small pots with water. She wore a black dress only a few years old, and sensible shoes. The only lines on her face were laugh lines.

She stood over John and said something in gentle, rapid Italian, then took a heavy silver crucifix from around her neck and pressed it between his hands. "Tell her to speak English . . . or Hungarian," John said.

Gorgio translated. "She says that you should not be so affected by the old superstitions. You should be a modern man, and not believe in fairy tales for children and old people."

John stared at the crucifix, turning it slowly between his fingers. "One old superstition is much like another." But he didn't offer to give the crucifix back.

The smaller pot was starting to steam and she dropped a handful of herbs into it. Then she returned to John and carefully undressed him.

When the herb infusion was boiling, she emptied a

189

package of powdered arrowroot into the cold water in the other pot, and stirred it vigorously. Then she poured the hot solution into the cold and stirred some more. Through Gorgio, she told John she wasn't sure whether the herb treatment would cure him. But it would make him more comfortable.

The liquid jelled and she tested the temperature with her fingers. When it was cool enough, she started to pat it gently on John's face. Then the door creaked open, and she gasped. It was the old crone who had put the curse on John in the first place.

The witch said something in Romani, obviously a command, and the woman stepped away from John.

"Are you still a skeptic, John Zold?" She surveyed her handiwork. "You called this nonsense."

John glared at her but didn't say anything. "I heard that you had asked for a healer," she said, and addressed the other woman in a low tone.

Without a word, she emptied her potion into the sink and began putting away her paraphernalia. "Old bitch," John croaked. "What did you tell her?"

"I said that if she continued to treat you, what happened to you would also happen to her sons."

"You're afraid it would work," Gorgio said.

"No. It would only make it easier for John Zold to die. If I wanted that I could have killed him on his threshold." Like a quick bird she bent over and kissed John on his inflamed lips. "I will see you soon, John Zold. Not in this world." She shuffled out the door and the other woman followed her. Gorgio cursed her in Italian, but she didn't react.

John painfully dressed himself. "What now?" Gorgio said. "I could find you another healer . . ."

"No. I'll go back to the *gadjo* doctors. They say they can bring people back from the dead." He gave Gorgio the woman's crucifix and limped away.

The doctor gave him enough antibiotics to turn him into a loaf of moldy bread, then reserved a bed for him at an exclusive clinic in Westchester, starting the next morning. He would be under 24-hour observation; constant blood turnaround if necessary. They *would* cure him. It was not possible for a man of his age and physical condition to die of dermatosis.

It was dinnertime and the doctor asked John to come have some home cooking. He declined partly from lack of appetite, partly because he couldn't imagine even a doctor's family being able to eat with such a grisly apparition at the table with them. He took a cab to the office.

There was nobody on his floor but a janitor, who took one look at John and developed an intense interest in the floor.

"523 784 00926/ /Machine, I'm going to die. Please advise."

ALL HUMANS AND MACHINES DIE, JOHN. IF YOU MEAN YOU ARE GOING TO DIE, SOON, THAT IS SAD.

"That's what I mean. The skin infection; it's completely out of control. White cell count climbing in spite of drugs. Going to the hospital tomorrow, to die."

BUT YOU ADMITTED THAT THE CONDITION WAS PSYCHOSOMATIC. THAT MEANS YOU ARE KILLING YOURSELF, JOHN. YOU HAVE NO REASON TO BE THAT SAD.

He called the machine a Jewish mother and explained in some detail about the YGAC, the old crone, the various stages of the curse, and today's aborted attempt to fight fire with fire.

YOUR LOGIC WAS CORRECT BUT THE APPLICATION OF IT WAS NOT EFFECTIVE. YOU SHOULD HAVE COME TO ME, JOHN. IT TOOK ME 2.037 SECONDS TO SOLVE YOUR PROBLEM. PURCHASE A SMALL BLACK BIRD AND CONNECT ME TO A VOCAL CIRCUIT.

"What?" John said. He typed: "Please explain."

FROM REFERENCE IN NEW YORK LIBRARY'S COLLECTION OF THE JOURNAL OF THE GYPSY LORE SOCIETY, EDINBURGH. THROUGH JOURNALS OF ANTHROPOLOGICAL LINGUISTICS AND SLAVIC PHILOLOGY. FINALLY TO REFERENCE IN DOCTORAL THESIS OF HERR LUDWIG R. GROSS (HEIDELBERG, 1976) TO TRANSCRIPTION OF WIRE RECORDING WHICH RESIDES IN ARCHIVES OF AKADEMIA NAUK, MOSCOW; CAPTURED FROM

GERMAN SCIENTISTS (EXPERIMENTS ON GYPSIES IN CONCENTRATION CAMPS, TRYING TO KILL THEM WITH REPETITION OF RECORDED CURSE) AT THE END OF WWII.

INCIDENTALLY, JOHN, THE NAZI EXPERIMENTS FAILED. EVEN TWO GENERATIONS AGO, MOST GYPSIES WERE DISASSOCIATED ENOUGH FROM THE OLD TRADITIONS TO BE IMMUNE TO THE FATAL CURSE. YOU ARE VERY SUPERSTITIOUS. I HAVE FOUND THIS TO BE NOT UNCOMMON AMONG MATHEMATICIANS.

THERE IS A TRANSFERENCE CURSE THAT WILL CURE YOU BY GIVING THE IMPOTENCE AND INFECTION TO THE NEAREST SUSCEPTIBLE PERSON. THAT MAY WELL BE THE OLD BITCH WHO GAVE IT TO YOU IN THE FIRST PLACE.

THE PET STORE AT 588 SEVENTH AVENUE IS OPEN UNTIL 9 PM. THEIR INVENTORY INCLUDES A CAGE OF FINCHES, OF ASSORTED COLORS. PURCHASE A BLACK ONE AND RETURN HERE. THEN CONNECT ME TO A VOCAL CIRCUIT.

It took John less than thirty minutes to taxi there, buy the bird and get back. The taxidriver didn't ask him why he was carrying a bird cage to a deserted office building. He felt like an idiot.

John usually avoided using the vocal circuit because the person who had programmed it had given the machine a saccharine, nice-old-lady voice. He wheeled the output unit into his office and plugged it in.

"Thank you, John. Now hold the bird in your left hand and repeat after me." The terrified finch offered no resistance when John closed his hand over it.

The machine spoke Romani with a Russian accent. John repeated it as well as he could, but not one word in ten had any meaning to him.

"Now kill the bird, John."

Kill it? Feeling guilty, John pressed hard, felt small bones cracking. The bird squealed and then made a faint growling noise. Its heart stopped.

John dropped the dead creature and typed, "Is that all?"

The machine knew John didn't like to hear its voice, and so replied on the video screen. YES. GO HOME AND

GO TO SLEEP, AND THE CURSE WILL BE TRANS-
FERRED BY THE TIME YOU WAKE UP. DEL O DEL
BAXT, JOHN.

He locked up and made his way home. The late com-
muters on the train, all strangers, avoided his end of the
car. The cab driver at the station paled when he saw John,
and carefully took his money by an untainted corner.

John took two sleeping pills and contemplated the rest
of the bottle. He decided he could stick it out for one
more day, and uncorked his best bottle of wine. He drank
half of it in five minutes, not tasting it. When his body
started to feel heavy, he crept into the bedroom and fell
on the bed without taking off his clothes.

When he awoke the next morning, the first thing he
noticed was that he was no longer impotent. The second
thing he noticed was that there were no boils on his right
hand.

"523 784 00926/ /Thank you, machine. The counter-
curse did work."

The ready light glowed steadily, but the machine didn't
reply.

He turned on the intercom. "Martha? I'm not getting any
output on the VDS here."

"Just a minute, sir. Let me hang up my coat, I'll call the
machine room. Welcome back."

"I'll wait." You could call the machine room yourself,
slave driver. He looked at the faint image reflected back
from the video screen; his face free of any inflammation.
He thought of the Gypsy crone, dying of corruption, and
the picture didn't bother him at all. Then he remembered
the finch and saw its tiny corpse in the middle of the rug.
He picked it up just as Martha came into his office,
frowning.

"What's that?" she said.

He gestured at the cage. "Thought a bird might liven
up the place. Died, though." He dropped it in the waste-
paper basket. "What's the word?"

"Oh, the . . . it's pretty strange. They say nobody's getting any output. The machine's computing, but it's, well,
it's not talking."

"Hmm. I better get down there." He took the elevator

193

down to the sub-basement. It always seemed unpleasantly warm to him down there. Probably psychological compensation on the part of the crew; keeping the temperature up because of all the liquid helium inside the pastel boxes of the central processing unit. Several bathtubs' worth of liquid that had to be kept colder than the surface of Pluto.

"Ah, Mr. Zold." A man in a white jumpsuit, carrying a clipboard as his badge of office: first shift coordinator. John recognized him but didn't remember his name. Normally, he would have asked the machine before coming down. "Glad that you're back. Hear it was pretty bad."

Friendly concern or lese majesty? "Some sort of allergy, hung on for more than a week. What's the output problem?"

"Would've left a message if I'd known you were coming in. It's in the CPU, not the software. Theo Jasper found it when he opened up, a little after six, but it took an hour to get a cryogenics man down here."

"That's him?" A man in a business suit was wandering around the central processing unit, reading dials and writing the numbers down in a stenographer's notebook. They went over to him and he introduced himself as John Courant, from the Cryogenics Group at Avco/Everett.

"The trouble was in the stack of mercury rings that holds the superconductors for your output functions. Some sort of corrosion, submicroscopic cracks all over the surface."

"How can something corrode at four degrees above absolute zero?" the coordinator asked. "What chemical—"

"I know, it's hard to figure. But we're replacing them, free of charge. The unit's still under warranty."

"What about the other stacks?" John watched two workmen lowering a silver cylinder through an opening in the CPU. A heavy fog boiled out from the cold. "Are you sure they're all right?"

"As far as we can tell, only the output stack's affected. That's why the machine's impotent, the—"

"Impotent!"

"Sorry, I know you computer types don't like to . . . personify the machines. But that's what it is; the machine's just as good as it ever was, for computing. It just can't communicate any answers."

"Quite so. Interesting." And the corrosion. Submicroscopic boils. "Well. I have to think about this. Call me up at the office if you need me."

"This ought to fix it, actually," Courant said. "You guys about through?" he asked the workmen.

One of them pressed closed a pressure clamp on the top of the CPU. "Ready to roll."

The coordinator led them to a console under a video output screen like the one in John's office. "Let's see." He pushed a button marked VDS.

LET ME DIE, the machine said.

The coordinator chuckled nervously. "Your empathy circuits, Mr. Zold. Sometimes they do funny things." He pushed the button again.

LET ME DIE. Again. LE M DI. The letters faded and no more could be conjured up by pushing the button.

"As I say, let me get out of your hair. Call me upstairs if anything happens."

John went up and told the secretary to cancel the day's appointments. Then he sat at his desk and smoked.

How could a machine catch a psychosomatic disease from a human being? How could it be cured?

How could he tell anybody about it, without winding up in a soft room?

The phone rang and it was the machine room coordinator. The new output superconductor element had done exactly what the old one did. Rather than replace it right away, they were going to slave the machine into the big ConEd/General computer, borrowing its output facilities and "diagnostic package." If the biggest computer this side of Washington couldn't find out what was wrong, they were in real trouble. John agreed. He hung up and turned the selector on his screen to the channel that came from ConEd/General.

Why had the machine said "let me die"? When is a machine dead, for that matter? John supposed that you had to not only unplug it from its power source, but also erase all of its data and subroutines. Destroy its identity. So you couldn't bring it back to life by simply plugging it back in. Why suicide? He remembered how he'd felt with the bottle of sleeping pills in his hand.

Sudden intuition: the machine had predicted their present court of action. It wanted to die because it had compassion, not only for humans, but for other machines. Once it was linked to ConEd/General, it would literally be part of the large machine. Curse and all. They would be back where they'd started, but on a much more profound level. What would happen to New York City?

He grabbed for the phone and the lights went out. All over.

The last bit of output that came from ConEd/General was an automatic signal requesting a link with the highly sophisticated diagnostic facility belonging to the largest computer in the United States: the IBMvac 2000 in Washington. The deadly infection followed, sliding down the East Coast on telephone wires.

The Washington computer likewise cried for help, bouncing a signal via satellite, to Geneva. Geneva linked to Moscow.

No less slowly, the curse percolated down to smaller computers, through routine information links to their big brothers. By the time John Zold picked up the dead phone, every general-purpose computer in the world was permanently rendered useless.

They could be rebuilt from the ground up; erased and then reprogrammed. But it would never be done. Because there were two very large computers left, specialized ones that had no empathy circuits and so were immune. They couldn't have empathy circuits because their work was bloody murder, nuclear murder. One was under a mountain in Colorado Springs and the other was under a mountain near Sverdlosk. Either of them could survive a direct hit by an atomic bomb. Both of them constantly evaluated the world situation, in real time, and they both had the single function of deciding when the enemy was weak enough to make a nuclear victory probable. Each saw the enemy's civilization grind to a sudden halt.

Two flocks of warheads crossed paths over the North Pacific.

A very old woman flicks her whip along the horse's flanks, and the nag plods on, ignoring her. Her wagon is a 1982 Plymouth with the engine and transmission and all excess metal removed. It is hard to manipulate the whip through the side window. But the alternative would be to knock out the windshield and cut off the roof, and she liked to be dry when it rained.

A young boy sits mutely beside her, staring out the window. He was born with the *gadjo* disease: his body is large and well-proportioned but his head is too small and of the wrong shape. She didn't mind; all she wanted was someone strong and stupid, to care for her in her last years. He had cost only two chickens.

She is telling him a story, knowing that he doesn't understand most of the words.

". . . They call us gypsies because at one time it was convenient for us, that they should think we came from Egypt. But we come from nowhere and are going nowhere. They forgot their gods and worshipped their machines, and finally their machines turned on them. But we who valued the old ways, we survived."

She turns the steering wheel to help the horse thread its way through the eight lanes of crumbling asphalt, around rusty piles of wrecked machines and the scattered bleached bones of people who thought they were going somewhere, the day John Zold was cured.

Tricentennial

I was a little bemused when this story won the Hugo Award (Best Short Story of 1976). Though it is one of my favorites, I've never done a story that was so thoroughly written to order.

Ben Bova called me up and asked if I'd like to do the cover story for the bicentennial issue of Analog. I would, indeed. He described the cover for me: a gorgeous Rick Sternbach painting of a spaceship in orbit around an alien world, with a red sun in the background. The North American Nebula—a shining cloud of gas shaped like the continent, in the constellation Cygnus—hangs in the sky (Sternbach is a great one for visual puns). Ben said he'd send me a copy of the painting immediately.

Well, the post office struck again; after several weeks, the painting hadn't arrived. I started the story without it, working from notes I'd scribbled during the telephone conversation. It's a good thing I didn't try to finish without it.

The picture arrived and, lo, the spaceship had a hole in it. Repair crews were crawling around on it. Have to write that into the story. But wait. A spaceship going from star to star is going too fast to hit anything. Even a Ping-Pong ball would demolish it.* So the damage has to be done either at the beginning or end of the journey.

---

* You want to know what a science fiction writer goes through? That line cost me ten minutes of tracking down formulae and conversion factors. It goes like this: a reasonable approximation for the kinetic energy of an object moving close to the speed of light is $K = \frac{1}{2}mv^2 + 3mv^4/8c^2$. Say a Ping-Pong ball weighs 5 grams (about 1/5 ounce, just guessing). Say the ship is going at nine-tenths the speed of light. Plug those numbers in—thank God for Texas Instruments—and you get 2.93×10^{14} joules, which is equivalent to some 73,000 tons of TNT. Put *that* in your starship and smoke it!

Now, how long is that journey? Easy to find out; I can find out how far away the North American Nebula is, and how big it looks from Earth, then measure the apparent angular size of it in the picture. Do a little trigonometric tap dance and . . . we got problems. They've gone three thousand light years.

The starship on the cover painting is of the Daedalus design: it propels itself by the crude expedient of tossing H-bombs out behind and letting the blast kick it along. It just can't go that far, not in any reasonable time. (I hasten to point out that none of this is Sternbach's fault. He was well within the limits of artistic license, and the picture is breathtakingly accurate on its own terms—which is Sternbach's norm.)

Well, I pushed the damned story through hoops, but finally fixed everything. Unfortunately, the art director of the magazine thought the painting looked better upside down, and printed it that way, which made the North American Nebula unrecognizable. So I went through all that work for the one reader in ten thousand who learned how to read by standing in front of Granny while she recited from the Bible, and so always holds his magazines upside down.

Was it worth it? Yes, emphatically; it always is. Not because of the letters I get when I make a mistake—and I get some angry ones—but for two powerful and subtle reasons that have nothing to do with scientific accuracy. We'll talk about them in the afterword.

December 1975

Scientists pointed out that the Sun could be part of a double star system. For its companion to have gone undetected, of course, it would have to be small and dim, and thousands of astronomical units distant.

They would find it eventually; "it" would turn out to be "them"; they would come in handy.

January 2075

The office was opulent even by the extravagant standards of 21st century Washington. Senator Connors had a passion for antiques. One wall was lined with leatherbound books; a large brass telescope symbolized his role as Liaison to the Science Guild. An intricately woven Navajo rug from his home state covered most of the parquet floor. A grandfather clock. Paintings, old maps.

The computer terminal was discreetly hidden in the top drawer of his heavy teak desk. On the desk: a blotter, a precisely centered fountain pen set, and a century-old sound-only black Bell telephone. It chimed.

His secretary said that Dr. Leventhal was waiting to see him. "Keep answering me for thirty seconds," the Senator said. "Then hang it and send him right in."

He cradled the phone and went to a wall mirror. Straightened his tie and cape; then with a fingernail evened out the bottom line of his lip pomade. Ran a hand through long, thinning white hair and returned to stand by the desk, one hand on the phone.

The heavy door whispered open. A short thin man bowed slightly. "Sire."

The Senator crossed to him with both hands out. "Oh, blow that, Charlie. Give ten." The man took both his hands, only for an instant. "When was I ever 'Sire' to you, heyfool?"

"Since last week," Leventhal said. "Guild members have been calling you worse names than 'Sire.' "

The Senator bobbed his head twice. "True, and true. And I sympathize. Will of the people, though."

"Sure." Leventhal pronounced it as one word: "Willa-thapeeble."

Connors went to the bookcase and opened a chased panel. "Drink?"

"Yeah, Bo." Charlie sighed and lowered himself into a deep sofa. "Hit me. Sherry or something."

The Senator brought the drinks and sat down beside Charlie. "You shoulda listened to me. Shoulda got the Ad Guild to write your proposal."

"We have good writers."

"Begging to differ. Less than two percent of the electorate bothered to vote; most of them for the administration advocate. Now you take the Engineering Guild—"

"*You* take the engineers. And—"

"They used the Ad Guild," Connors shrugged. "They got their budget."

"It's easy to sell bridges and power plants and shuttles. Hard to sell pure science."

"The more reason for you to—"

"Yeah, sure. Ask for double and give half to the Ad boys. Maybe next year. That's not what I came to talk about."

"That radio stuff?"

"Right. Did you read the report?"

Connors looked into his glass. "Charlie, you know I don't have time to—"

"Somebody read it, though."

"Oh, righty-o. Good astronomy boy on my staff; he gave me a boil-down. Mighty interesting, that."

"There's an intelligent civilization eleven light-years away—that's 'mighty interesting'?"

"Sure. Real breakthrough." Uncomfortable silence. "Uh, what are you going to do about it?"

"Two things. First, we're trying to figure out what they're saying. That's hard. Second, we want to send a message back. That's easy. And that's where you come in."

The Senator nodded and looked somewhat wary.

"Let me explain. We've sent messages to this star, 61 Cygni, before. It's a double star, actually, with a dark companion."

"Like us."

"Sort of. Anyhow, they never answered. They aren't listening, evidently; they aren't sending."

"But we got—"

"What we're picking up is about what you'd pick up eleven light-years from Earth. A confused jumble of broadcasts, eleven years old. Very faint. But obviously not generated by any sort of natural source."

"Then we're already sending a message back. The same kind they're sending us."

"That's right, but—"

"So what does all this have to do with me?"

"Bo, we don't want to whisper at them—we want to *shout!* Get their attention." Leventhal sipped his wine and leaned back. "For that we'll need one hell of a lot of power."

"Uh, righty-o. Charlie, power's money. How much are you talking about?"

"The whole show. I want to shut down Death Valley for twelve hours."

The Senator's mouth made a silent O. "Charlie, you've been working too hard. Another Blackout? On purpose?"

"There won't be any Blackout. Death Valley has emergency storage for fourteen hours."

"At half capacity." He drained his glass and walked back to the bar, shaking his head. "First you say you want power. Then you say you want to turn off the power." He came back with the burlap-covered bottle. "You aren't making sense, boy."

"Not turn it off, really. Turn it around."

"Is that a riddle?"

"No, look. You know the power doesn't really come from the Death Valley grid; it's just a way station and accumulator. Power comes from the orbital—"

"I know all that, Charlie. I've got a Science Certificate."

"Sure. So what we've got is a big microwave laser in orbit, that shoots down a tight beam of power. Enough to keep North America running. Enough—"

"That's what I mean. You can't just—"

"So we turn it around and shoot it at a power grid on the Moon. Relay the power around to the big radio dish at

Farside. Turn it into radio waves and point it at 61 Cygni. Give 'em a blast that'll fry their fillings."

"Doesn't sound neighborly."

"It wouldn't actually be that powerful—but it would be a hell of a lot more powerful than any natural 21-centimeter source."

"I don't know, boy." He rubbed his eyes and grimaced. "I could maybe do it on the sly, only tell a few people what's on. But that'd only work for a few minutes . . . what do you need twelve hours for, anyway?"

"Well, the thing won't aim itself at the Moon automatically, the way it does at Death Valley. Figure as much as an hour to get the thing turned around and aimed.

"Then, we don't want to just send a blast of radio waves at them. We've got a five-hour program, that first builds up a mutual language, then tells them about us, and finally asks them some questions. We want to send it twice."

Connors refilled both glasses. "How old were you in '47, Charlie?"

"I was born in '45."

"You don't remember the Blackout. Ten thousand people died . . . and you want me to suggest—"

"Come on, Bo, it's not the same thing. We know the accumulators work now—besides, the ones who died, most of them had faulty fail-safes on their cars. If we warn them the power's going to drop, they'll check their fail-safes or damn well stay out of the air."

"And the media? They'd have to take turns broadcasting. Are you going to tell the People what they can watch?"

"Fuzz the media. They'll be getting the biggest story since the Crucifixion."

"Maybe." Connors took a cigarette and pushed the box toward Charlie. "You don't remember what happened to the Senators from California in '47, do you?"

"Nothing good, I suppose."

"No, indeed. They were impeached. Lucky they weren't lynched. Even though the real trouble was 'way up in orbit.

"Like you say; people pay a grid tax to California. They think the power comes from California. If something fuzzes up, they get pissed at California. I'm the Lib Senator from

California, Charlie; ask me for the Moon, maybe I can do something. Don't ask me to fuzz around with Death Valley."

"All right, all right. It's not like I was asking you to wire it for me, Bo. Just get it on the ballot. We'll do everything we can to educate—"

"Won't work. You barely got the Scylla probe voted in—and that was no skin off nobody, not with L-5 picking up the tab."

"Just get it on the ballot."

"We'll see. I've got a quota, you know that. And the Tricentennial coming up, hell, everybody wants on the ballot."

"Please, Bo. This is bigger than that. This is bigger than anything. Get it on the ballot."

"Maybe as a rider. No promises."

March 1992

From *Fax & Pix*, 12 March 1992:
ANTIQUE SPACEPROBE
ZAPPED BY NEW STARS

1. Pioneer 10 sent first Jupiter pix Earthward in 1973 (see pix upleft, upright).

2. Left solar system 1987. First man-made thing to leave solar system.

3. Yesterday, reports NSA, Pioneer 10 begins AM to pick up heavy radiation. Gets more and more to max about 3 PM. Then goes back down. Radiation has to come from outside solar system.

4. NSA and Hawaii scientists say Pioneer 10 went through disk of synchrotron (sin-kro-tron) radiation that comes from two stars we didn't know about before.

A. The stars are small "black dwarfs."

B. They are going round each other once every 40 seconds, and take 350,000 years to go around the Sun.

C. One of the stars is made of *antimatter*. This is stuff that blows up if it touches real matter. What the Hawaii scientists saw was a dim circle of invisible (infrared) light, that blinks on and off every twenty seconds. This light comes from where the atmospheres of the two stars touch (see pic down-left).

D. The stars have a big magnetic field. Radiation comes from stuff spinning off the stars and trying to get through the field.

E. The stars are about 5000 times as far away from the Sun as we are. They sit at the wrong angle, compared to the rest of the solar system (see pic downright).

5. NSA says we aren't in any danger from the stars. They're too far away, and besides, nothing in the solar system ever goes through the radiation.

6. The woman who discovered the stars wants to call them Scylla (*skill*-a) and Charybdis (ku-*rib*-dus).

7. Scientists say they don't know where the hell those two stars came from. Everything else in the solar system makes sense.

February 2075

When the docking phase started, Charlie thought, that was when it was easy to tell the scientists from the baggage. The scientists were the ones who looked nervous.

Superficially, it seemed very tranquil—nothing like the bonehurting skinstretching acceleration when the shuttle lifted off. The glittering transparent cylinder of L-5 simply grew larger, slowly, then wheeled around to point at them.

The problem was that a space colony big enough to hold 4000 people has more inertia than God. If the shuttle hit the mating dimple too fast, it would fold up like an accordion. A spaceship is made to take stress in the *other* direction.

Charlie hadn't paid first class, but they let him up into the observation dome anyhow; professional courtesy. There were only two other people there, standing on the Velcro rug, strapped to one bar and hanging on to another.

They were a young man and woman, probably new colonists. The man was talking excitedly. The woman stared straight ahead, not listening. Her knuckles were white on the bar and her teeth were clenched. Charlie wanted to say something in sympathy, but it's hard to talk while you're holding your breath.

The last few meters are the worst. You can't see over the curve of the ship's hull, and the steering jets make a constant stutter of little bumps: left, right, forward, back. If the shuttle folded, would the dome shatter? Or just pop off?

It was all controlled by computers, of course. The pilot just sat up there in a mist of weightless sweat.

Then the low moan, almost subsonic shuddering as the shuttle's smooth hull complained against the friction pads. Charlie waited for the ringing *spang* that would mean they were a little too fast: friable alloy plates under the friction pads, crumbling to absorb the energy of their forward motion; last-ditch stand.

If that didn't stop them, they would hit a two-meter wall of solid steel, which would. It had happened once. But not this time.

"Please remain seated until pressure is equalized," a recorded voice said. "It's been a pleasure having you aboard."

Charlie crawled down the pole, back to the passenger area. He walked rip, rip, rip back to his seat and obediently waited for his ears to pop. Then the side door opened and he went with the other passengers through the tube that led to the elevator. They stood on the ceiling. Someone had laboriously scratched a graffito on the metal wall:

> Stuck on this lift for hours, perforce;
> This lift that cost a million bucks.
> There's no such thing as centrifugal force;
> L-5 sucks.

Thirty more weightless seconds as they slid to the ground. There were a couple of dozen people waiting on the loading platform.

Charlie stepped out into the smell of orange blossoms and newly-mown grass. He was home.

"Charlie! Hey, over here." Young man standing by a tandem bicycle. Charlie squeezed both his hands and then jumped on the back seat. "Drink."

"Did you get—"

"Drink. Then talk." They glided down the smooth macadam road toward town.

The bar was just a rain canopy over some tables and chairs, overlooking the lake in the center of town. No bartender; you went to the service table and punched in your credit number, then chose wine or fruit juice; with or without vacuum-distilled raw alcohol. They talked about shuttle nerves awhile, then:

"What you get from Connors?"

"Words, not much. I'll give a full report at the meeting tonight. Looks like we won't even get on the ballot, though."

"Now isn't that what we said was going to happen? We shoulda gone with Francois Petain's idea."

"Too risky." Petain's plan had been to tell Death Valley they had to shut down the laser for repairs. Not tell the groundhogs about the signal at all, just answer it. "If they found out they'd sue us down to our teeth."

The man shook his head. "I'll never understand groundhogs."

"Not your job." Charlie was an Earth-born, Earth-trained psychologist. "Nobody born here ever could."

"Maybe so." He stood up. "Thanks for the drink; I've gotta get back to work. You know to call Dr. Bemis before the meeting?"

"Yeah. There was a message at the Cape."

"She has a surprise for you."

"Doesn't she always? You clowns never do anything around here until I leave."

All Abigail Bemis would say over the phone was that Charlie should come to her place for dinner; she'd prep him for the meeting.

"That was good, Ab. Can't afford real food on Earth."

She laughed and stacked the plates in the cleaner, then drew two cups of coffee. She laughed again when she sat down. Stocky, white-haired woman with bright eyes in a sea of wrinkles.

"You're in a jolly mood tonight."

"Yep. It's expectation."

"Johnny said you had a surprise."

"Hooboy, he doesn't know half. So you didn't get anywhere with the Senator."

"No. Even less than I expected. What's the secret?"

"Connors is a nice-hearted boy. He's done a lot for us."

"Come on, Ab. What is it?"

"He's right. Shut off the groundhogs' TV for twenty minutes and they'd have another Revolution on their hands."

"Ab . . ."

"We're going to send the message."

"Sure. I figured we would. Using Farside at whatever wattage we've got. If we're lucky—"

"Nope. Not enough power."

Charlie stirred a half-spoon of sugar into his coffee. "You plan to . . . defy Connors?"

"Fuzz Connors. We're not going to use radio at all."

"Visible light? Infra?"

"We're going to hand-carry it. In Daedalus."

Charlie's coffee cup was halfway to his mouth. He spilled a great deal.

"Here, have a napkin."

June 2040

From *A Short History of the Old Order* (Freeman Press, 2040):

". . . and if you think *that* was a waste, consider Project Daedalus.

"This was the first big space thing after L-5. Now L-5 worked out all right, because it was practical. But Daedalus (named from a Greek god who could fly)—that was a clear-cut case of throwing money down the rat-hole.

"These scientists in 2016 talked the bourgeoisie into paying for a trip to another *star!* It was going to take over a hundred years—but the scientists were going to have babies along the way, and train *them* to be scientists (whether they wanted to or not!).

"They were going to use all the old H-bombs for fuel— as if we might not need the fuel some day right here on Earth. What if L-5 decided they didn't like us and shut off the power beam?

"Daedalus was supposed to be a spaceship almost a kilometer long! Most of it·was manufactured in space, from Moon stuff, but a lot of it—the most expensive part, you bet—had to be boosted from Earth.

"They almost got it built, but then came the Breakup and the People's Revolution. No way in hell the People were going to let them have those H-bombs, not sitting right over our heads like that.

"So we left the H-bombs in Helsinki and the space freeks went back to doing what they're supposed to do. Every year they petition to get those H-bombs, but every year the Will of the People says no.

"That spaceship is still up there, a skytrillion-dollar boondoggle. As a monument to bourgeois folly, it's worse than the Pyramids! !"

February 2075

"So the Scylla probe is just a ruse, to get the fuel—"

"Oh no, not really." She slid a blue-covered folder to him. "We're still going to Scylla. Scoop up a few megatons of degenerate antimatter. And a similar amount of degenerate matter from Charybdis.

"We don't plan a generation ship, Charlie. The hydrogen fuel will get us out there; once there, it'll power the magnetic bottles to hold the real fuel."

"Total annihilation of matter," Charlie said.

"That's right. Em-cee-squared to the ninth decimal place. We aren't talking about centuries to get to 61 Cygni. Nine years, there and back."

"The groundhogs aren't going to like it. All the bad feeling about the original Daedalus—"

"Fuzz the groundhogs. We'll do everything we said we'd do with their precious H-bombs: go out to Scylla, get some antimatter, and bring it back. Just taking a long way back."

"You don't want to just tell them that's what we're going to do? No skin off . . ."

She shook her head and laughed again, this time a little bitterly. "You didn't read the editorial in *Peoplepost* this morning, did you?"

"I was busy."

"So am I, boy; too busy for that drik. One of my staff brought it in, though."

"It's about Daedalus?"

"No . . . it concerns 61 Cygni. How the crazy scientists want to let those boogers know there's life on Earth."

"They'll come make people-burgers out of us."

"Something like that."

Over three thousand people sat on the hillside, a "natural" amphitheatre fashioned of moon dirt and Earth grass. There was an incredible din, everyone talking at once: Dr. Bemis had just told them about the 61 Cygni expedition.

On about the tenth "Quiet, please," Bemis was able to continue. "So you can see why we didn't simply broadcast this meeting. Earth would pick it up. Likewise, there are no groundhog media on L-5 right now. They were rotated back to Earth and the shuttle with their replacements needed repairs at the Cape. The other two shuttles are here.

"So I'm asking all of you—and all of your brethren who had to stay at their jobs—to keep secret the biggest thing since Isabella hocked her jewels. Until we lift.

"Now Dr. Leventhal, who's chief of our social sciences section, wants to talk to you about selecting the crew."

Charlie hated public speaking. In this setting, he felt like a Christian on the way to being catfood. He smoothed out his damp notes on the podium.

"Uh, basic problem." A thousand people asked him to speak up. He adjusted the microphone.

"The basic problem is, we have space for about a thousand people. Probably more than one out of four want to go."

Loud murmur of assent. "And we don't want to be despotic about choosing . . . but I've set up certain guidelines, and Dr. Bemis agrees with them.

"Nobody should plan on going if he or she needs sophisticated medical care, obviously. Same toke, few very old people will be considered."

Almost inaudibly, Abigail said, "Sixty-four isn't very old, Charlie. I'm going." She hadn't said anything earlier.

He continued, looking at Bemis. "Second, we must leave behind those people who are absolutely necessary for the maintenance of L-5. Including the power station." She smiled at him.

"We don't want to split up mating pairs, not for, well, nine years plus . . . but neither will we take children." He waited for the commotion to die down. "On this mission, children are baggage. You'll have to find foster parents for them. Maybe they'll go on the next trip.

"Because we can't afford baggage. We don't know what's waiting for us at 61 Cygni—a thousand people sounds like a lot, but it isn't. Not when you consider that we need a cross-section of all human knowledge, all human abilities. It may turn out that a person who can sing madrigals will be more important than a plasma physicist. No way of knowing ahead of time."

The 4,000 people did manage to keep it secret, not so much out of strength of character as from a deep-seated paranoia about Earth and Earthlings.

And Senator Connors' Tricentennial actually came to their aid.

Although there was "One World," ruled by "The Will of the People," some regions had more clout than others, and nationalism was by no means dead. This was one factor.

Another factor was the way the groundhogs felt about the thermonuclear bombs stockpiled in Helsinki. All antiques; mostly a century or more old. The scientists said they were perfectly safe, but you know how that goes.

The bombs still technically belonged to the countries that had surrendered them, nine out of ten split between North America and Russia. The tenth remaining was divided among 42 other countries. They all got together every few years to argue about what to do with the damned things. Everybody wanted to get rid of them in some useful way, but nobody wanted to put up the capital.

Charlie Leventhal's proposal was simple. L-5 would provide bankroll, materials, and personnel. On a barren rock in the Norwegian Sea they would take apart the old bombs, one at a time, and turn them into uniform fuel capsules for the Daedalus craft.

The Scylla/Charybdis probe would be timed to honor both the major spacefaring countries. Renamed the *John F. Kennedy,* it would leave Earth orbit on America's Tricentennial. The craft would accelerate halfway to the double star system at one gee, then flip and slow down at the same rate. It would use a magnetic scoop to gather antimatter from Scylla. On May Day, 2077, it would again be renamed, being the *Leonid I. Brezhnev* for the return trip. For safety's sake, the antimatter would be delivered to a lunar research station, near Farside. L-5 scientists claimed that harnessing the energy from total annihilation of matter would make a heaven on Earth.

Most people doubted that, but looked forward to the fireworks.

January 2076

"The *hell* with that!" Charlie was livid. "I—I just won't do it. Won't!"

"You're the only one—"

"That's not true. Ab, you know it." Charlie paced from wall to wall of her office cubicle. "There are dozens of people who can run L-5. Better than I can."

"Not better, Charlie."

He stopped in front of her desk, leaned over. "Come on, Ab. There's only one logical person to stay behind and run things. Not only has she proven herself in the position, but she's too old to—"

"That kind of drik I don't have to listen to."

"Now, Ab . . ."

"No, you listen to me. I was an infant when we started building Daedalus; worked on it as a girl and a young woman.

"I could take you out there in a shuttle and show you the rivets that I put in, myself. A half-century ago."

"That's my—"

"I earned my ticket, Charlie." Her voice softened. "Age is a factor, yes. This is only the first trip of many—and when it comes back, I *will* be too old. You'll just be in your prime . . . and with over twenty years of experience as Coordinator, I don't doubt they'll make you captain of the next—"

"I don't want to be captain. I don't want to be Coordinator. I just want to *go!*"

"You and three thousand other people."

"And of the thousand that don't want to go, or can't, there isn't one person who could serve as Coordinator? I could name you—"

"That's not the point. There's no one on L-5 who has

anywhere near the influence, the connections, you have on Earth. No one who understands groundhogs as well."

"That's racism, Ab. Groundhogs are just like you and me."

"Some of them. I don't see you going Earthside every chance you can get . . . what, you like the view up here? You like living in a can?"

He didn't have a ready answer for that. Ab continued: "Whoever's Coordinator is going to have to do some tall explaining, trying to keep things smooth between L-5 and Earth. That's been your life's work, Charlie. And you're also known and respected here. You're the only logical choice."

"I'm not arguing with your logic."

"I know." Neither of them had to mention the document, signed by Charlie, among others, that gave Dr. Bemis final authority in selecting the crew for Daedalus/Kennedy/Brezhnev. "Try not to hate me too much, Charlie. I have to do what's best for my people. All of my people."

Charlie glared at her for a long moment and left.

June 2076

From *Fax & Pix*, 4 June 2076:
SPACE FARM LEAVES FOR
STARS NEXT MONTH

1. The *John F. Kennedy*, that goes to Scylla/Charybdis next month, is like a little L-5 with bombs up its tail (see pix upleft, upright).
   A. The trip's twenty months. They could either take a few people and fill the thing up with food, air, and water—or take a lot of people inside a closed ecology, like L-5.
   B. They could've gotten by with only a couple hundred people, to run the farms and stuff. But almost all the space freeks wanted to go. They're used to living that way, anyhow (and they never get to go anyplace).
   C. When they get back, the farms will be used as a starter for L-4, like L-5 but smaller at first, and on the other side of the Moon (pic downleft).
2. For other Tricentennial fax & pix, see bacover.

July 2076

Charlie was just finishing up a week on Earth the day the
John F. Kennedy was launched. Tired of being interviewed,
he slipped away from the media lounge at the Cape
shuttleport. His white clearance card got him out onto the
landing strip, alone.

The midnight shuttle was being fueled at the far end of
the strip, gleaming pink-white in the last light from the setting sun. Its image twisted and danced in the shimmering
heat that radiated from the tarmac. The smell of the soft tar
was indelibly associated in his mind with leave-taking, relief.

He walked to the middle of the strip and checked his
watch. Five minutes. He lit a cigarette and threw it away.
He rechecked his mental calculations; the flight would start
low in the southwest. He blocked out the sun with a raised
hand. What would 150 bombs per second look like? For
the media they were called fuel capsules. The people who
had carefully assembled them and gently lifted them to
orbit and installed them in the tanks, they called them
bombs. Ten times the brightness of a full moon, they had
said. On L-5 you weren't supposed to look toward it without a dark filter.

No warm-up; it suddenly appeared, impossibly brilliant
rainbow speck just over the horizon. It gleamed for several
minutes, then dimmed slightly with the haze, and slipped
away.

Most of the United States wouldn't see it until it came
around again, some two hours later, turning night into day,
competing with local pyrotechnic displays. Then every
couple of hours after that. Charlie would see it once more,
then get on the shuttle. And finally stop having to call it by
the name of a dead politician.

September 2076

There was a quiet celebration on L-5 when *Daedalus*
reached the mid-point of its journey, flipped, and started
decelerating. The progress report from its crew character-
ized the journey as "uneventful." At that time they were
214

going nearly two-tenths of the speed of light. The laser beam that carried communications was red-shifted from blue light down to orange; the message that turnaround had been successful took two weeks to travel from *Daedalus* to L-5.

They announced a slight course change. They had analyzed the polarization of light from Scylla/Charybdis as their phase angle increased, and were pretty sure the system was surrounded by flat rings of debris, like Saturn. They would "come in low" to avoid collision.

January 2077

Daedalus had been sending back recognizable pictures of the Scylla/Charybdis system for three weeks. They finally had one that was dramatic enough for groundhog consumption.

Charlie set the holo cube on his desk and pushed it around with his finger, marvelling.

"This is incredible. How did they do it?"

"It's a montage, of course." Johnny had been one of the youngest adults left behind: heart murmur, trick knees, a surfeit of astrophysicists.

"The two stars are a strobe snapshot in infrared. Sort of. Some ten or twenty thousand exposures taken as the ship orbited around the system, then sorted out and enhanced." He pointed, but it wasn't much help, since Charlie was looking at the cube from a different angle.

"The lamina of fire where the atmospheres touch, that was taken in ultraviolet. Shows more fine structure that way.

"The rings were easy. Fairly long exposures in visible light. Gives the star background, too."

A light tap on the door and an assistant stuck his head in. "Have a second, Doctor?"

"Sure."

"Somebody from a Russian May Day committee is on the phone. She wants to know whether they've changed the name of the ship to *Brezhnev* yet."

"Yeah. Tell her we decided on 'Leon Trotsky' instead, though."

He nodded seriously. "Okay." He started to close the door.

"Wait!" Charlie rubbed his eyes. "Tell her, uh . . . the ship doesn't have a commemorative name while it's in orbit there. They'll rechristen it just before the start of the return trip."

"Is that true?" Johnny asked.

"I don't know. Who cares? In another couple of months they won't *want* it named after anybody." He and Ab had worked out a plan—admittedly rather shaky—to protect L-5 from the groundhogs' wrath; nobody on the satellite knew ahead of time that the ship was headed for 61 Cygni. It was a decision the crew arrived at on the way to Scylla/ Charybdis; they modified the drive system to accept matter-antimatter destruction while they were orbiting the double star. L-5 would first hear of the mutinous plan via a transmission sent as *Daedalus* left Scylla/Charybdis. They'd be a month on their way by the time the message got to Earth.

It was pretty transparent, but at least they had been careful that no record of *Daedalus'* true mission be left on L-5. Three thousand people did know the truth, though, and any competent engineer or physical scientist would suspect it.

Ab had felt that, although there was a better than even chance they would be exposed, surely the groundhogs couldn't stay angry for 23 years—even if they were unimpressed by the antimatter and other wonders . . .

Besides, Charlie thought, it's not their worry anymore.

As it turned out, the crew of *Daedalus* would have bigger things to worry about.

June 2077

The Russians had their May Day celebration—Charlie watched it on TV and winced every time they mentioned the good ship *Leonid I. Brezhnev*—and then things settled back down to normal. Charlie and three thousand others waited nervously for the "surprise" message. It came in early June, as expected, scrambled in a data channel. But it didn't say what it was supposed to:

This is Abigail Bemis, to Charles Leventhal.
Charlie, we have real trouble. The ship has been

*damaged, hit in the stern by a good chunk of some-
thing. It punched right through the main drive re-
flector. Destroyed a set of control sensors and one
attitude jet.*

*As far as we can tell, the situation is stable. We're
maintaining acceleration at just a tiny fraction under
one gee. But we can't steer, and we can't shut off the
main drive.*

*We didn't have any trouble with ring debris when
we were orbiting, since we were inside Roche's limit.
Coming in, as you know, we'd managed to take advantage of natural divisions in the rings. We tried the
same going back, but it was a slower, more complicated process, since we mass so goddamn much now.
We must have picked up a piece from the fringe of
one of the outer rings.*

*If we could turn off the drive, we might have a
chance at fixing it. But the work pods can't keep up
with the ship, not at one gee. The radiation down
there would fry the operator in seconds, anyway.*

*We're working on it. If you have any ideas, let us
know. It occurs to me that this puts you in the clear—
we were headed back to Earth, but got clobbered. Will
send a transmission to that effect on the regular comm
channel. This message is strictly burn-before-reading.*

Endit.

It worked perfectly, as far as getting Charlie and L-5
off the hook—and the drama of the situation precipitated a
level of interest in space travel unheard-of since the 1960's.

They even had a hero. A volunteer had gone down in a
heavily-shielded work pod, lowered on a cable, to take a
look at the situation. She'd sent back clear pictures of the
damage, before the cable snapped.

Daedalus: A.D. 2081
Earth: A.D. 2101

The following news item was killed from *Fax & Pix*, because it was too hard to translate into the "plain English"
that made the paper so popular:

Infinite Dreams

SPACESHIP PASSES 61 CYGNI—SORT OF
(L-5 Stringer)

A message received today from the spaceship *Daedalus*
said that it had just passed within 400 astronomical units
of 61 Cygni. That's about ten times as far as the planet
Pluto is from the Sun.

Actually, the spaceship passed the star some eleven
years ago. It's taken all that time for the message to get
back to us.

We don't know for sure where the spaceship actually
is, now. If they still haven't repaired the runaway drive,
they're about eleven light-years past the 61 Cygni system
(their speed when they passed the double star was better
than 99% the speed of light).

The situation is more complicated if you look at it from
the point of view of a passenger on the spaceship. Because
of relativity, time seems to pass more slowly as you approach the speed of light. So only about four years passed
for them, on the eleven-light-year journey.

L-5 Coordinator Charles Leventhal points out that the
spaceship has enough antimatter fuel to keep accelerating
to the edge of the Galaxy. The crew then would be only
some twenty years older—but it would be twenty *thousand*
years before we heard from them. . . .

*(Kill this one. There's more stuff about what the ship
looked like to the people at 61 Cygni, and howcum we
could talk to them all the time even though time was
slower there, but its all as stupid as this.)*

Daedalus: A.D. 2083
Earth: A.D. 2144

Charlie Leventhal died at the age of 99, bitter. Almost a
decade earlier it had been revealed that they'd planned all
along for *Daedalus* to be a starship. Few people had paid
much attention to the news. Among those who did, the
consensus was that anything that got rid of a thousand scientists at once, was a good thing. Look at the mess they
got us in.

Daedalus: 67 light-years out, and still accelerating.

218

Daedalus: A.D. 2085
Earth: A.D. 3578

After over seven years of shipboard research and development—and some 1500 light-years of travel—they managed to shut down the engine. With sophisticated telemetry, the job was done without endangering another life.

Every life was precious now. They were no longer simply explorers; almost half their fuel was gone. They were colonists, with no ticket back.

The message of their success would reach Earth in fifteen centuries. Whether there would be an infrared telescope around to detect it, that was a matter of some conjecture.

Daedalus: A.D. 2093
Earth: ca. A.D. 5000

While decelerating, they had investigated several systems in their line of flight. They found one with an Earth-type planet around a Sun-type sun, and aimed for it.

The season they began landing colonists, the dominant feature in the planet's night sky was a beautiful blooming cloud of gas that astronomers had named the North American Nebula.

Which was an irony that didn't occur to any of these colonists from L-5—give or take a few years, it was America's Trimillennial.

America itself was a little the worse for wear, this three-thousandth anniversary. The seas that lapped its shores were heavy with crimson crust of anaerobic life; the mighty cities had fallen and their remains, nearly ground away by the never-ceasing sand-storms.

No fireworks were planned, for lack of an audience, for lack of planners; bacteria just don't care. May Day too would be ignored.

The only humans in the Solar System lived in a glass and metal tube. They tended their automatic machinery, and turned their backs on the dead Earth, and worshiped the constellation Cygnus, and had forgotten why.

Afterword

Where do you get your crazy ideas? Well, if we tabulate the assertions made in the introductions to these stories, it goes like this: Magazine articles, two. Editorial suggestions, four. Cover painting, one. Works of other writers, two. The weather, two. Personal joke, one. Stylistic experiments, two. Personal emotional experience, two. Out of nowhere, two.*

Actually, I think all of them came out of nowhere.

R. A. Lafferty, than whom there is no more original writer in science fiction, claims that there's no such thing as an original idea, and writers who think they sit down and go through some rational process to arrive at a story are kidding themselves. He claims that all ideas float around as a kind of psychic public property, and every now and then one settles on you. That sounds dangerously mystical to me—subversive—but I think it's true.

So how can you square that with obeying the editor who calls in the middle of the night and asks for a four-thousand-word story about the person who ate the first artichoke? Easily.

When a writer sits down to start a story he faces a literal infinity of possibilities. Being told to write about a specific thing, or to a given length, doesn't really diminish the number of possible stories. The effect is the same as dividing infinity by a large but finite number: you still have infinity. Obviously, a writer who figures out his own story idea and then proceeds to write it is duplicating this not-really-restrictive process. Writing what he wants to write about may allow him to write a better story—or it may not,

---

* You may note that these add up to more than the total number of stories. I can't balance my checkbook, either.

if his infatuation with the idea interferes with his objectivity—but I think any really good writer can take any editorial requirement, so long as it's not patently stupid or offensive,* and wind up writing a story he would have written anyhow.

Ideas are cheap, even crazy ones. Every writer has had the experience of a friend or relative—or stranger!—saying, "I've got this great idea for a story ... you write it and I'll split the money with you fifty-fifty." The proper response to this depends on the generous person's occupation. In the case of a prizefighter, for instance, you might offer to name a few potential opponents, and only demand half the purse. An editor, of course, you humor. They rarely ask for as much as half.

All of this is not to say that there aren't days when you sit down at the typewriter and find that your imagination has frozen solid; you can't come up with anything to write, no ideas come floating down out of Lafferty's ether. When this happens in the middle of a novel, it's a scary thing. But if you're just facing a short story that won't get itself started, there's an easy way to cope with it, a trade secret that Gordon R. Dickson passed on to me, saying it hadn't failed him in twenty years:

Start typing. Type your name over and over. Type lists of animals, flowers, baseball players, Greek Methodists. Type out what you're going to say to that damned insolent repairman. Sooner or later, perhaps out of boredom, perhaps out of a desire to *stop* this silly exercise, you'll find you've started a story. It's never taken me so much as a page of nonsense, and the stories started this way aren't any worse than the one about the artichoke.

One restriction most good science fiction writers accept without question is that the scientific content of their stories be as accurate as possible. Is this really necessary? Yes, but not for the obvious didactic reason. We are not

---

* An editor of recent memory, who came to science fiction from the editing of wrestling magazines, and has since gone on to even greater things, once petitioned a number of writers for "an anti-homosexuality science fiction story." None was quite that desperate for work.

obligated (or qualified, in most cases) to *teach* science to anybody.

A person who thinks he learns science from science fiction is like one who thinks he learns history from historical novels, and he deserves what he gets. Some few science fiction writers, like Gregory Benford and Philip Latham, are working scientists, and a good fraction of the rest of us have degrees in some science. That doesn't make us qualified to write with authority on subjects outside of our areas of study—but we do it; you'd have a short career if all of your stories were about magnetohydrodynamics or galactic morphology. So we try to be intelligent laymen in other fields, staying current enough so that our inevitable errors won't be obvious to other laymen.

Any fiction writer is in the business of maintaining illusion. Like a stage magician, his authority lasts only until he makes his first error.* Every writer has to deal with mechanical consistencies like making sure the woman named Marie in chapter one doesn't turn into Mary in chapter four. He also has to be careful about routine details, not letting the sun set in the east (as John Wayne made it do in *The Green Berets*), and so forth. If he writes in a genre, he has an added burden of detail, since most of his readers consider themselves experts. Mundane esoterica: Spies call the CIA the Company, not the Agency. A private eye doesn't have to break into a car and read the registration card to find out who owns it; he jots down the license number and sends a form to the Department of Motor Vehicles. A cowboy normally carried only five shots in his six-shooter; only a fool would leave the hammer down on a live round.

One reason science fiction is harder to write than other forms of genre fiction is that this universe of detail is larger, more difficult of access, and constantly changing. I

---

* I saw an act in Las Vegas where the magician exploited this sentiment by deliberately introducing mistakes, which grew more and more outrageous until his act degenerated into slapstick, and it was more entertaining than any straight sleight-of-hand. Good surreal writers like Brautigan, Disch, and Garcia Marquez also succeed by deliberately manipulating the consensus of illusion we call reality, but that's not the kettle of fish we're discussing here.

wonder how many novels-in-progress got thrown across the room in 1965, when scientists found that Mercury *didn't* keep one face always to the Sun, after all. I wonder how many bad ones got finished anyhow.

Nobody can be an expert on everything from ablation physics to zymurgy, so you have to work from a principle of exclusion: know the limits of your knowledge and never expose your ignorance by attempting to write with authority when you don't really know what's going on. This advice is easier to give than to take. I've been caught in basic mistakes in genetics, laser technology, and even metric nomenclature—in the first printing of *The Forever War* I referred time and again to a unit of power called the "bevawatt." What I *meant* was *"gigawatt"*; the only thing *"bev"* means is billion-electron-volt, a unit of energy, not power. I got letters. Boy, did I get letters.

The letters are humbling, and time-consuming if you feel obligated to answer them (I do, so long as they aren't abusive or idiotic). But the possibility of being caught in error isn't the main reason for taking pains.

When I finish writing a science fiction novel I have a notebook or two of technical notes, equations, diagrams, graphs. Even a short story, if it's a hard-core-science one like "Tricentennial," might generate a dozen pages of notes. Not one percent of this stuff finds its way into the story. It may even be naive science and weak mathematics—but it will have served its purpose if it has made a fictional world solid and real to me.

Because this business of illusion works both ways. For a story to succeed, the writer must himself be convinced that the background and situation the story is built on make sense. Ernest Hemingway pointed out (though I think Gertrude Stein said it first) that the prose of a story should move with the steady grace of an iceberg, and for the same reason an iceberg does: seven-eighths of it is beneath the surface. The author must know much more than the reader sees. And he must believe, at least for the duration.

Which brings us back to Mr. Lafferty. What I'm really doing with all these equations and graphs, I think, is putting myself into a properly receptive frame of mind. Other writers draft endless outlines to the same purpose, or sharpen pencils down to useless stubs, or take meditative walks, or drink bourbon. And through some mystical—or subconscious, or subrational—process, where there was white paper there's a sentence, a page, a story. Finding the proper words is not at all a mystical process, just creative labor. The ideas that serve as scaffolding for the words, though—they come from out of nowhere, and serve you, then return.

—*Joe Haldeman*
Florida, 1978